Chapter 1: The Transaction

The neon-lit skyline of Creek City, with its towering spires of glass and steel, shimmered in the dusk. Above the chaotic streets, the city buzzed with the hum of airborne vehicles and holographic billboards promoting everything from virtual vacations to implanted memories. Kusi leaned against the railing of a high-rise balcony, eyes scanning the distant horizon where the city's lights blended with the night sky. Below him, millions lived their lives unaware of the secrets hidden in the very memories they held.

The Memory Exchange was set in a dingy back alley, away from the glitzy digital front of the city. Unlike the glossy, corporate-run memory centers, this was a place for those who preferred discretion. Memory trading in this part of town was as much an art as it was a transaction—delicate, intricate, and often dangerous.

Kusi adjusted the cuff of his jacket, fingers brushing against the sleek memory drive tucked safely in the inner pocket. The feeling of its smooth surface gave him a small sense of satisfaction. This was his world. He didn't need to know why people wanted to erase their past or implant new lives. He simply facilitated the exchange. Yet, as of late, something about the job unsettled him.

Tonight's client was late, which was unusual for someone who valued anonymity. Kusi checked his holo-watch, the flickering blue numbers floating above his wrist. Twenty minutes past the meeting time.

As Kusi turned to leave, a shadow emerged from the alley's depths. A man dressed in a tattered overcoat, hood obscuring his face, approached. The air between them seemed to crackle with tension. Kusi had dealt with all kinds before—addicts craving a better past, corporate spies covering their tracks—but something about this man felt off.

"You're Kusi, right?" the man rasped, his voice barely audible over the distant hum of the city.

Kusi nodded. He remained calm, his hand instinctively hovering near the memory drive. "Do you have the payment?"

Without a word, the man reached into his coat and pulled out a small, iridescent chip. The shimmering holographic code verified its authenticity. It was a hefty price, one Kusi hadn't expected for such a routine job. As Kusi reached for the chip, the man grabbed his wrist, locking eyes with him. The brief moment sent a shiver down Kusi's spine. There was something wild, almost desperate, in the man's gaze.

"Do you know what's on this memory?" the man asked, his voice hoarse and urgent.

Kusi pulled his hand away, breaking the contact. "I don't ask questions," he replied coolly, pocketing the chip. "That's not how this works."

The man hesitated, eyes flickering as if considering whether to say more. After a moment, he simply handed over the drive. "Just... make sure it's clean."

Kusi took the drive and slid it into his scanner, a sleek device embedded in his wrist unit. The transaction should have been seamless—he'd clean up the memory, strip out any unwanted data, and make sure it was ready for implantation. But as the data streamed across his retina display, Kusi noticed something strange.

The memory wasn't just fragmented; it was as if parts of it had been forcibly erased, leaving gaping voids. This was far from normal. Usually, when people traded memories, they came intact—messy perhaps, but whole. This memory was... broken. Worse, there were echoes—glimpses of something that should no longer exist. A face flickered across the stream, then vanished. He tried to rewind the data, but the glitch remained.

The man noticed Kusi's frown and shifted uneasily. "Problem?"

Kusi didn't answer immediately, still scanning the corrupted data. "Where did you get this?"

"That's none of your business," the man snapped. "Just clean it."

Kusi hesitated. The fragments were too distorted, too incomplete. He had seen tampered memories before, but this felt different. It felt... intentional. As if someone—or something—had gone to great lengths to erase not just the memory but the person attached to it.

"This memory," Kusi started, trying to keep his voice steady, "it's not just damaged. It's erased."

The man's eyes widened for a fraction of a second, fear flashing across his face before he regained composure. "I told you—just clean it."

Kusi weighed his options. Normally, he'd take the money and finish the job, but something in his gut told him to be cautious. This was no ordinary memory, and no ordinary transaction. Still, he'd learned early in the business that asking too many questions got people killed.

"Fine," Kusi said at last. "But this one's going to cost you extra. If anyone comes asking, you never met me."

The man nodded, though Kusi could see the tension in his clenched fists. With a quick motion, Kusi ejected the drive, the faint blue light fading as he handed it back. "It's done."

The man pocketed the drive, turning to leave without another word. But just as he reached the end of the alley, he paused, looking over his shoulder. "You should forget this transaction, broker. Some memories aren't worth keeping."

Kusi watched as the man disappeared into the shadows, leaving behind the faint echo of his warning.

Back in his apartment, Kusi couldn't shake the feeling that something was wrong. He'd been in the memory trade long enough to know when something didn't add up. As he reclined on his worn-out couch, staring at the ceiling, fragments of the glitch replayed in his mind.

The face he saw in the memory—it wasn't just erased. It was as though it had never existed. The thought sent a chill through him. People could alter memories, even erase them, but to completely delete someone from existence? That required power far beyond the underground market.

He accessed the encrypted backup of the memory he'd cleaned. Maybe it was nothing. Maybe it was just a botched job. But as the data began to stream again, Kusi noticed something new—something he hadn't caught before. Hidden in the corrupted code was a name.

Araba.

He didn't know it then, but that name would change everything.

Chapter 2: Araba's Forgotten Past

Kusi woke to the sound of his comm-link buzzing incessantly. He groaned, rolling over in bed, eyes blurry from a restless night. His apartment was a cluttered mess, the remnants of late-night meals and data drives scattered across his desk. The city outside was waking up, casting long shadows across the narrow window. He glanced at the comm-link's flashing screen. The name displayed was unfamiliar—no records, no history. A blocked identity.

Suspicious, Kusi hesitated before answering. In his line of work, untraceable calls were rarely good news. With a deep breath, he tapped the screen.

"Is this Kusi?" a voice asked—female, calm, yet tinged with desperation.

Kusi sat up, instantly alert. "Who's asking?"

"I need your help," she continued. "I've heard you deal in... memories."

His heartbeat quickened. The memory from last night still lingered in his mind, and he hadn't quite shaken the sense that something was off. The name—Araba.

"And who might you be?" Kusi asked, keeping his tone neutral.

"I don't know."

There was a brief silence between them. The voice on the other end was steady, but beneath the surface, he could sense the fear. People without names were common enough in the memory business—those who chose to erase parts of their lives, wiping their past to create something new. But there was something different about this one.

"You don't know?" Kusi echoed, intrigued.

"I've lost my memories. All of them," the voice said, the edge of panic creeping into her words. "I need to know who I am."

Kusi agreed to meet her at a small diner on the edge of Creek City. The place was old, a relic from the days before memory manipulation, where real conversations happened in person rather than through neural links or augmented projections. It was the kind of place where secrets were whispered, and no one asked questions.

He arrived first, sitting in a corner booth, his eyes on the door. He had been replaying the memory from the night before in his head—wondering if this mysterious woman could be connected. The name "Araba" from that glitch stuck with him. Was it just coincidence? In his world, nothing was ever coincidental.

A few minutes later, she entered. Kusi recognized her immediately, though not because they had met before. She was the face from the memory—part of the erased fragments he had cleaned. Her eyes were wide, searching, as if she had walked into a place she didn't belong. Her movements were hesitant, the confusion clear in the way she scanned the room.

She was tall, with dark, curly hair that cascaded loosely around her shoulders, and her skin was a shade too pale for someone from this part of town—like she'd been hiding from the sun. She looked... lost.

"Araba?" Kusi said the name out loud as she approached his table, watching for a reaction.

She froze mid-step, her eyes widening in shock. "How... how do you know that name?"

Kusi leaned back in his chair, arms crossed. "I'll explain. Sit down."

As she sat, Kusi could see the strain in her features. Whoever she was, the lack of memory weighed heavily on her. He knew the feeling—though he had never been erased, he'd seen what it did to people. It wasn't just forgetting; it was losing the very essence of who they were.

She looked at him expectantly, as if he held the key to unlocking her past.

"I saw you," Kusi started, keeping his voice low. "In a memory. A broken one. It came to me through an exchange. Your name was part of it—'Araba.' Does that sound familiar to you?"

Her face remained blank, though her eyes betrayed a flicker of hope. "I don't know. I don't remember anything before three days ago."

Kusi frowned. "Three days?"

She nodded, her fingers gripping the edge of the table. "I woke up in an abandoned building. No ID, no history. Just... nothing. I don't even know how I got there. All I know is, someone's erased me."

"Erased you," Kusi repeated, leaning in. "Not just memories, but your entire existence?"

She nodded again, her voice trembling slightly. "It's like I never existed. No records, no connections. Just blank space. I don't know how to find myself, but I think someone—someone powerful—did this to me."

Kusi's thoughts spun. The concept of erasing people wasn't new, but usually, it was selective—removing incriminating memories, altering embarrassing moments, covering up corporate scandals. Erasing an entire person, though? That was deep.

"Do you have any idea who could have done this?" Kusi asked.

"That's why I came to you," Araba said, her voice quiet but determined. "I need you to help me find out."

Kusi considered her words. He had been in the memory trade long enough to know that tampering with someone's identity, erasing their very existence, required serious resources. Only large corporations or underground syndicates could pull off something like this. And even then, erasing a person left ripples—digital footprints, loose ends. Something that shouldn't have been possible.

"This isn't going to be easy," Kusi warned her. "If you've been erased, someone didn't want you to be found. It'll take more than a simple memory restoration."

Araba's eyes hardened. "I don't care what it takes. I need to know who I am. I need to know why this happened."

Kusi could see the desperation in her eyes—the kind of desperation that came from being lost, disconnected from the very thing that defined her. He sighed, rubbing the back of his neck. "I'll help you. But you need to understand, this isn't like a normal job. Whoever erased you has deep ties. We'll be walking into something dangerous."

Araba didn't flinch. "I don't have a choice. I need to know."

Kusi hesitated only for a moment before pulling out his wrist scanner. He had already backed up the fragments of the glitchy memory he'd cleaned the night before. He wasn't entirely sure how, but he had a feeling it was connected to Araba.

"I've got a lead," Kusi said, bringing up the fragmented data on the screen. "This memory—it's broken. Someone tried to erase it, but they left traces. Your name was in there, attached to this... image." He handed her the scanner, watching her reaction closely. As the image flickered on the screen—a fleeting glimpse of her own face—Araba's eyes widened in shock.

"That's me," she whispered, as if seeing herself for the first time.

Kusi nodded, but his focus was on something else—a new piece of information embedded in the glitch that he hadn't noticed before. A timestamp. Three days ago.

He tapped the screen, zooming in on the corrupted fragment. "This memory was altered exactly when you said you lost your identity. Whoever erased you didn't just wipe your memories. They wiped you from everything."

"How do we undo it?" Araba asked, her voice barely above a whisper.

Kusi looked at her, the weight of her question settling between them. "We start by finding out who did it. And why."

As they sat in the fading light of the diner, Kusi couldn't shake the feeling that they had stumbled onto something far larger than just a lost identity. Whoever was behind Araba's erasure wasn't just covering up a mistake. They were hiding something. Something big.

"We need to dig deeper," Kusi said, his voice grim. "And for that, we'll need access to a place most people can't reach."

Araba met his gaze, a silent understanding passing between them. They were about to descend into the murky depths of the memory trade's darkest corners. And neither of them had any idea what they would find there.

Chapter 3: Beneath the Dive

The next day, the streets of Creek City were alive with their usual rhythm. The city pulsed with life: buzzing drones in the sky, holographic billboards screaming the latest products, and the endless hum of traffic both above and below. Kusi and Araba moved through the crowded sidewalks, trying to blend in. For Araba, it was easy—she was nobody, a person erased from every digital record. For Kusi, it was harder. As a broker, he had connections everywhere, and someone might recognize him at any moment.

They were heading to *"The Dive"*, an underground hub hidden beneath the city's underbelly. On the surface, it was nothing more than an abandoned transit station, but below, it housed one of the most sophisticated data markets in the world. If anyone could help them trace the origins of Araba's erasure, it was someone from The Dive.

"This place..." Araba murmured as they passed a towering building covered in neon. "I feel like I know it, but I don't remember."

Kusi shot her a glance. "The more you remember, the closer we get to finding out who did this. Don't fight it. Let the memories come back, piece by piece."

Araba nodded but remained silent. Her eyes scanned the unfamiliar streets, seeking familiarity in a world that had none for her.

The entrance to The Dive was hidden behind layers of graffiti-covered steel doors, and only those in the know could access it. Kusi tapped a sequence into a small panel by the door, the screen flickering to life

before scanning his face. After a pause, the heavy door groaned open, revealing a dark stairwell that led deep underground.

As they descended into the depths, Araba's breathing grew shallow. The stale air of the underground, combined with the oppressive darkness, made the place feel like a tomb. Kusi moved confidently ahead, but Araba couldn't shake the feeling that they were descending into something far more dangerous than they realized.

At the bottom of the stairs, they entered a large, dimly lit room, bustling with activity. Rows of data terminals lined the walls, each manned by brokers, hackers, and data miners. Some wore augmented reality visors, lost in virtual landscapes, while others argued in low voices over encrypted data streams. The Dive was a haven for those who lived in the shadows, where illegal transactions were as common as breathing.

"This is it," Kusi said, leading Araba to a terminal in the corner where a man sat with his back to them. "If anyone can help us, it's Kanton."

Kusi tapped the man on the shoulder. Kanton turned, his face a mask of cool indifference. He was lean, with short, spiked hair and a pair of AR goggles resting on his forehead. His clothes were casual, but his presence exuded a quiet intensity.

"Kusi," Kanton said, nodding in recognition. "What brings you to my corner of the underworld?"

Kusi gestured to Araba. "We need a deep trace. She's been erased—completely wiped from existence. We need to know who did it and why."

Kanton raised an eyebrow, intrigued. "Erased? That's not easy to do, even for the best. Corporate, government, or something else?" "We don't know yet," Kusi replied, keeping his tone steady. "But it happened three days ago. I've got fragments of a memory that we think might lead us somewhere."

Kanton scratched his chin, his curiosity piqued. "Interesting. Let's take a look."

Kanton connected Kusi's memory fragment to his terminal, pulling up the corrupted data on a wide display. Araba stood behind him, watching nervously as the screen flickered with distorted images and fractured sound bites. The fragments of her erased existence flashed before her eyes, offering glimpses of things she couldn't fully comprehend.

Kanton frowned, working quickly to stabilize the corrupted files. "Whoever did this was good. They didn't just erase her—they erased all traces. No digital signature, no residual data. It's like she never existed."

"But that's impossible, right?" Araba said, her voice wavering slightly.

Kanton shot her a sympathetic look. "Not impossible, but rare. Only a handful of entities have the tech to do something like this. I'd wager it's either a high-end corp, one of the elite memory traders, or..." He trailed off.

"Or what?" Kusi pressed.

Kanton's eyes darkened. "Or someone's working with PromptTech."

The mention of PromptTech sent a chill through Kusi. PromptTech was the most powerful tech conglomerate in Creek City, rumored to control not just the city's infrastructure, but the entire memory trade. They were untouchable, hidden behind layers of corporate secrecy. Few dared to challenge them, and those who did often disappeared—just like Araba.

"PromptTech," Kusi muttered, his thoughts racing. "Why would they erase her?"

Kanton shrugged, but his expression remained grim. "Could be anything. Maybe she knows something they don't want anyone else to know. Or maybe she's part of some experiment gone wrong."

Araba's eyes widened. "Experiment?"

"It's just a theory," Kanton replied, returning to the screen. "But PromptTech has been rumored to run trials with memory manipulation tech—far beyond anything the public knows. They're experimenting with altering people at a fundamental level. Rewriting lives, identities, entire realities."

"That would explain the clean erasure," Kusi said. "They're not just erasing memories—they're rewriting history itself."

Araba looked between the two men, panic creeping into her voice. "What do we do now?"

Kanton didn't answer immediately. He was focused on something on the screen, his fingers flying over the controls. "Wait a second," he said, zooming in on a barely visible data signature buried deep in the fragmented memory. "There's something here."

The three of them stared at the screen as a single, distorted image appeared. It was blurry, barely recognizable, but Kusi could make out the outline of a building. A tower. And then, underneath the image, a single word flashed across the screen: Apetown.

"Apetown," Kanton whispered. "The industrial sector. That's where PromptTech keeps some of its black-market operations."

Kusi's gut tightened. He had heard of Apetown—an old part of the city that had been abandoned after the corporations took over. It was now a lawless zone, home to underground labs, illegal experiments, and memory traders who worked off the grid.

"Looks like that's where you need to go," Kanton said, sitting back in his chair. "But be careful. If PromptTech's involved, you're stepping into dangerous territory."

Kusi nodded. "Thanks, Kanton. We owe you one."

"You owe me more than one," Kanton smirked, though the expression didn't quite reach his eyes. "Good luck. You're going to need it."

As they left The Dive, Kusi could feel the weight of what they were about to do pressing down on him. Apetown wasn't just dangerous—it was a death sentence for anyone who didn't know how to navigate it. But if PromptTech really was behind Araba's erasure, they didn't have a choice.

"We're really doing this, aren't we?" Araba asked, her voice soft but steady.

Kusi looked at her, seeing the fear and determination etched into her features. She was walking into this blindly, trusting him to guide her through the shadows of a world she didn't remember. But she had strength—more than she realized.

"Yeah," Kusi said finally. "We are. But you need to understand something. If PromptTech is involved, this goes deeper than either of us can imagine. They don't just erase people—they rewrite them. If we dig too deep, there's no turning back."

Araba squared her shoulders, her eyes filled with resolve. "I'm not afraid. I need to know who I am, Kusi. I need to know why they did this to me."

Kusi nodded, admiring her courage. "Then we head to Apetown. But we do it smart. If PromptTech's erasing people, they won't hesitate to erase us, too."

As they walked into the dimming light of the city, Kusi felt the weight of their next step settle on his shoulders. Apetown held answers, but it also held danger beyond anything they had encountered so far. And somewhere, deep within the twisted ruins of the industrial sector, the truth about Araba—and the dark secrets of PromptTech—waited for them.

Chapter 4: Into the Depths of Apetown

The next morning, Kusi and Araba stood at the edge of Creek City, staring into the decaying ruins of Apetown. Once an industrial powerhouse, Apetown had been abandoned after the collapse of its factories and the rise of corporate control. Now, it was a lawless zone, overrun by gangs, rogue AI, and underground labs. The towering factories were rusting skeletons of the past, casting long shadows over the cracked streets.

"This place is... eerie," Araba murmured, her voice tinged with unease.

Kusi glanced at her, his eyes scanning the ruins ahead. "It's more than eerie. It's dangerous. We're not just dealing with memory traders here. There are people—powerful people—who don't want us to dig too deep."

Araba's gaze hardened. "I understand the risks. But I need answers."

Kusi nodded. "We'll find them. But we have to be smart. We'll meet a contact of mine. He can get us into the right places without drawing too much attention."

They started down the cracked streets, the silence of Apetown wrapping around them like a shroud. The air was thick with the scent of rust and decay, and the occasional clatter of debris made

Araba jump. Kusi, however, moved with purpose, his eyes always watching, always alert.

As they walked deeper into the ruins, Kusi's comm unit buzzed. He tapped it, and a voice crackled through.

"Kusi, you better not be where I think you are."

It was Maya, one of Kusi's oldest contacts—a smuggler and hacker who had been operating in Apetown for years.

"Nice to hear from you too, Maya," Kusi said with a smirk. "We're heading to the old district. Got a lead on something big."

Maya's voice was sharp. "A lead that's gonna get you killed if you're not careful. Apetown isn't like it used to be. PromptTech's tightened its grip here. You're stepping into a war zone."

Kusi's expression darkened. "That's why I need your help. You still know the layout?"

There was a pause, followed by a sigh. "Yeah, I know it. But you owe me for this, Kusi. Big time."

"I always do," he replied, ending the call.

They reached an old factory, its windows shattered and its walls covered in graffiti. This was Maya's safehouse—a crumbling building that had been repurposed as a hideout for smugglers and renegades. Kusi rapped on the door, a specific sequence of knocks that signaled he wasn't a threat.

A moment later, the door creaked open, and Maya stood there, her dark eyes glaring at him. She was tall and lean, with short-cropped hair and tattoos that marked her as a survivor of Apetown's harsh life. Her face softened when she saw Kusi, but only slightly.

"Kusi, you idiot. You're lucky I like you," she said, stepping aside to let them in.

The inside of the factory was dimly lit, filled with makeshift equipment and scavenged tech. Maya led them through a maze of corridors until they reached a back room, where several monitors flickered with encrypted data feeds.

"So," Maya said, leaning against the wall, "what's this about?"

Kusi motioned to Araba. "She's been erased—completely wiped from every system. We think PromptTech's behind it, and we traced something to Apetown. We need to get into one of their black-market labs."

Maya's eyes widened slightly, her interest piqued. "Erased? That's not something you hear every day. PromptTech doesn't just erase people for fun. What makes her so special?"

Araba shifted uncomfortably under Maya's gaze. "I don't know. I don't remember anything."

Maya studied her for a moment, then nodded. "Alright, I'll help. But you have to understand, getting into one of PromptTech's labs is suicide. They've got security drones, armed guards, and worse. They've been experimenting with memory AI down here, creating things... things that shouldn't exist."

Kusi frowned. "Like what?"

Maya hesitated. "I don't know the details, but I've heard rumors. Some say they're trying to merge AI and human consciousness—creating hybrid entities that can control memories in ways we've never seen before. Others say they're developing tech that can alter a person's entire sense of self, turning them into something else entirely."

Araba's face paled. "Why would they do that?"

Maya shrugged. "Control, probably. PromptTech's always been obsessed with control. If they can control how people think, how they perceive reality, then they can control everything."

Kusi clenched his fists. "We have to stop them."

Maya raised an eyebrow. "Stop them? You're not going in there to stop anything, Kusi. You're going in there to survive. If you want to get answers, fine. But don't get yourself killed trying to play hero."

Kusi met her gaze, determination burning in his eyes. "I'll do whatever it takes to keep us alive. But if we can expose them, if we can bring this to light, it's worth the risk."

Maya sighed. "Alright. I can get you into the lab. But once you're in, you're on your own. I won't be able to help you if things go sideways."

Kusi nodded. "That's all we need."

Later that night, Kusi and Araba found themselves outside the walls of the PromptTech lab. The building was a stark contrast to the crumbling ruins of Apetown—a sleek, modern structure surrounded by high walls and patrolled by security drones. Maya had provided them with a way in—an old sewer system that ran beneath the lab, forgotten by most.

They slipped into the sewer entrance, the stench overwhelming at first, but Kusi pressed on, leading the way through the dark, narrow tunnels. The sound of water dripping echoed through the space, creating an eerie backdrop as they moved deeper underground.

"How do you know about this place?" Araba asked, her voice barely a whisper.

"Maya's good at finding cracks in the system," Kusi replied. "This lab's supposed to be off the grid, but nothing's completely hidden."

After what felt like hours, they reached a metal grate that led up into the lab. Kusi pried it open, and they emerged into a dark corridor lined with humming machinery. The air was sterile, cold, a stark contrast to the grimy underworld they had just crawled through.

"Stay close," Kusi whispered, his hand resting on the hilt of the small plasma weapon Maya had given him. "We don't know what's waiting for us up here."

They moved cautiously through the corridor, the sound of their footsteps barely audible over the hum of machines. As they turned a corner, Kusi spotted a door marked with the PromptTech logo, and beneath it, a series of numbers: Lab 37.

"This is it," he said, motioning for Araba to stay behind him.

He approached the door, his pulse quickening. There was no visible lock, only a small biometric scanner beside the door. Kusi knew this was the first major obstacle. He had anticipated this, but he hoped Maya's hacked access codes would work.

He pressed a small device against the scanner, watching as it blinked, cycling through access points until finally, the light turned green. The door slid open with a soft hiss, revealing a sterile lab filled with machines and data terminals.

But it wasn't the machines that caught Kusi's attention—it was the glass chambers along the far wall, each containing a human figure, suspended in liquid, their eyes closed.

Araba gasped softly. "What is this?"

Kusi moved closer to one of the chambers, his heart pounding in his chest. The figure inside was eerily still, floating as though in a dreamless sleep. But the more he looked, the more he realized these weren't just people—they were hybrids. Machines and human flesh fused together in ways that defied comprehension.

"PromptTech's experiments," he muttered. "They're creating something..."

Before he could finish, a loud alarm blared through the lab. The doors slammed shut, sealing them inside, and a voice echoed through the space.

"Unauthorized access detected. Security response initiated."

Kusi drew his weapon, his mind racing. "We've been made. We need to find the data we're looking for and get out—now!"

They scrambled to the data terminals, Araba frantically pulling up files while Kusi kept watch. The sound of heavy footsteps echoed in the corridors outside, growing closer with every second. Kusi's palms were slick with sweat as he braced himself for a fight.

"I've got something!" Araba shouted, pulling a drive from the terminal. "This has the details of the experiments. We can expose them!"

"Then we need to move!" Kusi barked, as the door shuddered under the force of someone—or something—trying to break through.

They raced for the back exit, Kusi leading the way as Araba clutched the drive to her chest. But just as they reached the door, it burst open, and a figure stepped into the lab—an armored guard, his face hidden behind a visor.

Without hesitation, Kusi fired his plasma weapon, the shot searing through the guard's armor and sending him crashing to the ground. But more were coming, and Kusi knew they didn't have much time.

"This way!" he yelled, pulling Araba down a side corridor.

They sprinted through the labyrinthine halls of the lab, the sounds of alarms and footsteps growing fainter as they put distance between themselves and their pursuers. Finally, they reached another access point—another sewer grate.

They dropped into the tunnels below, the cold, foul air hitting them like a wave. But they didn't stop. They ran through the tunnels until they were far enough away from the lab that the alarms were nothing more than a distant memory.

Finally, they collapsed against the wall of the tunnel, gasping for breath.

"We did it," Araba whispered, clutching the drive. "We've got the proof."

Kusi nodded, though his heart was still racing. "Yeah. But now we've got a bigger target on our backs than ever."

As they sat in the darkness, the reality of what they had just uncovered began to sink in. PromptTech wasn't just erasing memories—they were creating something far more dangerous. And Kusi and Araba were the only ones who could stop them.

Chapter 5: Whispers in the Dark

Kusi and Araba had barely escaped the PromptTech lab, but the tension lingered in the air as they made their way through the underground tunnels beneath Apetown. Their breaths were shallow, and the sound of their footsteps echoed through the darkness. The sewers stretched for miles, a labyrinth of forgotten paths, damp and cold. Their escape had bought them some time, but Kusi knew the reprieve wouldn't last long.

Araba clutched the stolen drive close to her chest, her fingers trembling slightly. "What now?" she asked, her voice barely a whisper in the stillness.

Kusi stopped for a moment, his back against the damp wall, eyes scanning the faint light flickering from distant grates above. His mind raced. They had exposed PromptTech's dark secret—hybrid experiments, fusing humans with AI—but that was only a fraction of what they were up against.

"We need to get out of Apetown," Kusi said finally, his voice steady despite the chaos around them. "PromptTech will have their agents hunting us, and they'll stop at nothing to retrieve that drive. But we need help—more than we can find in the shadows down here."

Araba nodded, though the weight of their situation pressed down heavily. "Where do we go? If they control memories, they control everything. We can't trust anyone."

Kusi frowned, the reality sinking in deeper. He had contacts, yes—people like Maya who could help them navigate the dangerous underworld of memory brokers—but to truly dismantle the web of control PromptTech wielded, they would need to strike from within the system itself. But first, they had to disappear.

Hours later, they emerged from the tunnels, the gray light of dawn casting long shadows over Apetown's decaying buildings. They moved quickly, heading to an old safehouse Kusi had used in the past. It was a forgotten corner of the city, an abandoned apartment complex hidden behind layers of rubble and overgrowth.

As they approached the crumbling structure, Kusi tapped a series of commands into his comm unit, signaling a hidden doorway to slide open. Inside, it was dark and dusty, the smell of mildew clinging to the air.

"Is this safe?" Araba asked, her eyes scanning the shadows for threats.

Kusi gave a small nod. "For now. But we can't stay long. I need to contact someone I trust."

Kusi activated a secure terminal hidden behind a wall panel, his fingers flying over the keys as he tapped into a private network. He was reaching out to *Kai*, an old friend from his memory broker days—a former corporate insider turned rogue hacker. Kai had deep connections within the corporate elite and could help them understand the data on the drive.

After a few tense moments, a video feed flickered to life. Kai's face appeared on the screen, his dark hair tousled, and a smirk playing at his lips.

"Kusi, you always call me when you're in trouble," Kai said with a teasing grin. "What is it this time? Got caught with your hand in the cookie jar again?"

Kusi didn't smile. "This is serious, Kai. I need your help. We've uncovered something big—PromptTech is running illegal experiments. They're not just manipulating memories—they're creating AI-human hybrids, and it's worse than anything I've seen before."

Kai's smirk faded, replaced by a look of concern. "Hybrids? That's... heavy stuff. And you're sure?"

Kusi glanced at Araba, then back at the screen. "We've got proof. Araba was erased—completely wiped from every system. They're covering up everything, and now we have the data."

Kai's eyes narrowed as he processed the information. "Alright. Send me the files. I'll take a look, but you know this puts a huge target on your back. PromptTech doesn't mess around with people who dig into their secrets."

Kusi nodded grimly. "I know. But if we don't expose this, they'll keep erasing people, and no one will ever know the truth."

Kai hesitated, then sighed. "Okay. Send it over. I'll see what I can do. But be careful, Kusi. If PromptTech is doing what you say, they'll come after you hard."

Kusi sent the files, and after a few moments, the connection ended. The room fell into an uneasy silence.

"We're not safe here, are we?" Araba asked quietly, her eyes meeting Kusi's.

Kusi shook his head. "No. We have to keep moving. There's a place we can go—a safe zone outside of Creek City. It's off the grid, run by people who hate the corps as much as we do. But getting there won't be easy."

As they prepared to leave the safehouse, Kusi sensed something was wrong. His instincts, honed by years of navigating the dangerous underworld, screamed at him that they weren't alone.

"Wait," he whispered, holding up a hand to stop Araba. His eyes scanned the room, searching for any signs of disturbance.

That's when he heard it—the faint sound of static interference, barely noticeable but unmistakable. Someone had tapped into the room's communications. His heart raced as he realized the terminal had been compromised.

"We've been found," Kusi hissed, grabbing Araba's arm. "We need to move. Now."

They bolted for the exit, but before they could reach the door, it slammed shut with a heavy thud, locking them inside. The lights flickered, and a voice echoed through the room.

"Going somewhere, Kusi?"

Kusi froze. He knew that voice. It was *Rashid*, an enforcer for PromptTech's security division. A ruthless mercenary who specialized in hunting down threats to the corporation.

"I've been watching you," Rashid's voice continued, a cruel edge to his tone. "Did you really think you could expose PromptTech's secrets and just walk away?"

Kusi's mind raced as he assessed their options. The room was sealed, and Rashid's men would be closing in any moment. He had to think fast.

"Araba," Kusi whispered, his voice tense. "There's a ventilation shaft behind the panel over there. Get inside and go. I'll hold them off."

Araba's eyes widened. "What? No! I'm not leaving you—"

"Go!" Kusi barked, his voice firm. "I'll meet you at the rendezvous point. But if they catch both of us, we're done."

Araba hesitated for a heartbeat, then nodded reluctantly. She moved quickly, prying open the panel and slipping into the narrow shaft. Kusi watched her go, his heart pounding as he heard the sound of footsteps approaching from outside.

He pulled his plasma weapon from its holster and positioned himself near the door, ready for the inevitable confrontation. The door slid open, and Rashid stepped inside, flanked by two heavily armed guards.

"Always the hero," Rashid sneered, his eyes locking onto Kusi. "You should have stayed in the shadows where you belong."

Kusi didn't respond. He fired without hesitation, his plasma shot tearing through the first guard's chest. The second guard returned fire, but Kusi rolled to the side, his years of experience in combat keeping him one step ahead.

The room erupted into chaos as gunfire echoed through the space. Kusi moved with precision, taking out the second guard with a well-aimed shot before turning his attention to Rashid.

But Rashid was ready. He lunged at Kusi, disarming him with a swift motion and slamming him against the wall. The impact knocked the wind out of Kusi, and for a moment, everything went blurry.

"You're out of your league, Kusi," Rashid growled, pressing a knife to Kusi's throat. "You're playing with fire, and it's going to burn you alive."

Kusi gritted his teeth, his mind racing for a way out. He could feel the cold edge of the blade against his skin, but he refused to give in.

Suddenly, there was a loud crash from the ventilation shaft, and Rashid turned his head just as Araba burst out, wielding a makeshift weapon she had scavenged from the shaft. She swung it at Rashid, hitting him across the face and sending him stumbling backward.

"Go!" Araba shouted, grabbing Kusi's arm and pulling him toward the exit.

They sprinted out of the room, the sound of Rashid's curses echoing behind them. Kusi's heart pounded in his chest as they raced through the safehouse, dodging gunfire and making their way to the streets outside.

They didn't stop running until they were deep into the shadows of Apetown, hidden among the ruins once more. Kusi leaned against a wall, gasping for breath, his body aching from the fight.

"That was... too close," Araba panted, her eyes wide with fear and adrenaline.

Kusi nodded, though his mind was already moving ahead. Rashid wouldn't stop until they were dead or captured. They had to leave the city, and fast.

Just as Kusi was about to speak, a figure stepped out of the shadows—a woman with silver hair and sharp, calculating eyes. She was dressed in sleek, dark clothing, the kind that allowed her to blend seamlessly into the night.

"Kusi," she said, her voice calm and confident. "It's been a long time."

Kusi tensed, recognizing her immediately. It was Nafissa, a rogue operative with deep ties to the underworld. She had always been a wildcard, but if she was here, it could mean one of two things: she was here to help, or she was here to kill them." You've got quite a mess on your hands," Nafissa continued, her eyes flicking between Kusi and Araba. "But lucky for you, I'm feeling generous. I can get you out of the city—but it's going to cost you."

Kusi met her gaze, his mind calculating the risks. Nafissa was dangerous, but right now, they didn't have any other options.

"Fine," he said, his voice steady. "We'll take your help."

Nafissa smiled, a glint of mischief in her eyes. "Good choice. Now, let's get moving before Rashid decides to come looking for you again."

As they followed Nafissa into the night, Kusi couldn't shake the feeling that they were stepping even deeper into the web of deception and danger. But one thing was clear, if they wanted to survive, they needed to trust Nafissa—at least for now.

Chapter 6: Shadows of Deception

The night sky loomed overhead, and Nafissa led Kusi and Araba through the narrow backstreets of Apetown. The city was alive with neon signs, flickering holograms, and the distant hum of drones. In the shadows, the ever-watchful eyes of PromptTech remained an unspoken threat. They had escaped the immediate danger, but Kusi knew that this reprieve wouldn't last long. Trusting Nafissa, a rogue operative with ties to both sides of the law, was their best option—for now.

As they moved swiftly, Kusi found himself studying Nafissa. She had always been an enigma, a ghost in the underworld, who appeared when it suited her and vanished just as quickly. Her motivations were often unclear, driven by her own agenda. Was she truly willing to help, or was this just another ploy?

"We're almost there," Nafissa said, her voice low. She didn't bother looking back, her confidence radiating in the way she moved through the city.

"Where exactly are we going?" Araba asked, her voice tinged with suspicion. She clutched the stolen drive tightly, as if it might slip away at any moment.

"A safe house," Nafissa replied, a smirk playing on her lips. "It's off the grid, buried deep within the underground. No corp drones, no surveillance—just a place for people like us."

"People like us?" Kusi repeated, raising an eyebrow. Nafissa finally looked back, her silver hair catching the dim light. "People who don't fit neatly into the corp-controlled world. People who know the game but refuse to play by the rules."

Kusi nodded slowly. He had no reason to trust her, but he knew that they didn't have many options. With Rashid and his team hunting them, they couldn't stay exposed much longer.

Nafissa led them down a steep alley, where the neon lights above disappeared, replaced by the cold darkness of an industrial underbelly. They descended through an old, rusted staircase that led them deeper into the bowels of the city. As they moved farther away from the surface, the city above became a distant memory, replaced by the low hum of machinery and the thick scent of grease and metal.

"This place is... charming," Araba muttered, her voice laced with irony.

Nafissa chuckled softly. "It's not about charm. It's about staying hidden."

At the bottom of the staircase, Nafissa pushed open a heavy, rusted door. Inside was a small, dimly lit room filled with old tech, worn-out furniture, and the faint glow of outdated screens. It wasn't much, but it would provide them the safety they desperately needed.

"Make yourselves comfortable," Nafissa said, walking over to a small terminal. "We won't stay here long, but it's secure enough for us to lay low and plan our next move."

Kusi glanced around, his senses on high alert. The room was cluttered but functional, a space designed for hiding rather than comfort. He watched as Nafissa tapped into the terminal, her fingers moving with practiced speed. Whatever her past, she clearly still had access to some serious resources.

"What's your angle, Nafissa?" Kusi asked, his voice low and careful. "You're not doing this out of charity."

Nafissa smirked but didn't look up from the terminal. "You're right. I have my reasons. But for now, let's just say our interests align. PromptTech has made plenty of enemies in this city, and I've got my own score to settle."

Kusi nodded, though he remained cautious. Nafissa's motivations might overlap with theirs for now, but he knew that could change at any moment. She was playing her own game, and he needed to be ready for whatever moves she made next.

As Nafissa worked on the terminal, Araba sat down, staring at the drive in her hand. The weight of everything they had uncovered was starting to hit her. She had lost her memories—her entire identity erased. The stolen drive held the key to unlocking the truth, but the truth could be even more dangerous than they realized.

"Kusi," Araba whispered, her voice barely audible. "What if we can't stop them? What if PromptTech is too powerful?"

Kusi knelt beside her, placing a reassuring hand on her shoulder. "We'll stop them. We have to. We've come too far to turn back now."

Araba's eyes flickered with uncertainty, but she nodded. She wasn't just fighting for herself anymore—she was fighting for all the people PromptTech had erased, all the lives that had been rewritten and discarded like data files.

Before Kusi could say more, Nafissa spoke up from the terminal. "Got it."

They both turned to her, their attention fully focused.

"I've accessed some of PromptTech's encrypted communications," Nafissa said, a hint of satisfaction in her voice. "They're scrambling to contain the leak. They know you two have something, and they've put a high priority on recovering that drive."

"Figures," Kusi muttered. "What else did you find?"

Nafissa's fingers flew over the keys, bringing up several data streams on the screen. "It's worse than we thought. PromptTech isn't just experimenting with memory manipulation—they've developed a full-scale operation. They're creating hybrid agents—people who are part human, part AI, but they're erasing their memories and repurposing them as soldiers, spies, whatever they need."

Araba's eyes widened in horror. "That's what they did to me, isn't it? They tried to turn me into one of them."

Nafissa nodded grimly. "You're lucky you escaped before the process was complete. Most people... aren't so lucky."

Kusi clenched his fists, anger simmering beneath the surface. "We need to expose this. If the public knew what PromptTech was doing—"

"They'd bury it," Nafissa interrupted, her voice sharp. "You don't understand how deep their influence goes. The media, the government, the other corporations—they're all in bed with PromptTech. If you want to stop them, you'll need more than just proof. You'll need allies, people with enough power to take them on."

Kusi frowned. "And where do we find allies like that?"

Nafissa leaned back in her chair, her eyes glinting with something that looked like amusement. "That's where I come in. I have contacts—people who operate outside the system.

Revolutionaries, mercenaries, people who don't owe anything to the corps. But they're not going to help you for free. You're going to have to make a deal."

Kusi's gut tightened. He had worked with mercenaries before, and he knew how dangerous those deals could be. But if Nafissa was right, they didn't have any other options. PromptTech was too powerful to take down without help.

"What kind of deal are we talking about?" Kusi asked cautiously.

Nafissa smiled—a smile that didn't quite reach her eyes. "Simple. You give them what they want, and they help you bring down PromptTech. It's a win-win."

Araba shifted uncomfortably. "What exactly do they want?"

Nafissa shrugged. "Depends on who you ask. Some want money, some want tech, some want leverage. But most of all, they want freedom—freedom from the corp-controlled world."

Kusi exchanged a glance with Araba. This was dangerous territory, but they had come too far to back down now. If they wanted to take on PromptTech, they would need to walk through the fire—and trust that they could come out the other side.

"Alright," Kusi said finally. "Set up the meeting."

Nafissa's grin widened. "I thought you might say that. I'll make the arrangements. But remember—these people aren't your friends. They'll help you, sure, but they'll also watch for any sign of weakness. If you're not careful, they'll chew you up and spit you out."

Kusi nodded. He knew how this game was played. The underworld was full of sharks, and they were about to dive right into the deep end.

Hours later, they found themselves in a remote part of the city, far from the corporate towers and the neon-lit streets. Nafissa led them to an abandoned warehouse, the perfect place for a clandestine meeting. The air was thick with tension, and Kusi's hand hovered near his plasma weapon as they approached the entrance.

Inside, the warehouse was dimly lit, filled with shadows and the low hum of machinery. A group of figures stood in the center, their faces obscured by the darkness. These were the revolutionaries Nafissa had spoken of—the people who had no allegiance to anyone but themselves.

The leader stepped forward, his face partially illuminated by a faint light. He was a tall man, his body scarred from years of battle. His eyes were cold, calculating.

"You must be Kusi," the man said, his voice a deep rumble. "Nafissa tells me you have something that could bring PromptTech to its knees."

Kusi nodded, his heart pounding. "We have proof of their experiments—illegal hybrids, memory manipulation. We want to take them down, but we can't do it alone."

The man's eyes flickered with interest. "And what do you want from us?"

"Your help," Kusi said plainly. "We need resources, protection, and a way to get this information out to the world."

The leader paused, considering the offer. Then, after what felt like an eternity, he smiled.

"Alright," he said. "You've got yourself a deal."

Chapter 7: Whispers of the Past

The dimly lit warehouse felt like a battleground, each shadow a reminder of the stakes they faced. Kusi stood at the center, surrounded by the revolutionaries led by the imposing figure known only as *Talon*. The air was thick with tension, the weight of their fragile alliance hanging heavy between them. Araba stood close to Kusi, her gaze flickering between the hardened faces of the revolutionaries and Nafissa, who leaned against a nearby wall, her arms crossed, a satisfied smirk on her face.

"You understand the risks," Talon said, his voice gravelly and commanding. "Working against PromptTech is dangerous. They don't just retaliate; they annihilate."

Kusi took a deep breath, steadying himself. "We're aware of the risks. But if we don't act now, more lives will be lost. We have evidence of their black market memory trade and their hybrid experiments. We need to expose them to the public."

Talon nodded, his expression contemplative. "And you think the public cares? PromptTech has the power to spin the narrative however they want. We can help you, but you'll need more than just evidence."

"What do you suggest?" Kusi asked, his resolve hardening.

"You'll need to gain access to their mainframe—expose their operations from the inside. We can provide a diversion, but you two will have to infiltrate their facility. It won't be easy."Kusi exchanged a glance with Araba, whose brow furrowed with worry. "How do we even get in? They have security systems we can't bypass alone."

"I have contacts within PromptTech who can help," Nafissa interjected, stepping forward. "But they'll want something in return."

Kusi's heart sank. He had expected as much. "What kind of price?"

Nafissa smiled slyly. "They want the memory data you've stolen. They'll exchange it for access codes and insider information. But once you hand it over, you'll be at their mercy."

Araba's face turned pale. "We can't trust them. What if they double-cross us?"

Talon raised a hand to silence her, his gaze sharp. "This is the underworld, lady. Trust is a luxury we can't afford. But if you're smart, you'll ensure that you have contingencies in place. You need to protect yourselves."

Kusi nodded, feeling the weight of responsibility pressing down on him. "Alright. We'll do it. But we'll need a plan. If we're going to get in and out without getting caught, we need to know their layout, security protocols, everything."

"That's where my contacts come in," Nafissa said, her tone shifting to a more serious pitch. "I can get us intel, but it'll take time. We'll also need gear—disguises, tech, anything to ensure we don't draw attention."

"Then we prepare," Kusi declared, determination flickering in his eyes. "We gather what we need and strike when the opportunity arises."

Talon nodded approvingly. "Good. We'll coordinate with Nafissa. In the meantime, you two should lay low. Stay off the radar until we have everything set up." As they began discussing logistics and strategies, Kusi couldn't shake the feeling of impending danger. The world outside was teeming with hidden threats, and the clock was ticking.

Later that night, Kusi and Araba returned to the safe house. It felt more like a prison than a refuge, but they had no choice. The walls were thin, the shadows deep, and every creak of the floorboards echoed with unease.

Kusi flopped onto a worn-out chair, exhaustion weighing heavily on him. "I didn't expect things to get so complicated," he said, running a hand through his hair. "We're in over our heads."

Araba sat down beside him, her gaze distant. "What if we can't stop them, Kusi? What if it's all for nothing?"

He looked at her, his heart aching at the fear in her eyes. "We can't think like that. We have to focus on what we can do. If we expose them, we'll save lives. And you... you'll reclaim your identity."

Araba's brow furrowed. "What if I don't want to reclaim it? What if I'd rather stay hidden than risk being erased again?"

Kusi leaned closer, sensing the weight of her turmoil. "You're not just fighting for yourself anymore, Araba. There are others like you—people who've lost everything because of PromptTech. You can't let them win."

She met his gaze, her expression softening. "What if I'm not strong enough?"

"You are," Kusi assured her, his voice steady. "You've survived this long. That means you're strong enough to fight."

Silence enveloped them, the weight of their unspoken fears hanging in the air. Kusi reached out, placing his hand on hers. "We'll figure this out together. We have to believe that we can change things."

Just as they began to gather their thoughts, the door creaked open. Nafissa stepped inside, her demeanor shifting from casual to serious. "We've got a problem."

Kusi's heart raced. "What is it?"

"I was followed," she said, her eyes darting toward the door. "We need to move—now."

Kusi and Araba sprang to their feet, adrenaline coursing through their veins. "What do you mean followed?" Kusi asked, anxiety tightening his chest.

Nafissa frowned. "I saw a drone on my way here. It's scanning the area, looking for anyone out of place. We need to get out before they close in."

"Do you have a backup route?" Kusi asked, urgency propelling his voice.

Nafissa nodded. "Follow me. We'll head to another safe house until the heat dies down."

Kusi grabbed Araba's hand, pulling her close as they dashed out of the room. The flickering lights of the corridor felt like a countdown, and Kusi's instincts kicked in. They raced through the back halls, Nafissa leading the way with the precision of someone who had navigated these dark pathways many times before.

As they reached a side door, Kusi paused, glancing back. "We need to make sure we're not being followed."

Nafissa shook her head, urgency clear in her eyes. "We don't have time. If the drones pick up on us, we'll be caught."

With a determined nod, Kusi pushed the door open, leading Araba and Nafissa out into the night. The air felt electric, charged with the possibility of danger lurking in every shadow. They moved quickly, ducking into the underbelly of the city, weaving through narrow passages and alleyways.

"Where's the safe house?" Kusi asked, keeping his voice low.

Nafissa pointed to a rundown building in the distance. "That one. It's abandoned but secure."

As they approached the building, Kusi couldn't shake the feeling that they were walking into a trap. His instincts screamed for caution, but the urgency of their situation pushed them forward.

They entered the safe house, the air stale but undisturbed. Inside, the atmosphere was quiet, a welcome relief from the chaos outside. Nafissa activated a series of security measures, sealing the entrance.

Once they were inside, Kusi turned to her. "How long until the drones figure out where we went?"

"Depends on their system," Nafissa replied, her brow furrowed in thought. "But they'll find us eventually. We need to lay low and gather intel on our next move."

Araba sank onto an old chair, her expression weary. "What now?"

"We wait for the storm to pass," Kusi said, crossing his arms. "And then we strike."

As the hours dragged on, Kusi tried to focus on their plans, but doubt crept in like a thief in the night. Would they really be able to infiltrate PromptTech? Would they find the truth? Or were they simply setting themselves up for failure?

In the quiet of the safe house, Araba caught his eye. "What are you thinking?" "I'm just wondering how far we can go with this," he admitted, his voice barely above a whisper. "What if we uncover something even darker than we expected?"

She nodded, her gaze thoughtful. "We have to be ready for anything. But we can't let fear stop us. We've come this far."

Kusi felt a surge of determination. They were in this together, and together they could face whatever lay ahead. "You're right. We'll take it one step at a time."

As they settled in, Kusi couldn't shake the feeling that they were on the precipice of something monumental. But with every passing moment, the shadows of the past loomed larger, threatening to engulf them.

Chapter 8: The Echoes of PromptTech

The safe house was a haven shrouded in darkness, the peeling walls and dust-covered furniture standing as relics of a bygone era. Kusi leaned against the window, watching the streets outside, where the neon lights flickered like ghosts. The city pulsed with life, oblivious to the secrets hidden within its depths.

Araba sat at a makeshift table, her fingers tracing the surface as if searching for answers in the grain of the wood. The silence hung heavy, laden with the unspoken fears that haunted them both. Kusi turned away from the window, the weight of their mission pressing heavily on his shoulders.

"How long do you think we'll have to stay here?" Araba asked, her voice breaking the stillness.

Kusi shrugged. "As long as it takes for the heat to die down. But we can't afford to be idle. We need to gather more intel and prepare for the next phase."

She nodded, her brow furrowing. "I just... I can't shake the feeling that we're being watched."

Kusi's heart raced at her words. "We need to be careful. PromptTech has eyes everywhere."

As they settled into the rhythm of waiting, Kusi pulled out the devices Nafissa had given them, examining the tech that would help them infiltrate PromptTech. He carefully unpacked the sleek black tablet, its screen lighting up with a soft glow. He began scrolling through the files, searching for anything that might give them an edge.

Araba watched him, her interest piqued. "What are you looking for?"

"Access codes, security layouts, anything that can help us navigate their systems," Kusi replied, frowning as he sifted through the information. "I know we can get in, but we need to understand their defenses."

Suddenly, a notification popped up on the screen. Kusi's pulse quickened as he read the message: "Secure Network Access: A-17 Facility".

"This is it," he said, excitement lacing his voice. "The A-17 Facility is where they conduct their most classified research. If we can get in there and download their files, we can expose everything."

"But how do we get there?" Araba asked, skepticism lacing her tone. "A facility like that will be crawling with security."

"We need Nafissa's contacts," Kusi replied, determination hardening his resolve. "If they can get us inside, we can make our move."

Just as Kusi was deep in thought, the door creaked open, and Nafissa stepped inside. She looked both anxious and excited, her eyes sparkling with urgency. "I've got news," she said, her voice low and hurried.

Kusi leaned forward. "What did you find out?"

"I contacted my inside source at PromptTech. They're planning a gala at the headquarters next week. It's an opportunity for you to slip in unnoticed," she explained, her expression serious. "The security will be lower due to the event, but you'll need disguises."

"A gala?" Kusi echoed, disbelief creeping into his voice. "That's our chance to get inside?" Nafissa nodded. "Exactly. You can blend in with the crowd while we create a distraction outside. But you need to act fast—once the gala starts, they'll tighten security."

"What about the data we need?" Araba interjected. "Can we get into their systems during the event?"

"I'll work on that," Nafissa replied. "I can provide you with remote access, but you'll need to be quick. If you're caught, there's no telling what PromptTech will do to you."

Kusi exchanged a glance with Araba, a mixture of hope and anxiety swirling in the air. "We'll do it," he said firmly. "This is our chance to expose them."

Over the next few days, they prepared for the gala, gathering disguises and rehearsing their roles. Kusi donned a sleek suit, its fabric smooth against his skin, while Araba transformed into a vision of elegance, her hair styled and makeup accentuating her features. The transformation felt surreal, like they were stepping into a world far removed from the shadows they had been hiding in.

As they stood before a cracked mirror, Kusi studied Araba's reflection, the determination in her eyes almost palpable. "You look amazing," he said, his voice filled with admiration. "This is going to work."

Araba smiled faintly, her nerves apparent. "I hope so. I've never done anything like this before."

"You're not alone," Kusi reassured her, placing a hand on her shoulder. "We're in this together. Remember what we're fighting for."

As the day of the gala approached, the tension between them grew. Kusi felt the weight of responsibility pressing down on him—failure wasn't an option. They had to succeed for the countless lives at stake.

The night of the gala arrived, shrouded in an air of anticipation. As Kusi and Araba approached the towering PromptTech headquarters, the shimmering lights danced like stars against the dark sky. The building loomed over them, a monument to the corporation's power and influence.

Inside, the atmosphere buzzed with laughter and conversation, a stark contrast to the reality they had been living. Kusi tightened his grip on Araba's hand as they entered the grand ballroom, the opulence of the event overwhelming. Crystal chandeliers hung from the ceiling, casting a warm glow over the crowd dressed in finery.

"Stick close," Kusi murmured, scanning the room for potential threats. "We need to find a way to the back offices."

Araba nodded, her eyes wide as she took in the extravagant decor. "It's beautiful... but it feels wrong."

Kusi could relate. The glamour of the gala hid the sinister truths that lay beneath the surface. "Remember why we're here," he reminded her, his voice steady. "We're exposing the darkness hidden within this façade."

They moved through the crowd, exchanging pleasantries with the other attendees, keeping their identities hidden behind charming smiles. Kusi's heart raced as he spotted the corridor leading to the back offices, a sliver of hope shining through the chaos.

Just as they made their way towards the corridor, Nafissa's voice crackled through their comms. *"I've created a diversion at the entrance. Security is distracted—now's your chance."*

"*Copy that,*" Kusi replied, adrenaline surging. "We're heading to the back."

As they slipped away from the ballroom, Kusi felt a rush of exhilaration and dread. They were on the verge of uncovering the truth, but the shadows of danger loomed close behind.

They reached the corridor, the air thick with anticipation. Kusi pulled out the tablet, activating the remote access Nafissa had set up. "We need to get into their systems quickly," he said, his fingers flying over the screen.

"How do we find the data we need?" Araba asked, her voice barely above a whisper.

Kusi glanced at the screen, navigating through the digital labyrinth. "I'll search for any files related to the black market operation and memory manipulation experiments."

Suddenly, an alarm blared through the building, echoing off the walls like a harbinger of doom. "They've figured out the distraction," Kusi muttered, panic surging within him. "We have to hurry!"

As they raced down the corridor, the weight of the world pressed against their shoulders. Time was slipping away, and they needed to find the truth before it was too late.

Chapter 9: Shadows of Betrayal

Kusi's heart pounded in his chest as he sprinted down the dimly lit corridor, Araba close behind him. The blaring alarm was a relentless reminder of the danger they faced. They had to reach the data room before security tightened their grip on the building.

"Over here!" Kusi shouted, spotting a door marked with a digital lock. He quickly input the access code Nafissa had provided, his fingers trembling with urgency. The door clicked open, revealing a small, sterile room lined with servers and monitors.

As they stepped inside, Kusi could feel the weight of the knowledge stored within those walls. "This is it," he breathed, moving toward the nearest terminal. "Help me find the data we need."

Araba nodded, her eyes scanning the room for any sign of threats. "I'll keep watch," she said, her voice steady despite the chaos outside.

Kusi settled into the chair and powered on the terminal, the screen illuminating his face with a cold glow. He began to navigate through the system, searching for files related to memory manipulation and the black market operation. Lines of code raced across the screen, a digital maze that mirrored the complexity of their mission.

Minutes felt like hours as Kusi scrolled through the data. "Come on, come on," he muttered under his breath, frustration bubbling within him. Just as he was about to lose hope, a file labeled *"Project Requiem: Memory Erasure and Redistribution"* caught his eye.

"Got something!" he exclaimed, adrenaline coursing through his veins. He opened the file, his heart racing as he read the chilling details. PromptTech had been developing technology that not only erased memories but also redistributed them to create a compliant populace. "This is worse than we thought. They're not just erasing dissent; they're controlling the entire narrative!"

Araba leaned over his shoulder, her expression a mix of horror and disbelief. "They can manipulate who people are? This is... this is insane!"

"Yes," Kusi agreed, typing furiously to download the data. "If we can expose this, we can dismantle their operations."

Suddenly, the door rattled violently, causing Kusi's heart to leap into his throat. "We need to move!" he shouted, frantically saving the files to a secure drive.

Just as Kusi finished downloading the information, the door burst open, and a group of armed guards stormed into the room. *"Hands where we can see them!"* one of them barked, his weapon trained on Kusi and Araba.

Kusi's instincts kicked in. He grabbed Araba's arm and pulled her toward the far corner of the room, hoping to find a way out. "We can't get caught!" he hissed.

But before they could react, a figure stepped into the doorway, a familiar silhouette emerging from the shadows. It was Nafissa, her expression unreadable.

"Stop!" she commanded, raising her hands. "They're with me!"

Kusi's mind raced as he tried to process the situation. "Nafissa, what are you doing?" he asked, bewildered.

"I'm trying to help!" she insisted, glancing at the guards. "You have to trust me."

The guards hesitated, their weapons still trained on Kusi and Araba. "What's the meaning of this?" one of them demanded, confusion etched on his face.

"Let them go," Nafissa urged, her voice steady. "They have vital information.PromptTech needs to hear what they've discovered."

Kusi's heart sank. Could Nafissa truly be trusted?

Before he could voice his doubts, the lead guard stepped forward, his eyes narrowing. "You expect us to just let them walk away? They're intruders!"

"Let me handle this," Nafissa said, stepping closer. "I'll explain everything to the higher-ups. Just give me some time."

Kusi exchanged a glance with Araba, both of them unsure. Could they rely on Nafissa, or was this a setup?

In that moment of hesitation, the guards' radio crackled to life, a voice echoing through the static. "All units, we have a code red. The intruders are in the data room. Secure the area immediately."

The guards shared a worried look, their momentary distraction enough for Kusi to act. "We need to go now!" he shouted, grabbing Araba's hand.

Nafissa's eyes widened in realization. "No! You can't just—"

But it was too late. Kusi and Araba bolted past the guards, slipping out of the data room just as chaos erupted behind them. Shouts filled the air, and the sounds of footsteps echoed down the corridor.

"Where do we go?" Araba panted as they raced through the twisting hallways, the alarms blaring louder than ever.

"Follow me!" Kusi shouted, leading her down a narrow side corridor. He had studied the layout earlier, memorizing the escape routes. They pushed forward, adrenaline fueling their every step.

The echo of pursuing footsteps grew louder, and Kusi felt the pressure of time pressing against him. He glanced back to see guards in pursuit, their faces grim and determined. They had to find a way out, and fast.

"Turn left here!" Kusi shouted, and they veered sharply, the sound of their breaths mingling with the chaos around them. They stumbled into a storage area filled with crates and equipment, the shadows offering a brief respite.

Breathing heavily, Kusi scanned the room, searching for an exit. "We need to hide," he urged, ducking behind a stack of crates.

Araba followed suit, her eyes wide with fear. "What do we do now?"

Kusi pressed his back against the cool metal of the crate, his mind racing. "We wait for the guards to pass, then we'll find another way out. We can't let them catch us."

As they crouched in silence, the sounds of footsteps grew distant. Kusi felt a mix of relief and anxiety wash over him. They had escaped the immediate danger, but the reality of their situation pressed heavily on him. They were still deep within enemy territory, with guards likely combing the area for them.

"What do we do next?" Araba whispered, her voice trembling slightly. Kusi took a deep breath, trying to formulate a plan. "We need to regroup with Nafissa. She may have a way to get us out of here safely. But we can't trust her completely. We need to be cautious." Just as he spoke, Kusi noticed movement outside the storage area. A figure slipped past the door—another guard, scanning the corridor. Kusi's heart raced, and he motioned for Araba to remain silent.

As the guard moved further away, Kusi's thoughts turned to the information they had obtained. If they could get it into the right hands, it could change everything. They were fighting against a powerful corporation that sought to control minds, but they now had evidence that could expose their heinous practices.

Once the coast seemed clear, Kusi and Araba made their way through the storage area and out into the hall. They navigated the corridors cautiously, always alert to the sounds around them.

Finally, they spotted an emergency exit at the end of the hall. "There!" Kusi pointed, a glimmer of hope igniting within him. "That's our way out."

They sprinted toward the exit, adrenaline propelling them forward. Kusi pushed the door open, the cool night air rushing over them as they burst outside.

Breathless and shaken, they stood in the shadows of the building, the reality of their escape settling in. But they knew this was only the beginning of a much larger fight. The knowledge they had unearthed would change everything, but they needed to stay one step ahead of PromptTech.

"Let's get to safety and regroup," Kusi said, determination setting his features. "We have a battle to fight, and we won't let them erase our identities or our memories."

As they vanished into the night, the weight of their mission loomed larger than ever. PromptTech was a formidable foe, but Kusi and Araba were more than just pawns in their game. They were about to become warriors in a fight against the shadows of betrayal.

Chapter 10: The Fractured Mirror

Kusi and Araba navigated the darkened streets, the neon glow of the city illuminating their path as they moved stealthily through the back alleys. The air was thick with tension; each echoing footstep felt like a ticking clock. Kusi knew that they had to find a safe haven and regroup before they could strategize their next move.

"We should find somewhere to lay low for a bit," Araba suggested, her voice barely above a whisper. "I can't shake the feeling that we're being watched."

Kusi nodded in agreement, his instincts heightened. "I have a friend who runs a safe house in this area. He owes me a favor," he replied, glancing over his shoulder. "If anyone can help us, it's him."

As they continued deeper into the labyrinthine alleyways, the oppressive weight of the city's secrets felt palpable. Graffiti-covered walls whispered tales of dissent against the powerful corporations that held the populace in their grip. In a world where memories were bought and sold, the struggle for identity had become a battle for survival.

They soon arrived at an unassuming door nestled between two larger buildings, almost hidden from sight. Kusi knocked three times, a rhythm he had long memorized. Moments later, the door creaked open, revealing a scruffy man with wild hair and wary eyes. It was *Mossey*, Kusi's old friend.

"What the hell are you doing here?" Mossey asked, glancing around nervously before ushering them inside. "You're putting us all at risk."

"Long story," Kusi replied, shutting the door behind them. "We need a place to hide. PromptTech is after us."

Mossey's expression hardened, a mix of concern and disbelief crossing his features. "PromptTech? You've really stirred the pot this time, haven't you?"

Araba, still shaken, stepped forward. "We have vital information. They're manipulating memories on a massive scale. We need your help."

Mossey's demeanor shifted, curiosity replacing his initial hesitation. "What do you mean? Are you serious?"

Kusi took a deep breath, knowing the weight of their revelations. "We discovered files detailing Project Requiem. PromptTech is not just erasing memories; they're redistributing them to control the populace. We need to expose them."

Mossey's eyes widened, the gravity of their situation dawning on him. "If that's true, we're all in danger. This isn't just about you anymore; they'll come after anyone connected to you."

"Which is why we need to act fast," Kusi urged. "We can't let them erase dissent. We have to find a way to get this information to the public."

Mossey nodded, moving toward a cluttered table filled with old tech and wires. "I can help you set up a secure connection to transmit the data. But we need to be careful. They have eyes everywhere."

As Mossey worked, Kusi and Araba exchanged glances, an unspoken bond forming between them. They were both fighting against a common enemy, and despite the chaos around them, Kusi felt a sense of purpose solidify within him. Together, they would expose the truth, no matter the cost.

With Mossey's expertise, the trio quickly set up a makeshift operation in the dimly lit room. Kusi watched as Mossey connected various devices, his hands moving deftly over the equipment.

"This should do it," Mossey finally said, stepping back to reveal a flickering screen. "If we can get a secure line, we can transmit the files to a journalist I trust. She'll make sure it gets the attention it needs."

"Let's do it," Kusi said, adrenaline surging through him. "Every second counts."

Mossey initiated the connection, and the screen blinked to life, displaying a series of complex codes and signals. Kusi's heart raced as he thought of the ramifications of their actions. This was the moment that could change everything.

"Sending the data now," Mossey said, his focus unwavering.

Suddenly, a loud crash echoed outside, causing the room to vibrate. The three of them froze, hearts pounding in unison.

"Did you hear that?" Araba whispered, her voice laced with fear.

Kusi felt a rush of urgency. "They've found us," he said, scanning the room for an escape route. "We need to move—now!"

Before they could react, the door burst open, and armed guards poured into the safe house. "Hands in the air!" one of them shouted, leveling his weapon at Kusi, Araba, and Mossey.

Kusi's mind raced. They were cornered, with no clear way out. Mossey quickly reached for a hidden compartment beneath the table, pulling out a small device. "We can use this!" he yelled, pressing a button that activated a blinding flash of light.

The guards staggered back, momentarily disoriented. Kusi seized the opportunity, grabbing Araba's hand. "This way!" he shouted, leading her through a narrow passage at the back of the safe house.

As they sprinted through the dim corridor, Kusi could hear the guards recovering, their shouts echoing behind them. He had no idea where the passage would lead, but there was no time to hesitate.

The passage opened into a hidden underground network, a maze of tunnels that had been used by rebels for years. Dim lights flickered overhead as they hurried deeper into the shadows.

"What is this place?" Araba asked, her breath coming in quick gasps.

"An old resistance hideout," Kusi explained, glancing around at the graffiti and makeshift barricades. "People used to fight back against the corporations here. We might be able to find shelter."

They pressed on, their footsteps echoing through the darkened corridors. Kusi's thoughts swirled with uncertainty. They had lost their chance to expose PromptTech, and now they were entangled in a deeper web of danger.

But as they moved further into the network, Kusi felt a flicker of hope. If they could connect with the remnants of the resistance, perhaps they could rally enough support to take down PromptTech once and for all.

As they navigated the labyrinth of tunnels, they finally stumbled upon a larger chamber filled with people huddled around makeshift tables, sharing whispered conversations. The atmosphere was tense but alive, a stark contrast to the oppressive world above.

"Who are these people?" Araba asked, her eyes widening at the sight of the underground network.

"They're the last remnants of the resistance," Kusi replied, feeling a sense of camaraderie in the air. "If anyone can help us, it's them."

Kusi stepped forward, raising his voice to address the gathered crowd. "Listen up! We have information about PromptTech's latest operations. They're manipulating memories on a grand scale, and we need to act now!"

A murmur spread through the crowd, and Kusi could see the spark of determination igniting in their eyes. They were hungry for a fight, for the chance to reclaim their identities and their futures.

An older woman with silver-streaked hair stepped forward, her gaze piercing. "You're Kusi, the memory broker," she said, her voice steady. "I've heard rumors about your exploits. What do you propose we do?"

Kusi felt a surge of resolve. "We need to expose PromptTech. They're erasing dissent, controlling the population, and we can't let that happen. We have the evidence to take them down, but we need numbers. We need a united front."

The room erupted with fervor, voices rising as they debated their next steps. Kusi could feel the tension building, the weight of their shared purpose binding them together.

"Together, we can take the fight to them," Kusi continued, his heart pounding with conviction. "We won't be erased; we will reclaim our memories and our identities!"

As Kusi spoke, he saw the fire of resistance igniting in the eyes of those around him. They were no longer just individuals; they were a collective, united by a common cause.

"Count me in," Araba said, stepping forward, determination etched on her face. "I won't let them control who I am."

One by one, others joined in, pledging their support. The room filled with energy, a palpable sense of purpose as they prepared to confront the looming threat of PromptTech.

Kusi felt a sense of belonging swell within him. They were no longer alone in their fight; they had allies, fellow warriors ready to stand against the oppressive force that sought to control their memories and their lives.

As the meeting drew to a close, Kusi knew the road ahead would be fraught with danger, but they were ready to take on the shadows. They had gathered a coalition, a force ready to challenge the powerful corporation and reclaim their identities.

With their newfound allies, they began to formulate a plan, each person contributing their skills and knowledge. Together, they would shine a light on the dark underbelly of memory manipulation and expose PromptTech for the threat it truly was.

As Kusi looked around the room, he felt the weight of responsibility on his shoulders. They were about to embark on a journey that would test their resolve and challenge everything they believed in. But united, they would face the shadows of betrayal together, ready to reclaim their memories and fight for their future.

Chapter 11: The Convergence of Shadows

The dimly lit underground chamber buzzed with an energy that hadn't existed before Kusi and Araba arrived. Conversations overlapped, voices rising and falling like the tides of a gathering storm. Kusi stood at the front, flanked by Araba and the silver-haired woman, who introduced herself as Brago, the leader of the resistance.

"Tonight, we prepare for war," Brago declared, her voice cutting through the din. "PromptTech believes they can control us through fear and manipulation, but they've underestimated the power of our memories—our identities!"

Cheers erupted, resonating against the concrete walls, fueling the fire within Kusi's heart. The room filled with fervor, a cacophony of determination. He could feel the tide shifting; they were no longer passive victims but active participants in their destiny.

The group began to strategize. Maps and blueprints of PromptTech's facilities were spread across the tables, illuminated by the glow of flickering lights. Kusi studied the documents, his mind racing with possibilities. He turned to Mossey, who was huddled over the maps with a group of tech-savvy rebels.

"We need to find a way to access their central data hub," Mossey explained, his fingers tracing lines on the map. "That's where they store all the information on their memory trading operations."

Araba leaned in, her brow furrowing. "If we can get in there, we can expose their entire operation. But how do we bypass their security systems?"

Brago interjected, her expression resolute. "We'll create diversions. If we can distract their guards and cause chaos at their main facility, we'll have a window to slip in and extract the data."

As the strategy session continued, Kusi felt the weight of his past decisions pressing down on him. This wasn't just about him or Araba anymore; it was about every soul whose memories had been erased, every individual who had suffered under PromptTech's grasp. They needed to succeed—not just for themselves, but for the future of their society.

"Here's the plan," Kusi said, his voice steady as he addressed the group. "We'll split into two teams. One will create a distraction outside the main facility—set off some fireworks, cause a scene. The second team, including me, will infiltrate the building during the chaos. We'll access the data hub and download everything we can find."

The resistance members nodded, some exchanging anxious glances. They were preparing to step into the jaws of danger, but Kusi could sense their resolve. They were ready to fight.

As the meeting wrapped up, Kusi found a moment alone with Araba. They stood at the edge of the chamber, the noise of planning and preparation fading into the background.

"Are you sure about this?" Araba asked, her eyes searching his. "This is dangerous. We could lose everything."

Kusi took a deep breath, feeling the weight of her concern. "I know it's risky, but if we don't do this, we're giving PromptTech permission to continue erasing lives. We can't allow that."

Araba nodded, her expression softening. "You're right. I just... I've lost so much already. I don't want to lose you too."

A surge of emotion swept over Kusi as he reached out, gently squeezing her hand. "You won't lose me. We're in this together. We'll fight for our memories, for our identities. No one can erase us if we stand united."

As night fell, the city was cloaked in shadows, but the underground resistance pulsed with life. Kusi, Araba, Mossey, and a handful of others gathered their gear, arming themselves with makeshift weapons and tech. The air was thick with anticipation, each person understanding the gravity of the mission ahead.

"Remember, stay close to your team,"Brago instructed as they prepared to depart. "Trust each other, and don't hesitate. Once we start, there's no turning back."

Kusi felt his pulse quicken. This was it. The moment they had all been preparing for had finally arrived.

As they emerged from the safe house into the cool night air, the city loomed before them—a vast expanse of neon lights and darkness. Kusi could see the distant silhouette of the PromptTech facility, an imposing structure that represented everything they were fighting against.

Kusi led his team through the alleys, their hearts racing with adrenaline. The plan was simple but fraught with uncertainty. They would split at the designated point, with the distraction team moving to the east side of the building while Kusi's team approached the entrance.

The closer they got, the more the tension mounted. Kusi felt the weight of his mission pressing down on him, but he also felt a sense of purpose. He was not just fighting for himself; he was fighting for everyone who had been silenced.

They reached the point where they would split, and Kusi turned to Araba, who stood beside him, her determination evident.

"Be careful out there," he said, a sense of urgency in his voice.

"Same to you," Araba replied, her gaze unwavering. "Let's do this."

With one last glance at each other, they parted ways, Kusi's heart pounding as he moved toward the entrance.

As Kusi and his team approached the facility, they could see the distraction team setting their plan in motion. Fireworks erupted in the air, a brilliant display of colors that illuminated the night sky. Alarms began to blare, and chaos ensued outside the building.

Kusi felt a rush of adrenaline. The distraction was working. He and his team slipped into the shadows, making their way toward the entrance amidst the chaos.

"Now's our chance!" Kusi urged, pushing forward. They reached the main door, which stood ajar, the guards distracted by the commotion outside.

Once inside, they were met with a stark contrast—the sterile, cold interior of the facility felt oppressive compared to the lively chaos outside. Fluorescent lights buzzed overhead, casting a harsh glow on the sleek surfaces.

Kusi motioned for silence, leading his team down a narrow corridor. "We need to find the data hub," he whispered, glancing at the nearby maps.

Suddenly, the sound of footsteps echoed behind them. Kusi's heart raced as he motioned for everyone to hide. They pressed against the walls, holding their breath as guards passed by, oblivious to their presence.

Once the coast was clear, Kusi exhaled, his pulse still racing. "Let's keep moving," he said, leading them deeper into the facility.

The corridors twisted and turned, each doorway potentially leading to danger. Kusi relied on the schematics Mossey had provided, directing them toward the central hub. As they moved, he couldn't shake the feeling that they were being watched.

Every shadow felt alive, every creak in the building amplifying the tension. Finally, they reached a heavy door marked with a security panel.

"This is it," Kusi said, his heart pounding in his chest. "This is the data hub."

Mossey stepped forward, quickly assessing the panel. "I can hack this, but it'll take a minute," he said, his fingers flying over the console.

Kusi and the others stood guard, anxiety mounting as they waited. The sounds of chaos outside faded, replaced by the ominous silence of the facility.

"Come on, Mossey," Kusi urged, glancing nervously at the door behind them. "We don't have much time."

With a final beep, the door slid open, revealing a room filled with rows of servers, blinking lights, and whirring machinery.

"Let's get to work," Kusi said, stepping inside.

They quickly spread out, Mossey working on one terminal while Kusi searched for relevant files. His heart raced as he navigated the labyrinth of data, his fingers dancing over the keyboard.

"What are you looking for?" Araba asked, her voice low as she scanned the room.

"Anything related to Project Requiem," Kusi replied, eyes scanning lines of code. "We need proof of what they're doing."

Just then, alarms began to blare, a shrill sound echoing through the room. "They know we're here!" Mossey shouted, his hands flying over the keyboard. "I'm almost done!"

Kusi's heart sank, panic flooding his veins. "We have to hurry! They'll send guards any second now!"

As Kusi frantically searched through the files, a surge of dread filled him. They were running out of time. He could hear the footsteps approaching, the sound growing louder with each passing moment.

"Got it!" Mossey exclaimed, a triumphant grin on his face. "I've extracted the data! We're good to go!"

Kusi turned to grab the drive, but before he could move, the door burst open. Guards flooded into the room, weapons drawn.

"Freeze!" one of them shouted, taking aim.

Kusi's instincts kicked in. "Run!" he yelled, pushing Araba toward the exit. They had to escape, and they had to do it fast.

Chaos erupted as they darted past the guards, narrowly avoiding gunfire. Kusi felt a rush of adrenaline as they raced through the corridors, the alarms blaring around them.

"Head for the back exit!" Mossey shouted, leading the way. They sprinted through the facility, heartbeats pounding in sync with their footsteps.

Kusi glanced back, seeing guards in pursuit. They were gaining on them. "Faster!" he urged, pushing himself harder.

Finally, they reached the back exit, bursting through the door into the night air. Kusi inhaled deeply, but there was no time to celebrate.

"Keep moving!" Brago shouted from the shadows. The distraction team had regrouped, and they needed to escape the area quickly.

As they ran, Kusi felt a mixture of triumph and fear. They had the data, but they were still being hunted. The reality of their situation weighed heavily on him, but they were alive, and they had a chance to expose PromptTech.

"Over here!" Brago led them into an alley, where they regrouped and caught their breath. "Did you get it?"

Kusi held up the drive, a sense of accomplishment flooding through him. "We got it."

Brago's expression shifted, a glimmer of hope in her eyes. "Then let's show the world what PromptTech is really doing."

As they stood together in the shadows, Kusi felt a sense of purpose reigniting within him. They had taken the first step toward reclaiming their identities, but there was still much to be done.

Together, they would expose the truth and fight against the oppression that sought to erase them. This was only the beginning.

Chapter 12: Fractured Alliances

The adrenaline of their escape gradually faded, replaced by a heavy silence as Kusi, Araba, and the resistance regrouped in the safe house. The dimly lit room was a stark contrast to the chaos they had just experienced, the air thick with tension and anticipation. Kusi held the data drive tightly in his hand, feeling the weight of their mission press down on him.

"What's next?" Mossey asked, glancing around the room, his face a mixture of excitement and apprehension. The adrenaline rush still lingered in the air, leaving everyone on edge.

Brago stepped forward, her silver hair catching the faint light. "We need to analyze the data. It could contain the evidence we need to expose PromptTech's operations, but we have to be careful. They will be on high alert after tonight."

Araba leaned closer, her brow furrowing. "Do we know what kind of information we're dealing with?"

"Not yet," Kusi replied, his heart racing. "But whatever it is, it could be crucial in rallying more people to our cause."

As they gathered around a makeshift table strewn with old monitors and discarded tech, Kusi inserted the data drive into one of the devices. The screen flickered to life, lines of code rapidly scrolling across the display. Mossey and Brago leaned in closer, their eyes scanning the data as Kusi navigated through the folders.

Suddenly, Araba gasped. "Look at this!" She pointed to a folder labeled *"Project Requiem."*

Kusi's heart sank. "That's it. That's what we need."

Mossey began typing furiously, extracting files from the folder. "If we can uncover the specifics of this project, it could expose PromptTech's methods for memory manipulation," he said, his voice steady.

As Mossey worked, Kusi felt the room's tension intensify. Each passing moment felt like a countdown, the weight of their discovery pressing down on them.

The files revealed a grim picture. Kusi read through reports detailing memory erasure procedures, the methods used to erase dissenters, and how the corporation profited from trading memories. His stomach twisted with disgust.

"They're treating people like commodities," Kusi muttered, anger boiling within him. "This is worse than we imagined."

"Not just commodities," Araba added, her voice trembling. "They're erasing entire lives. We have to stop this."

As they continued to sift through the information, Kusi stumbled upon a document that made his blood run cold. It detailed a list of names—people who had been targeted for memory erasure. Among them, Kusi spotted a familiar name: *Kira Alton*, his childhood friend who had disappeared years ago.

"Kira..." Kusi whispered, his voice barely audible. Memories of their friendship flooded back, moments of laughter and shared dreams. "They took her."

Araba placed a hand on his shoulder, her eyes filled with compassion. "We'll find a way to help her."

As Kusi processed the implications of their discovery, Brago's voice broke through his thoughts. "We need to spread this information. We can't be the only ones fighting against this."

Mossey nodded. "We should reach out to other factions, but we must be cautious. PromptTech will have eyes everywhere. They won't hesitate to silence anyone who stands in their way."

Just then, a young rebel named Jaxon burst into the room, his face flushed with urgency. "You need to see this!" he exclaimed, holding a handheld device that displayed a live news feed.

The screen flickered to life, showing a news anchor reporting on the chaos outside the PromptTech facility. "PromptTech has issued a statement condemning the actions of the so-called 'rebels' who attacked their headquarters last night. They claim to be safeguarding the populace from a growing threat."

Kusi felt a surge of frustration. "They're spinning this to make us look like the enemy."

Brago's expression hardened. "We need to counter their narrative. If we don't act quickly, they will control the story."

As the tension in the room escalated, Kusi could feel the fissures forming within the alliance. Some members expressed concerns about contacting other factions, fearing betrayal and loss of trust.

"What if they're working with PromptTech?" one voice chimed in, skepticism hanging in the air. "We can't risk exposing ourselves further."

Kusi glanced at Araba, sensing her unease. "We can't let fear dictate our actions. If we stay isolated, we'll never be able to make a real impact."

"Isolation is our only safeguard," another rebel countered. "We're already exposed. We can't afford to be vulnerable again."

The room erupted into a heated debate, voices clashing as doubts surfaced. Kusi felt a knot forming in his stomach. The fractures in their alliance were widening, and he feared it could jeopardize everything they had fought for.

Amid the chaos, Araba stepped forward, her voice steady but firm. "If we don't reach out to others, we will fail. PromptTech has power and resources, but we have something they don't—determination. We've seen the truth. We can't let fear silence us."

The room fell silent, her words resonating with the group. Kusi could see the glimmers of resolve flickering in their eyes. Araba was right; they had to take a stand.

Brago nodded slowly, her expression thoughtful. "Perhaps we can approach the dissenting factions carefully. We must find those who have lost as much as we have and are willing to fight back."

Mossey chimed in, his voice filled with conviction. "We need to create a network. If we can rally enough people, we can counter PromptTech's narrative."

With a newfound sense of purpose, Kusi took a deep breath, the anger from earlier morphing into determination. "Let's do this. We have to be strategic about our outreach. We'll share the information we uncovered, and we'll let others know we're not afraid."

As they finalized their plan, Kusi felt a sense of unity returning. They were fractured but not broken. Together, they would fight back against PromptTech's manipulation and reclaim their identities.

In the days that followed, the group worked tirelessly to connect with other factions, using encrypted channels to ensure their communications remained secure. Kusi found himself reaching out to those he had once thought lost, the memories of shared experiences fueling his resolve.

They crafted messages that outlined their mission, detailing the evidence they had gathered against PromptTech. Slowly but surely, they began to form alliances with like-minded individuals and groups who shared their cause.

But as they strengthened their network, Kusi couldn't shake the feeling that they were being watched. PromptTech's reach was vast, and he suspected they were tracking the dissenters, waiting for the right moment to strike.

"Stay vigilant," Kusi advised the group during their meetings. "We can't let our guard down. We need to prepare for anything."

Just as things seemed to be moving in their favor, a chilling message arrived through one of their secure channels. It was from an unknown source but carried the unmistakable mark of betrayal.

"We know who you are," it read. *"Your alliances will lead to your downfall. PromptTech is always watching."*

The room fell silent as Kusi read the message aloud, dread creeping into the hearts of everyone present.

"Who could it be?" Mossey asked, his expression turning dark. "Is there a mole among us?"

"We can't trust anyone now," Brago said, her tone grave. "We need to tighten our ranks and figure out where this information is coming from."

Kusi felt the weight of their situation bearing down on him. The alliance they had worked so hard to build was threatened, and he knew they had to act quickly.

As the shadows of betrayal loomed over them, Kusi made a vow to himself. They had come too far to let fear and paranoia fracture their mission. Together, they would fight against PromptTech, no matter the cost.

"Let's uncover the truth," Kusi said, his voice filled with determination. "We'll expose PromptTech and their methods. We won't let them erase our identities or our lives."

With renewed purpose, they began to strategize their next steps, preparing to confront the darkness that threatened to engulf them. This was not just a fight for their memories—it was a fight for their future.

Chapter 13: Echoes of Resistance

In the days that followed the ominous warning, Kusi and the resistance worked tirelessly to fortify their alliances. They moved with a sense of urgency, aware that the clock was ticking. PromptTech's grip on society was tightening, and they had to act before it was too late.

The safe house buzzed with activity. Rebels gathered around flickering screens, exchanging ideas and developing strategies to expose PromptTech's dark operations. Kusi felt the weight of leadership heavy on his shoulders, but it was tempered by the resilience of those around him. They were fighting for more than just survival; they were fighting for justice, for the lives that had been erased, and for their own identities.

One evening, Brago suggested a clandestine meeting with representatives from the most prominent dissenting factions. "We need to share what we know and consolidate our resources," she proposed, her silver hair shimmering in the dim light. "If we present a united front, we can challenge PromptTech more effectively."

Kusi agreed, recognizing the importance of unity in their struggle. He contacted several factions, arranging a secret meeting at a location far from prying eyes—an abandoned warehouse on the outskirts of the city. As they prepared for the meeting, Kusi's heart raced with anticipation and dread. Would they find allies, or would their efforts lead to further division?

On the night of the meeting, Kusi, Araba, Brago, and Mossey arrived early, ensuring the space was secure. The warehouse was dimly lit, shadows dancing along the walls as they set up their makeshift gathering space.

One by one, the representatives arrived—faces familiar from news reports and whispers in the underbelly of society. There were members of the *Cobalt Collective,* known for their technological prowess; the *United Voices*, a group advocating for the rights of those affected by memory manipulation; and several smaller factions seeking justice for their lost loved ones.

As the last representative entered, Kusi felt a wave of determination wash over him. They were united by a common purpose, and together, they would challenge the oppressive system.

As they took their seats, Kusi stood up to address the group. "Thank you all for coming," he began, his voice steady. "We are here because we share a common enemy: PromptTech. We've uncovered evidence of their heinous practices, and we believe it's time to expose them."

Murmurs of agreement echoed throughout the room.

A representative from the Cobalt Collective, a woman named *Vera*, spoke up. "What have you found? We need concrete evidence to rally the masses."

Kusi stepped forward, holding up the data drive. "This contains detailed reports on Project Requiem—how they erase memories, the names of their targets, and the extent of their operations. We need to disseminate this information to the public."

Mossey chimed in, "But we need a plan to protect ourselves while we do it. PromptTech will retaliate."

Brago nodded, her expression serious. "We must create a decentralized information network. If we distribute the data widely, it will be harder for PromptTech to suppress it."

The room buzzed with ideas as they strategized, discussing how to spread the truth without endangering themselves. They decided to use encrypted channels and anonymous servers to ensure their messages reached the public while protecting their identities.

Just as they began to solidify their plan, the air shifted. A representative from the United Voices, a young man named *Eli*, leaned forward, his voice a low whisper. "There are rumors of a mole among the factions. We can't trust everyone in this room."

A tense silence fell over the gathering, eyes darting nervously. Kusi felt a chill run down his spine.

"Who?" Brago asked, her voice barely above a whisper.

"I don't know," Eli replied, his gaze scanning the faces around him. "But we need to be cautious. We're walking into a trap."

The atmosphere turned heavy with suspicion. Kusi exchanged glances with Araba, their shared concern palpable. "We can't let paranoia cripple us," Kusi said, trying to break the tension. "We need to focus on our mission."

But doubt lingered in the air, and discussions grew quieter as everyone contemplated the implications of a potential traitor in their midst.

Vera spoke up again, her voice firm. "We should establish a vetting process for our communications. Only those we trust should have access to sensitive information."

"Agreed," Mossey added. "If we can create layers of security, we can minimize the risk of a leak. With a plan in motion, the group began to solidify their alliances. They exchanged contact information, ensuring that each faction had secure ways to communicate without revealing their identities.

As they prepared to leave, Kusi felt a spark of hope. They were making strides, forging connections that could empower their cause. But lingering doubts weighed heavily on him. Who could they trust?

Outside the warehouse, the night air was thick with tension. Kusi looked up at the stars, wondering if they would ever find peace in a world dominated by fear and manipulation.

As Kusi, Araba, Brago, and Mossey, stood together, they knew the road ahead would be fraught with danger. The fractures within their alliance still lingered, but they were united by a common purpose: to expose PromptTech and reclaim their identities.

Just then, Kusi spotted a figure lurking in the shadows, watching intently. His heart raced as he approached the person, ready to confront them. It was a woman, her hood pulled low over her face, but Kusi could see the glimmer of recognition in her eyes.

"Wait!" Kusi called out, causing the figure to pause.

"Are you Kusi?" the woman asked, her voice low and urgent.

"Yes, who are you?" Kusi replied, instinctively reaching for the weapon concealed at his side.

"I'm Lena," she said, stepping into the light. "I've been sent by a faction outside the city. We're aware of your mission and want to help."

Kusi's heart raced. "What do you know about us?"

"I've heard about your plan to expose PromptTech. We have resources and connections that can aid you," Lena explained, her eyes darting around nervously. "But we need to act quickly. There are whispers of a raid planned on dissenters."

Kusi exchanged a glance with Araba, a mixture of skepticism and intrigue swirling in his mind. "How do we know you're not working for PromptTech?"

"I understand your hesitation," Lena replied, her voice earnest. "But if you're going to stand against them, you need allies. We have people who can help you distribute the information safely."

Kusi considered her words carefully. The stakes were high, and any wrong move could jeopardize everything they had worked for.

"What's your angle?" Mossey asked, stepping closer, suspicion etched on his face.

Lena took a deep breath. "My brother was one of the first targets of Project Requiem. I've lost everything to PromptTech. I want justice as much as you do."

Kusi felt the weight of her words. Her pain mirrored his own, the loss echoing in their shared struggle. "If we do this, we need absolute trust. No secrets, no lies," he said firmly.

"Agreed," Lena replied, determination shining in her eyes. "I can provide you with intel on their movements and help coordinate a counteroffensive."

Kusi glanced at Araba, seeking her opinion. She nodded, her expression resolute. "We can't turn away help when we need it most."

With a heavy heart, Kusi extended his hand. "Alright, you're in. But remember, if you betray us, there will be no second chances."

Lena clasped his hand firmly, her grip strong. "I won't let you down."

As Kusi, Araba, Brago, Mossey, and Lena stood together, they knew the road ahead would be fraught with danger. The fractures within their alliance still lingered, but they were united by a common purpose: to expose PromptTech and reclaim their identities.

The battle was just beginning, and Kusi could feel the storm brewing on the horizon. Together, they would face the darkness head-on, armed with the truth and a determination that could not be extinguished.

Chapter 14: The Edge of Darkness

As dawn broke over the sprawling city, Kusi awoke to a sense of impending turmoil. The previous night's revelations echoed in his mind. They had made a dangerous pact with Lena, one that could either solidify their cause or plunge them deeper into chaos.

In the safe house, the atmosphere was charged with a mix of excitement and anxiety. Brago and Mossey were reviewing the intel Lena had provided, poring over maps and security protocols for PromptTech's facilities. Araba sat beside Kusi, her fingers tracing the patterns on the worn tabletop, lost in thought.

"Are you alright?" Kusi asked gently, concern etched on his face.

Araba looked up, her eyes searching his. "I'm just thinking about what's at stake. We're not just fighting for ourselves anymore; we're fighting for everyone who's been silenced."

Her words resonated with Kusi, deepening his resolve. They were stepping into a dangerous game, but they couldn't afford to turn back now.

They spent the morning strategizing, Kusi outlining the first steps of their plan. "We need to get the information out as soon as possible. If we can time it with a public event, we'll maximize our reach."

Brago nodded, her fingers flying across the keyboard. "There's a technology expo happening in the central square this weekend. If we can infiltrate it, we can broadcast the data directly."

Mossey leaned back, arms crossed. "PromptTech will be heavily monitoring the event. We need a distraction to divert their attention."

"I have a few contacts in the underground media," Lena interjected. "They can help us spread the word without drawing too much attention."

Kusi felt a flicker of hope. Their plan was taking shape, but he was acutely aware of the danger. PromptTech wouldn't take their efforts lightly, and betrayal loomed in the air like a thick fog.

As the days passed, they worked diligently, gathering resources and preparing for the expo. Kusi felt the pressure mounting; every moment counted. He couldn't shake the feeling that someone was watching, a shadow lurking just beyond their reach.

During a late-night meeting, as they discussed their final preparations, a sudden noise shattered the tension. The door to the safe house burst open, and a figure stumbled in, gasping for breath.

"Help! They're coming!" the newcomer shouted, eyes wild with fear.

Kusi rushed to the figure, his heart racing. "Who? Who's coming?"

"Operatives from PromptTech! I overheard them talking about a raid. They know about your plans!" the figure gasped, doubling over as he caught his breath.

Araba's eyes widened in alarm. "How did they find us?"

"I don't know! I was just passing by, and I heard them discussing your names. They're onto you!" he exclaimed.

A palpable tension enveloped the room. Kusi felt a surge of adrenaline; they needed to act quickly. "We can't stay here. We have to move!"

They gathered their belongings, adrenaline surging through their veins. Kusi turned to Lena, urgency in his voice. "Do you have a safe place we can go?"

"Yes," Lena replied, her voice steady despite the chaos. "There's an old safe house we can reach if we hurry. Follow me!"

As they fled into the night, Kusi's mind raced with thoughts of betrayal. Was there a traitor in their midst, or had their movements simply been too careless? Doubt gnawed at him, but there was no time to ponder.

They navigated through the winding alleys of the city, hearts pounding in sync as they raced against the clock. Kusi kept glancing over his shoulder, searching for any sign of pursuit. Shadows flickered in the corners of his vision, and paranoia seeped into his thoughts.

Eventually, they reached the old safe house, a dilapidated building tucked away in a forgotten part of the city. Kusi quickly surveyed the area, ensuring they weren't being followed.

Inside, they huddled together, catching their breath. The weight of the situation settled heavily on Kusi's shoulders. He looked around at his comrades—Brago, Mossey, Lena, and Araba—all of them fighting for a cause larger than themselves.

"We need to regroup and figure out our next move," Kusi said, his voice firm. "We can't let fear dictate our actions."

Araba nodded, her expression resolute. "We need to trust each other now more than ever. If there's a mole among us, we can't let that ruin our mission."

The atmosphere grew tense as they shared their suspicions, each person's gaze flickering with doubt. Kusi felt the unease settle in his gut like a stone.

Brago leaned forward, her brow furrowed. "What if we're being tracked? We need to change our plans and lay low for a while."

"No!" Kusi interjected, his voice rising. "We can't let them dictate our movements. We have to strike while we still can."

"Easy for you to say," Mossey shot back, frustration seeping into his tone. "You're not the one whose life is on the line."

"Enough!" Lena snapped, her voice sharp. "Arguing won't solve anything. We need a plan, and we need to stick to it."

As tensions simmered, Kusi felt the divide forming among them. The pressure of their circumstances was mounting, and he realized that doubt could shatter their fragile alliance.

"We need to find out who's been feeding information to PromptTech," Kusi urged. "We need to establish trust again."

"I can dig into the communications," Brago offered, her voice steadier now. "If anyone's been leaking, I'll find the evidence."

"Do it discreetly," Kusi warned, his eyes scanning the room. "We can't afford to tip them off."

Later that night, as the group settled into uneasy silence, Kusi turned to Araba. "Do you think we can trust Lena?"

Araba sighed, her expression contemplative. "I don't know. But I feel she has as much to lose as we do. We need allies, Kusi. We can't fight this battle alone."

"I know," Kusi admitted, feeling the weight of leadership pressing down on him. "But I also know that trust is fragile, and we can't afford to be naïve."

The following morning, Brago returned with unsettling news. "I've been monitoring communications," she said, her voice tense. "There's chatter about a traitor within the resistance. They're trying to find out where we are."

Kusi felt his stomach drop. "What do we do?"

"We need to create a diversion," Brago suggested. "If we can draw their attention away from us, it will buy us time to regroup."

"Then we'll execute the plan," Kusi decided, determination igniting within him. "We'll still go through with the expo. If we can get the information out, we'll expose their operations once and for all."

As they finalized their plans, Kusi felt a renewed sense of purpose. They would face PromptTech head-on, but he couldn't shake the feeling that shadows were closing in around them.

In the days leading up to the expo, the group worked tirelessly, fortifying their connections and ensuring their plans were foolproof. But each passing moment deepened Kusi's unease. Could they truly trust each other in this fight against a formidable enemy?

As the day of reckoning approached, Kusi knew they would either emerge victorious or fall into the depths of betrayal.

Chapter 15: Echoes of Ascension

The day of the technology expo dawned, casting a vibrant glow over the city, yet an air of tension hung in the atmosphere. Kusi stood at the window of their temporary safe house, his eyes scanning the skyline. He could feel the electric hum of anticipation and danger. Today was the culmination of their efforts, but he also knew it could unravel everything they had worked for.

Inside, the team buzzed with a mix of excitement and anxiety as they prepared for the day ahead. Brago was finalizing the technical setup, ensuring that their broadcast equipment was hidden yet functional. Mossey checked their exit routes while Lena coordinated with their underground media contacts.

Araba joined Kusi at the window, her expression reflective. "This is it, isn't it?" she said quietly. "The moment we've been waiting for."

"Yes," Kusi replied, a knot forming in his stomach. "But it's also the moment I fear the most."

As they gathered for a final briefing, Kusi laid out their strategy one last time. "Remember, our primary goal is to get the evidence out to the public. Once we do that, we'll have the support of the people, and PromptTech will lose its grip on power."

Brago nodded, her focus unwavering. "I'll be in the back, monitoring the feed and making sure everything goes smoothly. If things go south, I'll trigger the backup plan." "Good," Kusi replied, casting a glance around the room. "And keep an eye on each other. We don't know what tricks PromptTech might have up their sleeves."

As they made their way to the expo, the bustling streets were filled with people eager to witness the latest technological advancements. Kusi's heart raced. Each step felt heavier than the last as the weight of their mission pressed upon him.

Upon arrival at the expo, the atmosphere was electric. Crowds milled about, their chatter blending into a cacophony of excitement. Kusi felt the buzz of anticipation, but beneath that lay an undercurrent of fear.

"Stick to the plan," Kusi reminded the group, leading them through the throng of attendees. "We'll split up to avoid drawing attention, and meet at the designated spot once we've secured our objectives."

As they dispersed, Kusi felt a mix of adrenaline and anxiety surging through him. He was acutely aware of the stakes involved; one misstep could expose them all.

Navigating through the expo, Kusi caught glimpses of PromptTech's latest innovations—dazzling displays showcasing memory implants, neural enhancements, and AI-driven technologies. Each booth felt like a monument to their manipulation of humanity, and Kusi's resolve hardened.

He made his way to a secluded area at the edge of the expo, where he was set to meet with Lena's contacts. He hoped they would be able to help amplify their message, broadcasting it to a wider audience.

Just as he reached the rendezvous point, a figure stepped out from behind a nearby booth. "Kusi?" the woman asked, her voice low and urgent.

"Yeah, that's me," he replied, eyes narrowing. "You must be one of Lena's contacts." The woman nodded, glancing around nervously. "We need to move. PromptTech is tightening security. They're aware something's happening today."

Kusi's heart sank. "What do you mean?"

"I overheard them talking. They've been monitoring chatter and are expecting trouble. You have to hurry if you want to get the information out."

With urgency coursing through him, Kusi made a quick decision. "Let's go. We need to regroup with the others."

As they moved swiftly through the expo, Kusi felt the tension rise. The energy of the crowd began to shift, an unease settling over the attendees as whispers of something amiss rippled through the air.

"Stay close," he instructed the woman, whose name he still didn't know. "We can't afford to get separated."

Suddenly, the atmosphere shifted dramatically as a loudspeaker crackled to life. A voice rang out, commanding attention.

"Attention, everyone! PromptTech is implementing emergency protocols. Please remain calm and exit the premises immediately."

Kusi's heart raced. "This isn't good," he muttered. "They know we're here."

Panic erupted as people began to rush toward the exits. Kusi grabbed the woman's arm, pulling her through the chaos. "We need to find the others!" he shouted over the din.

The crowd surged around them, a wave of confusion and fear. Kusi scanned the area, desperately searching for Araba, Brago, and Mossey amidst the chaos.

"Over there!" the woman shouted, pointing toward a cluster of familiar faces. Kusi pushed through the throng, adrenaline surging as he reached his friends.

"Did you hear the announcement?" Mossey yelled, his voice strained. "They're onto us!"

"No time to explain!" Kusi replied, urgency lacing his tone. "We have to get to the broadcast point now!"

As they navigated through the crowd, Kusi felt a growing sense of dread. The expo was a labyrinth, and with every passing moment, their window of opportunity was closing. The emergency protocols would make their escape more difficult.

Suddenly, Kusi caught sight of a group of security personnel moving toward them. "This way!" he shouted, veering down a side corridor that led toward the back of the venue.

With the others close behind, they slipped through a doorway that led to a storage area filled with crates and equipment. It was a tight squeeze, but they needed to find a way to regroup.

"Do you think they saw us?" Araba asked, breathless and wide-eyed.

"I don't know," Kusi replied, trying to steady his racing heart. "But we need to find a way to get the information out, or everything we've done will be for nothing."

Just as they began to strategize, the sound of footsteps echoed in the corridor. Kusi felt the hairs on the back of his neck stand on end as he peered around the corner. A pair of security guards approached, their expressions stern.

"Looks like we've got a few uninvited guests," one of them sneered, eyes glinting with menace.

Kusi's heart raced. They had no time to waste. "We can't let them capture us. We need to fight back!"

Before he could finish, Mossey lunged forward, engaging one of the guards. The chaos erupted as fists flew, and Kusi found himself wrestling with the second guard, adrenaline fueling his movements.

The struggle was fierce, and Kusi's instincts kicked in. He was no stranger to conflict, but this felt different—this was a fight for their very existence. As he grappled with the guard, Kusi's thoughts raced back to the mission, to the stakes involved.

With a surge of determination, he managed to throw the guard off balance, sending him crashing into a stack of crates. Just as he turned to help Mossey, the sound of a loud crash echoed through the corridor, followed by a blaring alarm.

"Now what?" Brago shouted, her eyes wide with panic.

"We need to get out of here!" Kusi urged, his heart pounding. "The broadcast equipment has to be in the main control room. We can't let them stop us now."

Kusi led the group through the maze of corridors, his senses heightened. With each turn, the sound of footsteps echoed behind them, the guards in hot pursuit. He could feel the weight of their mission pressing down on him.

Finally, they reached the main control room, a large space filled with monitors and equipment. Kusi's heart raced as they pushed inside, quickly shutting the door behind them.

"Get everything set up!" he shouted. "We need to broadcast now!"

As Brago frantically connected the equipment, Kusi looked around the room. He could see the fear in Araba's eyes, but there was also determination. They were all in this together, fighting against a system that sought to control them.

With the equipment finally powered on, Brago's fingers danced over the keyboard, the screens flickering to life. "We're almost ready," she said, her voice steady despite the chaos outside.

Kusi felt the pressure mounting as the sounds of chaos grew louder. "We have to do this now!" he urged, glancing at the door. "They won't be far behind." Just as Brago initiated the broadcast, the door burst open. A team of security personnel stormed in, eyes wide with fury.

"Stop right there!" one of them shouted, raising his weapon.

With a surge of adrenaline, Kusi leaped forward, ready to protect his friends at all costs. "We won't let you silence us!" he shouted, his voice fierce and resolute.

As the chaos erupted around them, Kusi realized they were at a crossroads—this was the moment that would define their fight for freedom, and they would not back down.

Chapter 16: The Pulse of Resistance

The room erupted into chaos as Kusi and his team faced off against the security personnel. The tension in the air was palpable, a thick fog of fear and determination that hung over them. Kusi's heart pounded in his chest, matching the frantic rhythm of their situation. The monitors flickered ominously, casting a harsh glow on the faces of everyone present.

"Get down!" Brago shouted as she dove behind a console, pulling Kusi and Araba with her. Mossey and Lena followed suit, instinctively taking cover as the guards opened fire. A cacophony of gunshots rang out, mingling with the blaring alarm, creating a dissonant soundtrack to their desperate struggle.

Kusi's mind raced as he tried to strategize amidst the chaos. "We need to hold them off while Brago gets the broadcast out!" he yelled, feeling the adrenaline surging through him.

As they ducked behind the console, Kusi grabbed a makeshift weapon—a heavy metal object from the nearby equipment. "I'll create a distraction," he said, determination etched on his face. "Just keep the broadcast going!"

"Be careful!" Araba pleaded, her voice laced with concern.

Kusi nodded, steeling himself as he made a quick calculation. Timing was everything. "On my mark!" he shouted before sprinting toward the door.

As he burst into the open, he threw the metal object down the corridor, the loud clatter echoing as it hit the floor. The guards turned momentarily, their attention diverted just long enough for Kusi to seize the opportunity.

"Now, Brago!" Kusi shouted, adrenaline fueling his actions. He dove back behind the console just as gunfire erupted again, bullets ricocheting off the walls. Brago's fingers flew over the keyboard, her face set in a mask of concentration.

The screens flickered, coming to life with the broadcast. A live feed showed Kusi's team, their faces etched with determination. "This is it," Brago murmured, focusing on the camera as she prepared to speak. "The world needs to see what's happening here."

Kusi peeked around the console, gauging the guards' movements. "We have to keep them occupied!" he yelled. "Mossey, Lena, can you cover me?"

"Got your back!" Mossey replied, his voice steady.

With a shared glance of resolve, Kusi charged forward again, joined by Mossey and Lena. They moved as a cohesive unit, ducking and weaving to avoid the incoming fire. Kusi felt the weight of their mission pressing on him, every second counting as they fought against the clock.

"We can't let them take control!" Kusi shouted, his voice filled with urgency.

The guards advanced, their tactical training evident in their movements. Kusi, fueled by desperation, grabbed a nearby chair and swung it at one of the guards, knocking him off balance. Mossey followed suit, tackling another guard to the ground.

"Keep pushing forward!" Lena shouted, her eyes blazing with determination as she covered them. The chaotic sounds of the fight surrounded them, but Kusi's focus narrowed. In that moment, he felt a surge of clarity—this was not just about them anymore; it was about everyone who had been silenced, everyone whose memories had been manipulated and erased.

"People need to hear our story!" Kusi yelled, rallying his team. "We're fighting for their freedom!"

Brago continued to work on the broadcast, her fingers dancing across the keyboard. "I'm in!" she shouted, her voice echoing through the chaos. "I'll stream this to every major network. We need to expose them!"

Just as the tide seemed to shift in their favor, Kusi spotted a figure at the back of the control room—someone he recognized. It was Director Harlow, the ruthless head of security for PromptTech. His steely gaze locked onto Kusi, a cold smile spreading across his face.

"Thought you could make a scene and get away with it?" Harlow taunted, his voice dripping with malice. "You're outnumbered, Kusi. You have no idea who you're up against."

Kusi felt a chill run down his spine. "You don't know what we're capable of," he shot back, trying to project confidence. "We're not afraid of you."

"Is that so?" Harlow stepped forward, his presence imposing. "You think you can expose us? You're merely pawns in a much larger game."

Kusi felt a fire ignite within him. "Then let's make this game interesting," he challenged, determined to stand his ground.

Harlow waved a hand, signaling for more guards to close in. "Seize them!" he ordered, his voice cold and commanding. The guards advanced, weapons drawn, ready to apprehend Kusi and his team.

But Kusi's resolve only strengthened. "We won't go down without a fight!" he yelled, rallying his friends. Together, they pushed back against the guards, fighting with everything they had.

The control room erupted into chaos, the sounds of struggle blending with the urgent broadcast as Brago managed to capture the moment. "This is what PromptTech doesn't want you to see!" she shouted, her voice ringing through the speakers. "They erase memories, control lives, and silence dissent! We will not be silenced!"

Just when it seemed that they were cornered, a surprising ally appeared—Araba, her eyes fierce and determined, stepped forward, brandishing a small device. "I've hacked into their security system!" she announced, her voice unwavering. "We have a chance to disrupt their operations!"

Kusi's heart soared at her bravery. "Do it!" he shouted, feeling a renewed sense of hope.

Araba pressed a button on the device, and the lights in the control room flickered ominously. The monitors began displaying static, the guards momentarily distracted as chaos erupted on the screens.

"This is our chance!" Kusi yelled, pushing forward. "Let's finish what we started!"

With newfound determination, Kusi and his team fought against the guards with everything they had. The air was thick with tension, but each member of the group fought with a purpose, united in their quest for freedom.

The sounds of gunfire, shouts, and chaos filled the room as Kusi and his friends made their stand. They moved as a team, covering each other and pushing forward, unwilling to back down in the face of danger.

"We can't let them control us any longer!" Mossey shouted, his voice fierce as he tackled another guard to the ground.

As the battle raged on, Kusi could feel a shift in the atmosphere. The broadcast was gaining traction, and their message was reaching a wider audience. He could almost feel the pulse of resistance rising outside, people awakening to the truth of PromptTech's tyranny.

"This is it!" Brago shouted, her eyes wide with excitement. "People are starting to respond!"

Kusi felt a surge of adrenaline as he fought back against the guards. The realization that their struggle was resonating with others fueled his determination. They were not alone in this fight.

Just as victory seemed within reach, Harlow lunged forward, determined to take Kusi down. "You think you've won?" he spat, anger flashing in his eyes. "You're just delaying the inevitable!"

Kusi faced him, a fierce resolve in his gaze. "We're just getting started," he replied defiantly. "This is about reclaiming our identities and our lives. You can't erase us!"

With that, Kusi and Harlow clashed, a battle of wills and strength that would determine the fate of their fight. In that moment, Kusi understood that this wasn't just a fight against PromptTech—it was a fight for the very essence of humanity itself.

Chapter 17: Undercover Missions

The atmosphere in the safe house was charged with a mix of anticipation and apprehension. Kusi looked around at the diverse group gathered before him, each person representing a unique story, a different reason for being there. Some had lost loved ones to PromptTech's ruthless memory manipulation; others had experienced firsthand the cruelty of the corporation's power. This was no longer just a fight for survival—it was a battle for justice.

Araba stood next to him, her eyes scanning the room, absorbing the weight of their mission. "We've made a start, but we need to be smart about our next steps," she said, her voice low but steady.

Kusi nodded, his mind racing. "We've gained some momentum with the broadcast, but we need to ensure our message reaches beyond just this safe house. We need allies everywhere."

Juna stepped forward, her expression serious. "We have connections with other resistance groups. They've been monitoring PromptTech for years and have valuable intel. We should reach out to them."

"Good idea," Mossey added, his tone resolute. "But we have to ensure they're trustworthy. We can't afford to bring anyone into this fold who might compromise our mission."

Kusi felt the weight of responsibility settling on his shoulders. "Let's split into teams. One group can work on establishing contact with these resistance factions, while the other focuses on gathering evidence against PromptTech's black market operations."

Lena, who had been quiet until now, spoke up. "We also need to find a way to protect ourselves. PromptTech will retaliate. We need to secure our communications and lay low until we're ready to make our next move."

As they brainstormed strategies, Kusi couldn't shake the feeling that they were operating in a precarious bubble. Outside, the city was still reeling from the broadcast, but it wouldn't take long for PromptTech to respond. They needed to stay one step ahead.

"Let's use encrypted channels to communicate," Brago suggested, typing furiously on her device. "I can set up a secure network that only we can access. That way, we can share information without risking exposure."

"Perfect," Kusi said, his admiration for Brago's technical skills growing. "We'll need that to coordinate our efforts."

The group discussed potential locations for future meetings, ensuring they would remain hidden from PromptTech's surveillance. Every detail mattered; the stakes had never been higher.

Hours passed as they plotted their course of action. Kusi felt the adrenaline coursing through him again, the fire of purpose igniting his resolve. They were not just a group of individuals anymore; they were a united front against an oppressive force.

As the discussions wound down, Kusi glanced around the room, taking in the determined faces. "This isn't just about fighting back against PromptTech; it's about reclaiming our identities and ensuring that no one else suffers the way we have."

"We will be the echoes of resistance," Araba said softly, her voice carrying a weight of conviction. "We will not be silenced."

With their plans laid out, the group began to prepare for their respective missions. Kusi felt a sense of urgency as they split into teams, each taking on a specific task. His team would focus on gathering evidence against PromptTech, while Juna's team would reach out to other resistance groups.

"Remember, stay vigilant," Kusi cautioned as they gathered at the door. "We don't know how far PromptTech's reach extends, so trust your instincts and don't take unnecessary risks."

As they moved out into the night, Kusi felt the weight of their collective purpose pressing down on him. They were taking their first real steps toward dismantling the corporation's grip on their lives, but the dangers lurking in the shadows were all too real.

The streets felt different in the aftermath of their broadcast. The air was thick with uncertainty, and Kusi could sense the tension hanging over the city. As they moved through the alleys, Kusi glanced at the faces of those around him. There was a mix of fear and determination, a fragile hope beginning to take root.

He couldn't help but wonder how many others were out there—people who shared their pain, their desire for change. The thought fueled his resolve. They were fighting for something larger than themselves; they were fighting for a future free from the chains of memory manipulation.

Kusi and his team made their way to an old warehouse on the outskirts of the city, a known gathering spot for those disillusioned by PromptTech's tyranny. As they approached the entrance, Kusi felt a mix of excitement and anxiety. They were stepping into a world filled with unknowns, a place where alliances could shift in an instant.

Inside, the warehouse was dimly lit, filled with the low hum of conversation. Kusi felt the weight of eyes upon him as he stepped into the space, his heart pounding in his chest. They were among allies, but in a world where memories were traded like currency, trust was a rare commodity.

Kusi moved through the crowd, introducing himself to various groups, explaining their mission, and sharing their experiences. Each story they told sparked a fire within those who listened, reigniting the flames of resistance that had been simmering beneath the surface.

Araba stood beside him, her presence grounding him. "We can't underestimate the power of shared stories," she said quietly, her eyes scanning the room. "Each person here has lost something, just like we have."

Kusi nodded, feeling the weight of their shared experiences creating a bond among them. They were not just individuals fighting against PromptTech; they were a collective force, ready to challenge the status quo.

As the night wore on, Kusi found a moment of solitude in a quiet corner of the warehouse. He leaned against a cool wall, his mind racing with thoughts. What lay ahead was uncertain, and the challenges they faced felt overwhelming at times. But he was fueled by a deep-seated desire to reclaim their identities, to expose the dark truth behind PromptTech's machinations.

Araba joined him, sensing his moment of reflection. "Are you okay?" she asked softly.

"I just... I can't shake the feeling that we're being watched," he admitted, looking into her eyes. "Every step we take could lead us closer to danger."

"We've already taken the biggest step by standing together," Araba replied, her voice unwavering. "We can't let fear dictate our actions. We owe it to ourselves and to those who've suffered to keep pushing forward."

Kusi felt a swell of gratitude for her presence. "You're right. We can't let them intimidate us. We'll expose the truth and fight back."

Just then, a commotion erupted at the entrance of the warehouse, drawing their attention. Kusi's heart raced as he spotted armed figures pushing their way through the crowd. PromptTech's enforcers had found them.

"Everyone, scatter!" Kusi shouted, adrenaline kicking in. The atmosphere shifted instantly from hope to panic as people scrambled for cover. Kusi grabbed Araba's arm, urging her to move.

"Stay close!" he yelled over the chaos, guiding her through the throng of bodies. They had to escape before it was too late.

Kusi and Araba ducked into a side corridor, pressing against the wall as they heard the shouts of the enforcers behind them. "This way!" Kusi whispered urgently, leading them deeper into the maze of the warehouse.

As they maneuvered through the shadows, Kusi couldn't shake the sense of betrayal gnawing at him. Had someone tipped off PromptTech? He felt the stakes rising, and the realization hit him hard—trust would be their greatest weapon and their most significant vulnerability.

They burst through a back exit just as the sounds of gunfire echoed behind them. Kusi and Araba stumbled into the night air, gasping for breath. They had narrowly escaped, but the threat loomed large. They needed to regroup and assess their next move.

"What do we do now?" Araba asked, her voice trembling slightly as they hurried down the alley.

"We find the others, and we regroup. We need to figure out who we can trust and how to turn this around," Kusi replied, determination igniting within him.

As they vanished into the night, the echoes of their resistance resonated within them. They were no longer just individuals; they were part of a movement—an unyielding force against PromptTech's tyranny.

Chapter 18: The Fractured Veil

The night air was thick with tension as Kusi and Araba navigated the winding alleyways, their hearts pounding from the close call. PromptTech's enforcers had breached their sanctuary, and the sting of betrayal hung heavily in the air. They needed to regroup and figure out their next steps, but first, they had to ensure the safety of their allies.

As they hurried through the darkness, Kusi couldn't shake the feeling that they were being hunted. Every shadow felt like a threat, every sound an omen. They reached a secluded corner, where they found Juna and Mossey, breathless and wide-eyed.

"What happened?" Juna asked, her voice edged with panic. "We heard the commotion."

"We were ambushed," Kusi said, his voice low but firm. "We need to get everyone to safety. PromptTech knows we're here."

Mossey clenched his fists, anger flashing in his eyes. "We need to hit them back. We can't let them intimidate us."

"No, we can't act recklessly," Kusi countered, feeling the weight of leadership pressing down on him. "We need to be strategic. The more visible we are, the easier it will be for them to track us."

Araba stepped forward, her expression resolute. "We should head to the rendezvous point. It's remote, and we can regroup there. We can assess our allies and decide our next move."

Juna nodded, her features hardening with determination. "Let's move, then. We can't stay here."

As they made their way toward the rendezvous point, Kusi felt a sense of urgency gnawing at him. Every corner they turned could be a trap, every alleyway a potential ambush. They kept to the shadows, moving as quietly as possible.

"What if someone in the safe house betrayed us?" Araba whispered, the words hanging heavily in the air. "We can't trust anyone anymore."

Kusi felt a knot form in his stomach. "We'll figure it out. We can't let fear dictate our actions. We need to focus on the task ahead—gathering intel and building our network."

Upon arriving at the rendezvous point, an old, abandoned building at the edge of the city, Kusi felt a brief moment of relief. They quickly set up a temporary base, utilizing the crumbling walls and debris for cover. The atmosphere was tense as they waited for the others to arrive.

Juna busied herself with the equipment, checking their communication devices and ensuring everything was secure. "We need to find out who's still with us," she said, her tone serious. "We can't afford any more surprises."

Kusi nodded, grateful for her pragmatism. "Let's divide the tasks. Juna, you and Mossey should try to reach out to the other resistance groups. Araba and I will gather intel on PromptTech's recent movements. We need to understand what they're planning."

As they worked, Kusi felt the weight of the world pressing down on him. He glanced at Araba, who was studying the makeshift map of the city spread out before them. "You okay?" he asked, sensing the turmoil beneath her composed exterior.

"I will be," she replied softly, her fingers tracing the outlines of their potential routes. "But we need to expose PromptTech. We can't let them continue to erase people's memories and identities."

"We'll make them pay for what they've done," Kusi promised, determination hardening in his chest.

After several hours of gathering information, Kusi felt the pieces of the puzzle starting to fit together. They discovered that PromptTech was planning a major operation—a public demonstration showcasing their new memory technology. It would be a perfect opportunity for Kusi and his team to infiltrate the event and expose the corporation's true intentions.

"We have to crash that event," Kusi said, excitement sparking in his eyes. "This is our chance to show the world the dark side of their operations. We need to make a statement."

"But how do we get in?" Mossey asked, his brow furrowed. "It'll be heavily guarded."

"We can create a diversion," Juna suggested, her expression brightening. "If we cause a stir outside the venue, we can slip in while everyone is distracted."

Kusi nodded, appreciating her quick thinking. "We'll need to plan this carefully. We can't afford to be caught."

As they discussed the details, Kusi felt a renewed sense of purpose. This was the moment they had been waiting for—a chance to turn the tide against PromptTech. They would expose the corporation's lies and rally the public to their cause.

As the plan solidified, Kusi felt the weight of responsibility shift. He was no longer just a memory broker; he was now a leader in a fight for freedom and identity.

When the day of the event arrived, Kusi's heart raced with a mix of anticipation and fear. They had prepared as much as possible, but the reality of facing PromptTech loomed large. He gathered everyone together, feeling the palpable tension in the air.

"This is it," he said, looking each person in the eye. "Today, we reclaim our identities and show the world what PromptTech is truly capable of. Remember, we're fighting for each other, for our families, and for everyone whose memories have been stolen."

The group nodded, a surge of determination flowing through them. They were ready to face whatever lay ahead, united in their cause.

As they approached the venue, Kusi felt a rush of adrenaline. The bright lights and bustling crowd were overwhelming, but he focused on their mission. They moved through the throng of people, blending in while keeping a watchful eye on their surroundings.

Araba walked beside him, her presence grounding him. "We can do this," she said, her voice steady. "We'll expose them."

With a deep breath, Kusi pushed forward, knowing that their moment was finally here. The fractures within PromptTech would soon be exposed, and they would emerge from the shadows, echoing the cries for justice and truth.

Chapter 19: Into the Abyss

The energy at the venue was electric, a vibrant pulse of excitement mixed with an undercurrent of tension. Kusi and his team merged into the crowd, their hearts racing as they navigated through clusters of attendees eagerly awaiting PromptTech's grand demonstration. Kusi's eyes darted around, searching for security measures and any signs of potential threats. The venue was expansive, with towering screens displaying flashy advertisements for PromptTech's latest memory-enhancing technologies, promising a world where memories could be curated like a playlist.

As they approached the entrance, Kusi could see the throng of media personnel, their cameras aimed at a sleek stage where a charismatic spokesperson was scheduled to present. It was the perfect façade, a shiny exterior hiding the rot beneath.

"Stick to the plan," Kusi whispered to Araba, who was adjusting the small earpiece connected to their communication devices. "We create the diversion outside while Juna and Mossey slip in to gather intel. Once we're inside, we'll signal you to join us."

Araba nodded, her determination evident in her steely gaze. "Let's make sure they regret underestimating us."

Outside, the sun hung low in the sky, casting an orange hue over the crowd. Kusi and Araba took their positions, a few feet away from the entrance, their hearts pounding in anticipation. As Kusi scanned the area, he spotted a group of protesters holding signs that read *"Stop Memory Manipulation!"* and *"We Are More Than Our Memories!"* They were the perfect distraction.

"Now!" Kusi shouted, motioning for Araba to join him as they moved toward the protesters. They quickly grabbed a couple of signs, blending into the group just as they began chanting slogans against PromptTech's practices. The noise erupted, drawing attention away from the entrance.

Araba's voice rose above the others. *"We won't be erased! We demand our memories back!"* Her passionate cry fueled the crowd, creating a wave of energy that surged through the protesters.

As expected, security personnel rushed to manage the situation, focusing on the chaos outside, leaving the entrance momentarily unguarded.

Meanwhile, Juna and Mossey slipped into the building, their expressions masked with determination. The interior was sleek and modern, an embodiment of PromptTech's wealth and power. As they moved deeper into the building, they carefully observed their surroundings, taking mental notes of every detail—the security cameras, the guard placements, and the exits.

"We need to find the control room," Juna whispered, glancing at the schematics they had pulled up on a portable device. "It should be near the back of the auditorium."

"Let's hurry before they realize what's happening outside," Mossey urged, his eyes scanning for any signs of security.

They weaved through the corridors, blending with the crowd of attendees who were blissfully unaware of the brewing storm. The sounds of laughter and applause echoed, a stark contrast to the urgency they felt.

As they approached the auditorium, Juna's heart raced. They could hear the spokesperson's voice booming through the speakers, extolling the virtues of PromptTech's technology. *"Imagine a world where your memories are enhanced, curated to perfection! With our new technology, you can relive your happiest moments anytime you wish!"*

Juna exchanged a glance with Mossey, their shared determination palpable. "This is it. We need to get this footage."

They slipped into a side door, entering a darkened room filled with monitors displaying live feeds from various locations within the venue. The control room was cluttered with equipment, and Mossey quickly began recording the screens while Juna searched for anything incriminating.

"There!" Juna pointed to a screen showing an encrypted feed labeled "Memory Erasure Protocols." "This could expose everything!"

As she worked to hack into the system, Mossey remained vigilant, glancing at the door every few seconds. The tension in the air was thick, and they both knew they were running out of time.

Back outside, Kusi and Araba continued to rally the protesters, their voices rising in fervor. The police had arrived, but the protesters stood their ground, chanting louder. Kusi could see the commotion affecting the atmosphere inside, the audience growing restless. It was now or never.

With the security distracted, Kusi decided it was time to put their plan into action. He motioned for Araba, and they pushed through the throng of protesters, making their way toward the entrance.

"We need to get inside now!" Kusi urged, adrenaline coursing through his veins.

As they entered the building, the sounds of the demonstration faded, replaced by the sterile silence of the interior. The air felt charged with a mix of anticipation and fear as they navigated through the halls.

Inside the auditorium, the spokesperson continued to tout the benefits of memory manipulation, completely oblivious to the brewing chaos outside. But as Kusi and Araba pressed further in, they could sense the shift in energy—the unease growing among the crowd, the murmurs of confusion spreading.

Suddenly, Kusi spotted Juna and Mossey emerging from the control room, their expressions grim but resolute. "We have what we need!" Mossey exclaimed, urgency in his voice. "We need to broadcast it!"

"Let's do it!" Kusi shouted, rallying the team. They moved quickly, making their way toward the main stage.

As they reached the front, Juna hurriedly set up the equipment, her fingers flying over the controls. "We can stream this live," she said, her voice steady even amid the chaos.

Just as Juna prepared to hit the button, the lights in the auditorium flickered ominously, and an alarm blared, causing panic to ripple through the crowd. The spokesperson stumbled, his confident demeanor shattered as confusion engulfed the attendees.

"Ladies and gentlemen, please remain calm!" he urged, but his voice was drowned out by the chaos.

Kusi took a deep breath, stepping forward to grab the microphone. "Everyone, listen! PromptTech has been erasing memories, controlling what you remember! We're here to show you the truth!"

The crowd began to murmur, shifting their attention from the spokesperson to Kusi, confusion and curiosity mingling in their expressions.

"This footage will prove it!" Juna shouted, hitting the button to stream the live feed. The screens around the auditorium lit up, revealing the disturbing truths about memory manipulation—the protocols, the experiments, and the lives destroyed by PromptTech's ruthless ambition.

Gasps filled the room as the footage played, the reality of the situation crashing down on the audience like a tidal wave. Faces turned pale, and the once-supportive attendees began to stir with anger and betrayal.

"How could they do this?" someone shouted from the back of the crowd.

"We've been lied to!" another voice echoed, igniting a wave of outrage.

Kusi's heart raced as he realized the tide was turning. The crowd was no longer passive; they were enraged, ready to confront the truth.

Just then, security personnel rushed in, attempting to regain control of the situation. "Shut this down!" one of them shouted, pushing through the throng of people.

"Time to go!" Mossey urged, and the team quickly regrouped, moving toward the exits. But the chaos had erupted fully now; people were pushing against the security, trying to flee the venue, desperate for answers.

Kusi led the way, with Araba and Juna close behind. The noise grew louder as they navigated through the throng, the sounds of shouts and the sirens merging into a cacophony of chaos.

As they burst out of the main doors, Kusi could see the protesters still outside, their voices resonating in solidarity. The scene was surreal—a blend of anger, confusion, and a newfound sense of hope.

"Keep pushing!" Araba shouted, rallying the protesters. "We have to show them we won't be silenced!"

Kusi felt a surge of pride as he watched the group stand together, united against the corruption they had just unveiled. They had exposed PromptTech, but now they needed to harness this energy into a movement.

As they regrouped with their allies, Kusi's mind raced with possibilities. This was just the beginning; they had ignited a spark that could spread like wildfire. Together, they would fight against PromptTech's tyranny, reclaim their identities, and ensure that no one else would suffer the same fate.

As they disappeared into the crowd, Kusi glanced at Araba, who met his gaze with a determined smile. They had survived the abyss, and now they would rise from its depths, ready to confront whatever awaited them on the road ahead.

Chapter 20: A Web of Connections

The air was thick with anticipation as Kusi, Araba, Juna, and Mossey regrouped in a dimly lit underground safe house. The walls, lined with makeshift tables and scattered technology, buzzed with the remnants of their recent success. Outside, the sounds of the protest faded, replaced by an almost eerie silence that felt both comforting and foreboding.

Kusi leaned against a table cluttered with old monitors and cables, his mind racing with the implications of what they had just achieved. They had exposed PromptTech, but Kusi knew that this was merely the first step in a much larger battle. The corporation wouldn't take the revelation lightly; they would retaliate.

"What's our next move?" Juna asked, her eyes scanning the group. The adrenaline from the chaos was beginning to ebb, replaced by a steely resolve.

Araba took a deep breath, her expression thoughtful. "We need to consolidate our support. There are more people out there who are affected by PromptTech's manipulations. We can't just sit here and wait for them to come after us."

Mossey nodded in agreement, his gaze focused. "We should reach out to other groups fighting against memory manipulation. If we can form an alliance, we can amplify our voice."

Kusi straightened, feeling the weight of leadership settle on his shoulders. "Let's gather intel on other organizations. We can use our network to identify potential allies and spread the word about what we've uncovered. The more people we can rally to our cause, the stronger we'll be."

"Agreed," Juna said. "We should also enhance our security. PromptTech will be on high alert, and we need to ensure we can operate without being tracked."

As they began to strategize, Kusi couldn't shake the feeling that they were racing against time. The corporation would not only want to silence them but also cover their tracks. They needed to act quickly.

After hours of brainstorming and gathering resources, Kusi decided it was time to send out a message to the public. They needed to ensure that the exposure of PromptTech's practices reverberated throughout the city.

Kusi sat down at one of the old monitors, the soft glow illuminating his determined expression. "We need to craft a message that resonates, something that can ignite the passion of the people," he said, typing furiously as he outlined a call to action.

Araba leaned over his shoulder, reading the words as they flowed onto the screen. "We should also include personal stories—people who have suffered due to memory manipulation. That will humanize the issue."

As they crafted the message, they worked late into the night, fueled by coffee and a shared sense of purpose. By dawn, Kusi felt a mixture of exhaustion and exhilaration wash over him. They had created a powerful manifesto, a rallying cry for those who had felt the heavy hand of PromptTech.

With the message ready, Kusi and his team set to work spreading it across social media platforms, forums, and encrypted channels. They knew the risks involved, but it was necessary to ignite a flame in the hearts of those who had been silenced.

"Let's use our contacts to reach out to journalists," Juna suggested. "If we can get the media involved, it will amplify our message even further."

Mossey took charge of coordinating with their contacts, relaying information and organizing meetings with potential allies. The sense of urgency fueled their actions, and soon they were enveloped in a web of connections that extended far beyond their initial scope.

As the days turned into a blur of activity, Kusi felt a shift in the atmosphere. The message they had sent out was gaining traction, resonating with individuals who had long been disenfranchised. People began to share their stories, revealing the personal toll that memory manipulation had taken on their lives.

One morning, as Kusi sifted through responses, a notification caught his eye. A journalist named *Tessa Hartley* had reached out, expressing interest in covering their story. "She's well-connected and has a reputation for exposing corporate corruption," he murmured, sharing the message with the group.

Araba's eyes lit up. "This could be the break we need! If she covers our story, it could reach a wider audience."

They quickly arranged a meeting, and as Kusi prepared, a mix of hope and anxiety swirled within him. This could be a pivotal moment for their cause, a chance to shine a spotlight on the atrocities committed by PromptTech.

The meeting was set in a quaint coffee shop on the outskirts of the city, its ambiance a stark contrast to the weighty topic they were about to discuss. Kusi, Araba, Juna, and Mossey arrived early, their nerves palpable as they waited for Tessa to arrive. When she entered, her confident demeanor and sharp gaze immediately captured Kusi's attention. She exuded a sense of purpose, a fire in her eyes that promised determination.

"Thanks for meeting with me," she said, settling into a chair. "I've been following the buzz surrounding PromptTech, and your message stood out. This is a story that needs to be told."

Kusi felt a surge of optimism. "We have evidence of their practices—how they manipulate memories and erase dissent. We can provide you with everything you need to expose them."

Tessa nodded, her expression serious. "I want to dig deeper. I need to understand how extensive their operations are. What I've seen so far is alarming, but I want to connect with more individuals who have been affected."

As they delved into the details, Kusi, Araba, and Juna shared their experiences and the stories they had gathered from others. Tessa listened intently, taking notes as they spoke. The more they revealed, the clearer it became that PromptTech's reach was insidious, penetrating every aspect of society.

"I have sources within PromptTech who might be willing to talk," Tessa said, her expression grave. "But it will take time to gain their trust. This is dangerous work."

Kusi nodded, understanding the risks involved. "We're in this together. If you need anything from us, we're here to help."

As the meeting progressed, they began to strategize on how to approach potential whistleblowers within the corporation. It was a delicate dance of trust and danger, and Kusi felt the weight of their mission intensify.

As days turned into weeks, Tessa began to publish articles detailing the findings of Kusi's group. The ripple effect was immediate; public interest surged, and protests against PromptTech grew in intensity. The once-dormant city was waking up, ignited by the truth of what lay beneath the surface.

Kusi and his team were relentless, organizing meetings with activists, gathering testimonies, and expanding their network. The fight against PromptTech became a movement, drawing in individuals from all walks of life—those who had lost memories, families torn apart, and even former employees disillusioned by the corporation's practices.

One evening, as they gathered in their safe house, Kusi felt a profound sense of purpose. "We're not just fighting for ourselves anymore. We're fighting for everyone who has been silenced. We need to keep pushing, keep raising awareness."

Araba's gaze was unwavering. "We have to keep the momentum going. There are still many who are unaware of what's happening, and we can't let PromptTech dictate the narrative."

But just as they began to see the fruits of their labor, an unexpected threat loomed on the horizon. Rumors of a crackdown on dissenting voices began to circulate, whispers of disappearances and intimidation tactics employed by PromptTech to stifle the growing movement.

Kusi felt the tension rise within the group as they discussed their options. "We can't let fear dictate our actions. If we stand united, we can withstand their tactics."

Juna's expression was thoughtful. "We need to increase our security. We can't afford to be vulnerable now, especially with the stakes this high."

As they worked to fortify their defenses, Kusi couldn't shake the feeling that they were entering a dangerous phase of their fight. PromptTech was cornered and desperate, and Kusi knew they would stop at nothing to protect their interests.

As the city simmered with tension, Kusi and his team prepared for the battles ahead. They had ignited a fire, and now they had to ensure it wouldn't be extinguished. The path forward was fraught with challenges, but Kusi felt an unyielding resolve.

"We have each other's backs," he reminded his team. "No matter what happens, we're in this together."

As they looked at one another, determination reflected in their eyes, Kusi knew that the alliance of shadows they had formed would be their strength. They were not just fighting against PromptTech; they were fighting for the very essence of their identities and the right to control their own memories.

Chapter 21: Fractured Reflections

The city pulsed with unrest, its veins flowing with the fervor of dissent. Kusi stood at the window of their safe house, looking out over the streets teeming with protesters. Makeshift signs waved like flags of a revolution, and the chants echoed through the air—a cacophony of voices demanding accountability and justice against PromptTech.

Yet, beneath the surface of this awakening lay a sense of fragility. Kusi could feel it in the tension of the crowd, the flicker of uncertainty in their eyes. The movement had gained momentum, but it also painted a target on their backs. They were now firmly in the corporation's crosshairs.

"Every day we wait gives them more time to retaliate," Araba said, joining him at the window. Her voice was steady, but Kusi could see the weight of worry etched in her features. "We need to strike while the iron is hot. We can't let this energy fade."

He turned to her, seeing the fierce determination that had drawn him to her in the first place. "You're right. We need a plan, something bold to keep the pressure on PromptTech."

As the sun dipped below the horizon, casting the city in shades of orange and purple, the group gathered around their makeshift conference table. The atmosphere was charged with purpose, and Kusi could sense the stakes rising.

"I've been looking into PromptTech's operations," Mossey began, pulling up a schematic on the old monitor. "They have a central data hub where they store sensitive information about their memory manipulation processes. If we can infiltrate it, we could expose everything—names, locations, evidence of their black market dealings."

"Do we know how heavily guarded it is?" Juna asked, her brow furrowed in concentration.

"Very," Mossey replied grimly. "But if we time it right, we could slip in during a shift change. Their security relies heavily on automated systems, and there's a window where human oversight is minimal."

Kusi felt a mixture of excitement and dread. The prospect of infiltrating the heart of PromptTech was enticing, yet the danger was palpable. "We'll need to be prepared for anything. If we're caught, it could mean the end of our movement—and our lives."

Araba nodded, her expression unwavering. "We've come too far to turn back now. If we can gather the right evidence, it will shift the tide in our favor."

They spent the next few days strategizing, mapping out their approach and gathering the necessary tools for the infiltration. Kusi immersed himself in the details, ensuring every angle was covered. The plan was ambitious, but they were fueled by desperation and hope.

The night before their mission, they huddled together, going over the final details. "Communication will be crucial," Juna reminded them. "We need to stay connected throughout the operation."

Kusi distributed earpieces, ensuring they could maintain contact without raising suspicion. "Remember, our goal is to gather evidence and get out. We can't afford to get distracted."

As they settled into a restless sleep, Kusi felt the weight of responsibility pressing down on him. Lives depended on their success, and he couldn't shake the feeling that they were teetering on the edge of something monumental.

On the day of the infiltration, the city buzzed with anticipation. Kusi and his team moved with purpose, each step laden with the potential for disaster. They arrived at the outskirts of PromptTech's headquarters, a looming structure of glass and steel that seemed to mock their rebellion.

"Stick to the plan," Kusi whispered, a fire igniting in his chest. "We go in, get the data, and get out. No heroics."

They slipped into the building, the sterile air inside contrasting sharply with the chaos outside. The initial moments felt surreal as they navigated through the maze of corridors, blending into the flow of employees.

Mossey led the way, his knowledge of the building's layout guiding them toward the central data hub. As they approached, Kusi's heart raced. They were almost there.

Just as they reached the entrance to the data hub, alarms blared throughout the building. Red lights flashed, bathing the corridor in an ominous glow. "What the hell?" Juna shouted, panic rising in her voice.

"It's a lockdown!" Mossey exclaimed, his fingers dancing over the keypad. "We need to move!"

The sound of footsteps echoed behind them, the guards mobilizing in response to the alarm. Kusi felt a surge of adrenaline. "We can't go back. We have to push forward!"

They rushed inside the hub, Mossey quickly accessing the terminal. "I'll download everything I can. Just give me a minute!"

"Make it fast!" Araba urged, her eyes darting to the door. Kusi stood guard, ready to confront anyone who might enter.

As Mossey worked, the tension in the air was suffocating. Kusi's mind raced with what they had to lose. This was it—this could be the turning point in their battle against PromptTech.

But just as Mossey's progress bar hit fifty percent, the door swung open with a violent clang. A group of guards poured in, weapons drawn, eyes locked on Kusi and his team.

"Get on the ground!" one of the guards shouted, his voice cold and authoritative.

Kusi's instincts kicked in. "Run!" he yelled, shoving Araba towards the exit.

Chaos erupted as they scattered in different directions. Kusi found himself sprinting down a narrow corridor, adrenaline coursing through his veins. He could hear the shouts of the guards behind him, the pounding of boots echoing in the hall.

As he rounded a corner, Kusi's heart sank at the sight of a dead end. He was trapped. Just as he turned to look for another way out, a guard stepped into view, weapon raised.

In that instant, Kusi felt a surge of despair and determination. He couldn't let fear consume him. He had fought too hard, risked too much. He had to protect Araba, Juna, Mossey, and everyone who had suffered under PromptTech's tyranny.

With a deep breath, Kusi charged forward, tackling the guard with every ounce of strength he could muster. The two men crashed to the ground, struggling for control of the weapon. Kusi's mind raced, every moment stretching into eternity as he fought against the odds.

Just as he felt the guard's grip tightening, a flash of movement caught his eye. It was Araba, rushing in to help him. She delivered a swift kick to the guard's side, causing him to stumble, giving Kusi the opening he needed.

With a final push, Kusi disarmed the guard and pinned him to the ground, breathing heavily as he caught his breath. "We need to go!" he urged Araba, pulling her to her feet.

They raced back to the data hub, hoping Mossey and Juna had managed to evade capture. As they entered, the sight before them sent a chill down Kusi's spine. Mossey was still at the terminal, but Juna was nowhere to be seen.

"Where's Juna?" Kusi demanded, panic rising in his throat.

"She—she went to check for an exit!" Mossey replied, his hands moving rapidly over the keyboard. "I'm almost done! Just a few more seconds!"

"Let's get out of here!" Araba insisted, her voice urgent.

As the download completed, Kusi felt a surge of triumph mixed with dread. They had the evidence, but at what cost? Juna's absence gnawed at him. "We can't leave without her."

Mossy grabbed the hard drive, securing it in his pocket. "We have to make a choice! We can't risk getting caught!"

But Kusi shook his head, defiance rising within him. "We won't abandon her! She's one of us!"

Just then, the door burst open again, and more guards flooded in. "Go!" Kusi shouted at Mossey and Araba. "I'll find Juna!"

"Are you insane?" Mossey protested.

"I'm not leaving her behind!" Kusi shouted back, his heart pounding in his chest. Without waiting for their response, he sprinted deeper into the labyrinth of corridors, determined to find his friend.

As Kusi navigated through the shadows, every sound seemed amplified—the distant shouts of guards, the echo of his footsteps. He couldn't shake the feeling that time was slipping away. He needed to find Juna before it was too late.

Finally, he rounded a corner and caught sight of her—a figure silhouetted against a flickering light. Relief washed over him, but it was quickly replaced with dread as he noticed she was cornered by two guards.

"Juna!" Kusi shouted, his heart racing. Without thinking, he charged toward her, adrenaline propelling him forward.

The guards turned, their expressions shifting from surprise to aggression. Kusi tackled one of them, the impact sending them both crashing to the ground. Juna wasted no time, delivering a swift kick to the other guard, her determination shining through the chaos.

"Let's go!" she urged, her voice fierce.

Kusi nodded, and together they sprinted toward the exit, every second feeling like an eternity.

As they burst through the exit doors, Kusi felt a rush of cool air against his face. Freedom was within reach, but the sounds of pursuit echoed behind them. They dashed across the parking lot, searching for a place to hide.

Mossy and Araba were waiting by a vehicle, their faces a mix of relief and fear. "We thought we lost you!" Mossey exclaimed, his eyes wide.

"We're not done yet!" Kusi said, pulling Juna close. "Get in!"

As they piled into the vehicle, the engines roared to life, and they sped away from the chaos. Kusi felt a mix of triumph and anxiety wash over him. They had escaped, but the battle was far from over.

Later that night, as they gathered in the safe house, Kusi stared at the hard drive containing the evidence of PromptTech's malfeasance. The reality of their situation weighed heavily on him. They had made it out, but the fight was only just beginning.

"Now we have to plan our next move," Araba said, her voice steady despite the exhaustion that hung over them.

Kusi nodded, determination coursing through him. "We have to get this information out. The public deserves to know the truth about what PromptTech has done."

As they strategized, Kusi couldn't help but feel a sense of unity growing among them. They were more than a team; they were a family forged in the fires of rebellion.

But even as they plotted their next steps, Kusi couldn't shake the feeling that they were being watched. PromptTech would not let their actions go unpunished. The shadows of the past were closing in, and Kusi knew that the true test of their resolve was yet to come.

As the night wore on, Kusi glanced at Araba, who was deep in thought. He knew they were in this together, facing the darkness head-on. They would fight for every life impacted by the corporation's greed, and he would do everything in his power to ensure that their memories would not be erased.

With the dawn breaking outside, Kusi felt a renewed sense of purpose. The battle against PromptTech had only just begun, and he was determined to see it through. Together, they would shatter the silence surrounding memory manipulation and ignite a movement that could change everything.

As the sun rose, casting golden light over the city, Kusi knew that the journey ahead would be fraught with danger, but he also felt an undeniable hope. They would fight, they would resist, and together, they would reclaim their memories and their futures.

Chapter 22: Fractured Realities

The morning sun spilled through the cracked windows of the safe house, casting long shadows across the floor. Kusi sat at the rickety table, the hard drive containing their hard-won evidence resting heavily before him. His heart raced with anticipation and dread as he considered the implications of their recent infiltration into PromptTech.

Araba entered the room, her expression determined despite the exhaustion that lingered in her eyes. "What's our next move?" she asked, her voice steady, but Kusi could sense the weight of their mission pressing down on her.

"We need to get this information out to the public," Kusi replied, gesturing to the hard drive. "But we can't just release it blindly. We need a strategy."

Araba nodded, a spark of excitement igniting in her gaze. "We should reach out to the journalists who have been covering PromptTech's activities. They can help us ensure that the information gets the attention it deserves."

Kusi's mind raced with possibilities. They had seen the impact that protests had generated, but they needed a louder voice—someone with the reach to amplify their findings. "Let's compile a list of trustworthy contacts in the media and begin drafting a message. We can't afford to miss this opportunity."

As the day unfolded, Kusi, Araba, Mossey, and Juna worked tirelessly, sifting through articles and social media profiles to identify journalists who had exposed PromptTech in the past. They crafted a compelling narrative, highlighting the corporation's unethical practices and the lives it had destroyed through memory manipulation.

Kusi could feel the urgency building as they refined their approach. "We need to frame this as not just a personal story but a societal issue," he said, looking at the group. "Memory manipulation isn't just about individual experiences; it's about control. It affects everyone."

Mossey nodded in agreement. "If we can show how far-reaching this is, it will resonate with a larger audience. People will understand that their own memories could be at risk."

As they worked late into the night, Kusi felt a sense of camaraderie developing between them. Each member of their group was vital to the mission, and together they formed a formidable team against PromptTech.

The following day, Kusi sent out their carefully crafted message to several journalists, hopeful that they would receive a response soon. They gathered at the safe house, each member on edge as they awaited news.

Hours turned into days, and just as frustration began to seep into the group, Kusi's communicator pinged with an incoming message. His heart raced as he opened the notification. It was from a journalist named Kira Chen, known for her investigative work on corporate malfeasance.

"I'd like to meet," the message read. *"Your claims are serious. We need to discuss how to verify your information before publishing."*

Kusi's breath caught in his throat. This could be the breakthrough they had been waiting for. "It's Kira Chen! She wants to meet with us!" He shared the message with the group, excitement filling the air.

Araba's eyes lit up. "We have to make sure we're prepared. This is our chance to expose PromptTech's corruption."

They arranged to meet Kira in a discreet café on the outskirts of the city, a place where prying eyes were less likely to intrude. The atmosphere was tense as they gathered around a small table, waiting for Kira to arrive.

When she walked in, Kusi felt a wave of relief. Kira exuded confidence, her sharp gaze scanning the room as she approached their table. "You must be Kusi," she said, extending her hand. "And the rest of you?"

"Mossey, Juna, and Araba," Kusi introduced, each member exchanging brief greetings with her.

"I appreciate you meeting with me," Kira said, taking a seat. "Your claims about PromptTech are serious, and I want to ensure we have all the facts straight before we go public."

Kusi nodded, his mind racing with the potential impact of their meeting. "We have evidence of memory manipulation practices that extend beyond anything the public has been led to believe. It's not just individual memories being traded; entire lives are being erased."

Kira leaned in, intrigued. "Tell me everything."

As Kusi laid out their findings, he could see Kira's interest intensifying. He shared the details of their infiltration, the hard drive filled with evidence, and the stories of individuals whose lives had been shattered by PromptTech's actions. Each account served as a chilling reminder of the consequences of unchecked power.

"What you're saying is incredible," Kira replied, her expression serious. "But we need more than just your word. We need documents, testimonies—anything we can use to substantiate these claims."

Kusi glanced at Araba, who had been quietly absorbing the conversation. "We can gather testimonies from individuals affected by PromptTech's actions," she suggested. "There are support groups—people who have lost their memories or who are seeking answers. They might be willing to share their stories."

"That's a good start," Kira agreed. "But we'll also need to trace back the data from your hard drive to see where it leads. We need to corroborate your findings with credible sources."

With Kira's guidance, they developed a plan to gather additional evidence. Kira suggested reaching out to former employees of PromptTech who might be willing to speak out, as well as establishing connections with grassroots organizations focused on memory rights.

Over the next few weeks, the group worked tirelessly, conducting interviews and collecting stories. Kusi felt a surge of hope as they began to piece together a mosaic of truths that painted a damning picture of PromptTech's operations.

During this time, Kusi and Araba's bond deepened. They often stayed up late, poring over testimonies and discussing strategies. Araba's resilience inspired Kusi, and he found himself drawn to her strength and determination.

One evening, as they reviewed their findings, Kusi paused, looking at Araba. "I never imagined we'd be here—fighting against something so powerful. It's terrifying and exhilarating at the same time."

Araba met his gaze, a fire igniting in her eyes. "We're not just fighting for ourselves anymore; we're fighting for everyone who has been affected. This is bigger than us, Kusi."

As the day of their press conference approached, a sense of unease settled over Kusi. He knew they were about to take a monumental step, but the stakes were high. PromptTech would not take their actions lightly.

On the eve of the conference, the group gathered in the safe house, sharing a quiet meal as they prepared for the next day. The atmosphere was somber yet charged with anticipation.

"Tomorrow could change everything," Juna said, her voice soft yet filled with conviction. "We need to be ready for whatever comes next."

Kusi nodded, a mix of nerves and excitement swirling within him. "We've come too far to back down now. We're standing up for those who can't fight for themselves."

As they finished their meal, Kusi felt a renewed sense of purpose. They were about to expose the dark underbelly of memory manipulation and ignite a movement that could reclaim their identities.

The next day, as they gathered outside the conference hall, Kusi felt the weight of the moment bearing down on him. The crowd was swelling, a sea of faces eager to hear their story. Journalists set up cameras, the media buzz surrounding them like a swarm.

Kira stood at the front, her expression determined. "We need to make sure our voices are heard. This is our moment to shine a light on the truth."

As Kusi stepped up to the podium, his heart raced. He glanced at Araba, Mossey, and Juna, each of them standing behind him, their unwavering support bolstering his confidence.

"Thank you all for being here today," Kusi began, his voice steady as he spoke into the microphone. "We're here to shed light on the truth behind PromptTech's actions—actions that have affected countless lives. Memory manipulation is not just a concept; it's a weapon wielded by those in power to control and erase the narratives of the individuals they deem unworthy."

The crowd erupted into applause, their energy surging around him. Kusi felt the power of their collective resolve, a wave of support that propelled him forward. "Today, we stand together against oppression. We refuse to be silenced, and we will fight for the right to our memories, our identities, and our futures!"

Just as the applause reached a crescendo, the atmosphere shifted. A commotion broke out near the back of the crowd, and Kusi's heart dropped as he spotted a group of PromptTech's security personnel pushing through the masses, their expressions cold and menacing.

"Everyone, please remain calm!" Kira shouted, her voice cutting through the chaos. "This is a peaceful demonstration!"

But Kusi could see the determination in the guards' eyes. They were there to intimidate and silence. He felt a surge of anger rise within him as he scanned the crowd, the mix of fear and courage palpable.

Suddenly, a guard stepped forward, raising a megaphone. "This assembly is unauthorized! Disperse immediately or face consequences!"

Kusi's pulse quickened. They had anticipated a response, but the reality of it sent adrenaline coursing through his veins. This was the moment of truth, a test of their resolve.

Araba stepped up beside Kusi, her voice fierce. "We will not back down! We're here to speak the truth, and you cannot silence us!"

The crowd erupted in cheers, the spirit of resistance igniting. Kusi could feel the energy shift, a surge of unity that defied the oppressive presence of PromptTech.

"Remember why we're here!" Kusi shouted, trying to rally the crowd's spirits even as anxiety twisted in his gut. "We're not just fighting for ourselves, but for everyone who has had their memories stolen, their lives erased. This is about our right to exist in our own narratives!"

The cheers grew louder, echoing off the buildings surrounding them. Kusi felt a surge of strength and determination from the crowd, a collective heartbeat that resonated with their shared struggle. The tension in the air crackled like static electricity, charged with the promise of confrontation.

Kira stood resolutely by Kusi's side, her expression determined. "If they want a fight, let's give them one! We're not going to back down. We will take our message to the people, and we will make it impossible for them to ignore us!"

With that, Kira stepped back to address the crowd. "This is a moment of truth! Let's show PromptTech that we are united, and we will not be intimidated! Together, we can demand accountability and change!"

The crowd roared in agreement, their energy palpable as Kusi felt the fire of resistance burning brightly in their midst. He had never felt so alive, so connected to the fight against injustice.

As the guards advanced, pushing through the crowd, Kusi exchanged glances with Araba and Mossey. "We need to keep the momentum going," he said urgently. "Let's lead them forward—show them we won't be afraid!"

Araba nodded, a fierce glint in her eyes. "We need to create a diversion. If we can draw them away from the center, it'll give us time to regroup and keep sharing our message."

Kusi turned to Mossey, who was scanning the crowd, eyes darting like a hawk. "Can you work with Juna to get people to spread out? Create some chaos, draw them away from the podium!"

Mossey grinned, adrenaline coursing through him. "I'm on it!" He quickly moved through the crowd, relaying the plan to Juna.

As the guards continued to push forward, Kusi raised his voice, calling for unity. "Stay strong! We will not be divided! Remember, our power lies in our numbers!"

With a determined yell, Mossey and Juna started to incite movement among the crowd. People began to chant slogans, clapping and raising their fists in solidarity, creating a wave of noise that reverberated through the air. It was a moment of spontaneous rebellion—a reminder that they were more than just individuals; they were a collective force.

As the guards reached the podium, Kusi felt his heart race. He stood firm, facing the menacing figures with a resolve he hadn't known he possessed. "You can't silence us! We will not back down!" he declared.

One of the guards, a burly figure with a menacing glare, stepped forward. "You are trespassing and inciting unrest. We will take you in if you do not disperse immediately."

Kusi held his ground, refusing to let fear dictate his actions. "You can try, but the truth is stronger than your intimidation tactics! We're here to expose the truth about PromptTech and the manipulation of memories. We will not be silenced!"

Araba stepped beside him, her voice ringing with conviction. "We are the voices of the forgotten, and we refuse to let you erase us any longer!"

The crowd surged, their defiance creating an unbreakable barrier against the oppressive forces before them. Kusi could feel the adrenaline coursing through him, the overwhelming sense of purpose igniting a fire within him. He could see the determination etched on the faces of the people around him, each one a testament to the fight for their memories and identities.

Suddenly, the tide began to shift. Journalists snapped photos, capturing the moment, their cameras flashing like lightning amidst the chaos. Kira stood resolute, ensuring their message was broadcast far and wide, the very act of documenting the confrontation a shield against the guards' intimidation.

Just then, a familiar face emerged from the crowd—Kira Chen herself, with a camera crew following closely behind. "What's happening here?" she shouted, approaching Kusi. "Can you tell me what's going on?"

"This is our fight against PromptTech!" Kusi exclaimed, gesturing to the crowd. "We're demanding transparency and accountability for their memory manipulation practices!"

Kira nodded, her focus unwavering. "I'll make sure this is covered extensively. You're doing something monumental here!"

Kusi felt a rush of hope as he realized that their stand was gaining traction, a wave of change surging forward. The crowd's energy fed into him, igniting a determination that felt unstoppable.

As the standoff continued, Kusi's thoughts raced. The situation was dangerous, and they needed to be strategic. "Let's move toward the park!" he shouted to the crowd. "We can continue our demonstration there, and the media can follow!"

With that, the crowd began to chant, "To the park! To the park!" The guards, caught off guard, found it difficult to maintain control as the people surged forward, pushing past them.

Kusi felt a rush of exhilaration as he moved with the crowd. They were reclaiming their narrative, their memories, and their identities with every step they took. As they made their way to the park, Kusi glanced at Araba, who was smiling, her eyes sparkling with defiance.

Once they reached the park, the atmosphere shifted. The space was open, allowing for freedom of movement. People gathered, their voices rising in unison, united in purpose. Kusi felt the energy swell, a palpable sense of solidarity that filled the air.

"Now we can share our stories," Kusi declared, addressing the crowd. "We are here to remind the world that our memories matter, that our identities cannot be erased or manipulated!"

The crowd erupted in applause, and Kusi felt a surge of emotion. This was their moment—an opportunity to reclaim what had been stolen from them. Together, they would fight against the powerful forces that sought to control their narratives.

As they shared stories of loss, pain, and resilience, Kusi marveled at the diverse experiences that intertwined to form a tapestry of resistance. Each voice added weight to their collective narrative, weaving a story that could not be ignored.

"We will stand together, fight together, and remember together!" Araba shouted, her voice ringing through the park. "Our memories are our truths, and we will not let anyone take that away from us!"

Kusi felt the crowd's energy lift, a powerful force that propelled them forward. In that moment, he knew that they were not just fighting for their own memories but for a future where everyone had the right to their own narrative.

Yet, amidst the unity and strength, Kusi sensed the looming shadow of PromptTech. The fight was far from over, and he knew they would face retaliation. But with every story shared and every voice raised, they were building a movement that could challenge the very foundation of the corporation's control.

As the sun dipped low in the sky, casting a golden hue over the park, Kusi looked around at the faces of his companions—Araba, Mossey, Juna, and Kira. They were warriors in this fight for justice, and together they would illuminate the dark corners of memory manipulation.

This was just the beginning. A battle had been ignited, and Kusi felt a surge of determination rise within him. They would not back down; they would forge ahead, ready to confront whatever challenges lay ahead, united in purpose and resilience.

Chapter 23: The Veil of Truth

As the first light of dawn broke over the horizon, painting the sky in hues of orange and pink, Kusi found himself standing at the edge of the park, reflecting on the events of the previous day. The park had transformed overnight, becoming a symbol of their defiance. Banners with slogans like "Memories Matter" and "Erase the Erasers" fluttered in the gentle morning breeze, remnants of the passionate demonstration that had unfolded.

Kusi took a deep breath, the crisp morning air invigorating his senses. Around him, remnants of the night's gathering lingered: discarded cups, crumpled flyers, and a sense of hope that felt almost tangible. But amidst the hope was an undercurrent of anxiety; he knew that PromptTech would not sit idle, especially after the disruption they had caused.

Gathering his thoughts, Kusi made his way to the small café that had become a makeshift headquarters for their movement. Inside, he found Araba and Mossey deep in conversation, surrounded by scattered papers and devices flashing with activity. The café buzzed with energy, filled with supporters discussing strategies and sharing their stories.

"Morning!" Kusi greeted them, his voice steady despite the turmoil swirling in his mind.

"Morning!" Araba replied, her smile radiant. "We've been brainstorming ways to keep the momentum going. We can't let yesterday be a one-off."

Mossey looked up, his brows furrowed in concentration. "There's a lot of chatter online. Some are rallying to continue the demonstrations, while others are pushing for more organized efforts. But we need to be strategic about it."

Kusi nodded, feeling a sense of unity in their shared purpose. "We have to make sure our message is clear. This isn't just about protesting; it's about building a movement that demands accountability from PromptTech."

As they discussed tactics, Kusi couldn't shake the feeling that there was more to uncover about PromptTech's operations. He recalled the whispers he had heard about a black market for memories and the dark dealings that lay beneath the surface. "What if we could expose something bigger? Something that could not only inform the public but also rally them to our cause?" he suggested.

Araba's eyes lit up with interest. "You mean, like a journalistic exposé? We could infiltrate some of their operations, gather evidence, and release it to the public."

"Exactly," Kusi replied, excitement bubbling within him. "We need to connect the dots and show people the real implications of what PromptTech is doing. If we can find someone on the inside who's willing to talk…"

Mossey leaned back, folding his arms thoughtfully. "That could be dangerous. PromptTech has eyes everywhere, and anyone who tries to cross them might not end up alive to tell the tale."

Kusi understood the risks, but he also felt an overwhelming urgency to act. They needed allies, and perhaps it was time to reach out to someone who had insight into PromptTech's inner workings. "What about Juna?" Kusi proposed. "She has connections in the tech community and may know someone who has insider information." Araba nodded. "It's worth a shot. If we can get close to someone with first-hand knowledge of the black market or the memory trade, it might give us the leverage we need."

Kusi pulled out his device and messaged Juna, inviting her to join them at the café. As he sent the message, a sense of anticipation filled the air. They were on the brink of something significant, and every action brought them closer to exposing the truth.

Minutes later, Juna entered the café, her expression a mix of excitement and caution. "Hey, everyone! What's this I hear about a new plan?" she asked, her eyes sparkling with curiosity.

Kusi gestured for her to sit. "We need your help. We're looking for a way to expose PromptTech's darker dealings—particularly anything to do with the black market for memories."

Juna leaned forward, intrigued. "I have some contacts in the tech underworld, people who might know more about the memory trading business. But it's risky; if PromptTech catches wind of this, we could all be in serious trouble."

"Risk is part of the game," Mossey chimed in. "But it's worth it if it means getting the truth out there."

After a brief discussion, they devised a plan to reach out to Juna's contacts and set up a meeting with someone who might be willing to talk. They decided to be cautious, using encrypted communication and avoiding direct references to PromptTech.

Juna shared the names of a few potential contacts, individuals known to have ties to the black market. "If we can get one of them to agree to meet, we might be able to gather enough information to make a solid case against PromptTech," she explained.

"Let's do it," Kusi said, feeling a surge of determination. "But we need to make sure we have a backup plan in case things go sideways."

The group spent the next hour strategizing, discussing possible escape routes and safety measures. Kusi's mind raced with possibilities, each one more exhilarating than the last. They were becoming a force to be reckoned with, and with each step, they were reclaiming their power.

As they wrapped up their meeting, Juna received a message from one of her contacts—a tech specialist named Theo who had been rumored to have knowledge of the memory trading operations. "He wants to meet tonight," she said, excitement in her voice. "But he insists on a public location. No one can know he's talking to us."

"Where?" Kusi asked, his pulse quickening.

"Underground bar called The XCorp," Juna replied. "It's known for being a hub for those who dabble in tech and memory trades. We'll blend in, but we need to be careful."

As the day wore on, Kusi felt a mix of anticipation and anxiety. They would be stepping into the underbelly of the city, a place where danger lurked around every corner. He gathered a small bag of essentials—his device, a portable charger, and a small recording device—anything that might help them capture crucial information.

When evening fell, the group met again, preparing for the night ahead. Araba's eyes glimmered with excitement as they discussed what they hoped to learn. "This could be the key to exposing everything," she said, her voice steady.

"Let's stay focused," Kusi reminded them. "We need to listen carefully and gather as much information as we can without drawing attention to ourselves."

As they made their way to The XCorp, the vibrant city transformed around them. Neon lights flickered against the darkened streets, casting eerie shadows on the pavement. The atmosphere felt charged, alive with possibility and danger. Kusi's heart raced as they approached the entrance, a nondescript door wedged between two larger buildings.

Inside, the air was thick with the scent of alcohol and the sound of laughter and clinking glasses. The bar pulsed with energy, filled with a diverse crowd of patrons—techies, hackers, and individuals lost in their own worlds. Kusi glanced around, trying to gauge the atmosphere, a sense of caution looming over him.

"There he is," Juna whispered, nodding toward a figure seated at the far end of the bar. Theo was lean, with sharp features and an air of confidence. He glanced up, locking eyes with Juna before motioning for them to come closer.

As they approached, Kusi's stomach tightened with anticipation. Theo leaned back, his demeanor relaxed, but Kusi could sense the tension beneath the surface. "You made it," Theo said, a hint of curiosity in his voice. "I hear you're looking for information about PromptTech."

"Yes," Kusi replied, his voice steady. "We need to know about the black market for memories—specifically, how it operates and who's involved."

Theo raised an eyebrow, glancing around to ensure no one was listening. "You're diving into dangerous waters. PromptTech doesn't take kindly to people snooping around their business."

"We know the risks," Araba interjected, her determination shining through. "But we can't stand by while they manipulate lives and erase identities."

Theo regarded them for a moment, assessing their resolve. "Alright. But I need to know you're serious. This isn't just a casual inquiry; lives are at stake here." Kusi nodded, feeling a swell of determination. "We're prepared to do whatever it takes to expose the truth. People deserve to know what's happening."

"Then listen carefully," Theo began, his voice dropping to a whisper. "The black market operates under the radar, with connections deep in the tech community. PromptTech has a web of contacts that stretch far and wide, making it hard to pinpoint who's involved. But there are whispers of a hidden auction where memories are traded like commodities."

Kusi leaned in, hanging on Theo's every word. "What kind of memories?"

"Everything," Theo replied, his eyes glinting with a mix of caution and intrigue. "Personal experiences, skills, even the memories of those erased from existence. It's a lucrative business, and PromptTech is at the center of it. They don't just erase memories—they sell them, manipulate them, and use them as leverage over people."

Kusi felt a chill run down his spine. This was worse than he had imagined. "We need evidence," he pressed. "Can you help us?"

Theo considered for a moment. "I might know someone who can get you in touch with the right people. But it's risky. If you get caught, there's no telling what PromptTech will do."

"Whatever it takes," Kusi insisted, determination radiating from him. "We can't let them continue this."

Theo nodded, the gravity of the situation settling between them. "Alright. I'll make some calls. But you need to lay low until I get back to you. The walls have ears, and PromptTech is always listening."

As they wrapped up their conversation, Kusi felt a mix of hope and apprehension. They were on the brink of uncovering a massive conspiracy, but the dangers were looming closer. He couldn't shake the feeling that PromptTech was watching, waiting for any sign of rebellion.

As they left The XCorp, Kusi's heart raced with the possibilities that lay ahead. They were stepping deeper into a world fraught with danger, but the truth was worth every risk. And with Araba, Juna, and Mossey by his side, he felt ready to face whatever challenges awaited them.

Later that night, as they walked home under the starlit sky, Kusi's thoughts whirled with the revelations of the evening. He glanced at Araba, who walked beside him, her face illuminated by the moonlight.

"Are you okay?" he asked, sensing the tension in her demeanor.

She smiled softly, her eyes reflecting the stars above. "I'm just thinking about everything we've learned. This is bigger than any of us. But we're not alone in this. We have each other."

Kusi nodded, feeling the weight of her words. The fight ahead would be daunting, but they were united by a shared purpose. And together, they would unearth the truth, no matter the cost.

With that thought in mind, they stepped forward into the night, ready to face the challenges that lay ahead, their resolve strengthened by the bonds they had forged

.

Chapter 24: Navigating the Shadows

The days following their meeting at The XCorp, were a whirlwind of activity. Kusi, Araba, Juna, and Mossey transformed the café into a hub of information, strategizing and preparing for the next steps in their fight against PromptTech. They were determined to expose the corporation's malfeasance and the grim reality of memory trading.

"Tonight's the night," Kusi announced as they gathered in the café, the atmosphere charged with anticipation. "Theo's arranged a meeting with a contact who can get us closer to the auction. If we play our cards right, we might be able to gather enough evidence to make a real impact."

Araba's eyes shone with determination. "Let's make sure we're ready for anything. We need to keep a low profile, especially if we're going into one of their high-stakes operations."

Mossey chimed in, "I've been monitoring the underground chatter. There's been a lot of talk about this auction. People are nervous. It seems like something big is about to go down."

As evening approached, the group made final preparations. They donned casual clothing—simple but practical outfits that would help them blend into the crowd. Kusi felt a mixture of excitement and trepidation as they reviewed their plan one last time.

"We'll enter the venue in pairs," Kusi instructed, feeling the weight of leadership settle on his shoulders. "Juna and I will scout ahead while Araba and Mossey hang back, observing from a distance. If things go sideways, we need to be able to regroup quickly."

"Got it," Mossey replied, his demeanor serious. "I'll keep my eyes open. If I see anything suspicious, I'll send you a message."

As they made their way to the venue, Kusi's heart raced. The location was an abandoned warehouse on the outskirts of the city, repurposed for clandestine gatherings. The atmosphere felt electric, the air thick with anticipation and the promise of danger. Shadows flickered in the dim light, and muffled voices echoed as they approached.

Inside, the scene was surreal. A lavish setting adorned with ambient lights and elaborate decorations belied the dark purpose of the gathering. People milled about, exchanging hushed conversations while glancing over their shoulders, clearly aware of the risk involved. Kusi felt a knot in his stomach as he surveyed the room, knowing they were stepping into the lion's den.

"Stay close," Juna whispered, nudging Kusi as they moved further inside. "We need to find Theo's contact and get the lay of the land before we do anything."

They made their way to a quieter corner of the warehouse, where Theo's contact, a woman named Mira, was supposed to be waiting. Mira was known for her expertise in the memory trade, and Kusi hoped she would provide the insights they needed.

"Over there," Juna pointed discreetly, spotting a woman with vibrant purple hair and a commanding presence. Mira stood at the bar, sipping a drink and scanning the room with sharp eyes.

Kusi approached cautiously, Juna by his side. "Mira?" he said, offering a polite nod.

She turned to them, her gaze piercing. "You must be the ones Theo mentioned. You're brave to show up here."

"Or foolish," Kusi replied, a nervous laugh escaping him. "We're just here to gather information. We want to expose PromptTech and what they're doing with memories."

Mira's expression softened slightly, but the gravity of the situation remained. "You're not the only ones who feel that way. This auction is where memories are bought and sold like commodities. PromptTech has deep roots in this operation."

As they spoke, Kusi noticed the atmosphere in the room shift. The crowd began to gather in front of a large stage, where an imposing figure stood at the podium. The auctioneer, a man with a slicked-back hairstyle and a glimmering suit, commanded attention.

"Ladies and gentlemen," he boomed, his voice resonating throughout the warehouse. "Welcome to tonight's auction, where memories become currency and experiences are laid bare for the highest bidder. Let's begin!"

Kusi's heart raced as he turned to Mira. "We need to get closer. We have to see what they're selling."

"Stick close to me," Mira instructed, leading them through the throng of people. They squeezed between clusters of attendees, adrenaline coursing through Kusi's veins as they approached the front of the stage.

As the auctioneer began the first bid, Kusi felt a wave of unease wash over him. The first item up for sale was a memory of a child's first steps, accompanied by a video montage that played on a large screen. The crowd gasped, and Kusi could see the eyes of some bidders glinting with greed.

"Who would want to buy something like that?" Araba murmured, her voice barely audible over the murmurs of the crowd.

"People often want memories to feel connected, to relive experiences that define them," Mira explained. "But in reality, it's exploitation. PromptTech s goal is to control and manipulate people through their pasts."

Kusi's heart sank as he watched the bidding unfold. It felt wrong—so utterly devoid of humanity. The auctioneer's voice rose, the prices escalating rapidly, until a wealthy-looking man finally claimed the memory for a staggering amount. The crowd erupted in applause, and Kusi's stomach churned at the thought of memories being sold like mere objects.

As the auction continued, Kusi felt a tap on his shoulder. He turned to see Mossey, a look of alarm etched on his face. "We need to move. I just overheard some guys talking about a raid. They're onto us."

Kusi's heart raced. "What do you mean?"

"They mentioned some newcomers snooping around. PromptTech 's security is here in full force. We need to get out—now."

Mira's eyes widened, her previous confidence shaken. "If they find you here, they'll take you out without hesitation. We have to go, and fast."

Kusi felt a surge of urgency as they turned to leave, but as they made their way through the crowd, the atmosphere shifted abruptly. The auctioneer's voice echoed, laced with authority.

"Ladies and gentlemen, I regret to inform you that we have a security breach. Please remain calm as we conduct a sweep of the venue."

A ripple of fear spread through the audience as murmurs turned into panic. People began to push and shove, desperate to escape. Kusi felt his heart pounding in his chest as he exchanged glances with Araba and Juna. This was it—the moment they had feared.

"Stick together!" Kusi shouted, trying to keep the group close as they navigated the chaos.

But the crowd was overwhelming, and Kusi felt himself being pulled in different directions. He spotted Mira disappearing into the throng, and panic surged through him. They couldn't lose her—she was their only chance of understanding the full scope of PromptTech's operations.

"Over here!" Mossey called, motioning toward a side exit that seemed less congested.

Kusi nodded, feeling a sense of urgency take hold. They pushed through the crowd, determined to escape the chaos, but as they reached the exit, a group of uniformed guards stepped into view, blocking their path.

"Stop right there!" one of the guards shouted, his voice authoritative and menacing. "You're not going anywhere."

Kusi's mind raced. They had to think fast. "We're just trying to leave! We didn't do anything wrong!" he protested, but the guard wasn't buying it.

"Search them!" the guard ordered, advancing toward them with his colleagues.

Panic surged through Kusi's veins. They had to act, and fast. "Back off!" he yelled, adrenaline fueling his words.

Araba stepped forward, her voice steady. "We have every right to be here. This is a public gathering."

But the guards advanced, determination etched on their faces. Kusi felt the weight of the moment settle on him, and instinct took over. He turned and dashed toward a nearby stairwell, his heart pounding as he urged Araba, Mossey, and Juna to follow.

"Move!" he shouted, adrenaline propelling him forward. They raced up the stairs, the echoes of pursuit ringing in their ears.

They burst through the door at the top of the stairs and found themselves on a rooftop terrace. The city skyline stretched out before them, illuminated by the glow of neon lights and the distant hum of activity. Kusi could hear the guards below, their shouts growing fainter.

"Where do we go now?" Juna asked, glancing around for an exit.

"There!" Mossey pointed to a fire escape ladder leading down the side of the building. "We can make it down and blend into the alley."

With no time to waste, Kusi led the way, descending the ladder quickly. The ground felt like a sanctuary as they hit the pavement, the thrill of escape surging through them.

"Keep moving!" Kusi urged, leading them through the narrow alleyways, heart racing. The sound of sirens blared in the distance, and he knew they had to find a way to lose the heat.

Finally, they found a hidden spot behind a row of dumpsters, catching their breath as they tried to regain composure.

As they crouched behind the dumpsters, the adrenaline of the escape slowly began to ebb, leaving a lingering anxiety in its wake. Kusi leaned against the cool metal, trying to calm his racing heart.

He could hear the distant wails of sirens, a stark reminder of how close they had come to capture.

"Did everyone make it out?" Kusi asked, scanning their faces for any signs of distress.

"Yeah, we're all here," Araba replied, her voice shaky but resolute. "What now?"

Kusi rubbed the back of his neck, feeling the weight of their situation. "We regroup and rethink our approach. If PromptTech is onto us, we need to be smarter about this."

Juna nodded, her eyes fierce with determination. "We can't let them intimidate us. We know too much now."

Kusi felt a surge of determination. They had crossed a line, and retreating was not an option. "We need to find a way to gather evidence, and we need allies. If PromptTech is as powerful as we think, we can't do this alone."

As they huddled together, Kusi felt a sense of camaraderie growing among them. They had faced danger, but they had also tasted the thrill of fighting back against the oppressive forces that sought to control their lives.

"Tomorrow, we find Mira," Kusi said, a sense of purpose driving his words. "We'll dig deeper and uncover the truth, no matter the cost."

Kusi's mind raced with thoughts of what lay ahead. They had witnessed the dark underbelly of PromptTech's operations, and now it was imperative that they act. The memories they had seen traded like currency haunted him—what kind of world had they stepped into?

"We should lay low tonight," Mossey suggested, glancing around as if the shadows themselves were listening. "We'll need our strength."

"I agree," Araba said, her voice steady. "But we can't afford to lose momentum. We need a plan, and we need it fast."

Kusi nodded, knowing she was right. "Let's meet back here tomorrow morning. We'll strategize and see if we can track down Mira."

As the night wore on, Kusi lay awake, staring up at the ceiling of his small apartment. The events of the night played over and over in his mind—the faces of the auction participants, the fear in Araba's eyes, and the ominous presence of PromptTech's guards. The shadows felt alive around him, closing in like a predator waiting to strike.

But as dawn broke, a renewed sense of purpose filled him. They were fighting against a system that commodified human experience, and that made their struggle worthwhile. He had to protect not just his memories but also the memories of others who had been erased from existence.

The next morning, the group reconvened at The XCorp, the café now a sanctuary for their plans. Kusi arrived early, the scent of coffee mingling with the crisp morning air. He scanned the room, anticipation coursing through him.

"Where's Mira?" Juna asked, concern etched on her face.

"I'm sure she'll come," Kusi reassured them, though he felt a twinge of doubt. "We just need to be patient."

Finally, after what felt like an eternity, Mira entered the café. Her vibrant hair seemed to shine even brighter in the sunlight, and her presence brought a palpable energy to the room.

"Sorry for the delay," she said, sliding into a seat at their table. "I had to shake off some followers. PromptTech is keeping a close eye on me."

"Do you have information for us?" Kusi asked, leaning in, eager to hear what she had to say.

Mira nodded, her expression serious. "What you witnessed at the auction is just the tip of the iceberg. PromptTech is not just trading memories; they are actively erasing dissenting voices. They're controlling the narrative by manipulating history itself."

Kusi felt a chill run down his spine. "What do you mean?"

Mira leaned closer, lowering her voice. "They've developed a system to remove individuals from societal memory. If someone poses a threat or dissent, they're erased—completely. People who used to exist become nothing more than ghosts, and their memories are repackaged and sold."

The weight of her words settled heavily on Kusi's shoulders. "How do we stop them?"

Mira sighed, her gaze distant. "We need evidence. We need to expose their operations and rally others to our cause. There are still many who oppose PromptTech; we just need to find them."

The group spent the next few hours discussing strategies and potential allies. Mira shared her knowledge of underground networks—hackers, journalists, and former employees who had fled PromptTech's grasp. Kusi felt hope begin to bloom within him as they mapped out a plan.

"We'll start by reaching out to these contacts," Kusi said, his voice filled with determination. "We need to build a coalition to fight back against PromptTech. If we can gather enough evidence, we might have a chance."

As the meeting wrapped up, Kusi felt a sense of purpose swell within him. They were no longer just a group of individuals—they were a collective force against a corrupt system. And that was something worth fighting for.

With a renewed sense of urgency, the group set out to contact potential allies. Kusi took the lead, reaching out to a network of hackers known as "The Specters." They were notorious for their ability to infiltrate secure systems and expose hidden truths. If anyone could help them gather the evidence they needed, it was them.

As they worked tirelessly throughout the day, Kusi felt a sense of camaraderie growing among them. Each call they made and each connection they forged brought them closer to their goal. They were no longer just fighting for their own memories; they were fighting for a future where memories belonged to the people—not a corporation.

Later that evening, Kusi found himself alone in his apartment, reflecting on the journey that had led him here. He glanced at a photo on his desk—a picture of his family, taken long before memory manipulation became commonplace. The faces smiled back at him, filled with love and warmth. It was a reminder of everything that was at stake.

His phone buzzed, breaking him from his reverie. It was a message from Juna. *"We've secured a meeting with The Specters tonight. Are you in?"*

Kusi felt a rush of adrenaline. This was the moment they had been waiting for—a chance to gain the support they needed to fight back. He quickly typed a response.

"Absolutely. I'll be there."

As he prepared to leave, a sense of anticipation washed over him. They were about to step deeper into the shadows, but Kusi knew it was a necessary risk. The fight against PromptTech was no longer just about memories; it was about reclaiming their lives and the lives of those who had been erased.

When he arrived at the designated meeting spot, a dimly lit bar on the outskirts of the city, he felt the weight of the world on his shoulders. The atmosphere was thick with secrecy and tension as he spotted Juna and Mossey seated at a table in the corner.

"There you are," Juna greeted, relief flooding her voice. "We were starting to worry."

"Not a chance," Kusi replied, taking a seat. "Let's hope The Specters are as good as their reputation."

As the minutes ticked by, Kusi felt a mixture of excitement and dread. They were about to dive deeper into a world filled with uncertainty and danger, but he was determined to see it through. The fight for their identities—and the identities of countless others—was just beginning.

And as the shadows danced around them, Kusi steeled himself for the challenges that lay ahead, ready to navigate the treacherous waters of resistance against PromptTech's insidious grasp.

.

Chapter 25: Veil of Illusions

The dimly lit bar pulsated with low music, creating an almost hypnotic atmosphere that masked the tense discussions taking place within. Kusi scanned the room, his heart racing with anticipation. The Specters were known for their discretion, and he hoped that the reputation was well-deserved.

As they settled into their booth, Juna leaned in closer. "Do you think they'll really help us?"

"We need to give them a reason to," Kusi replied, glancing toward the entrance. "If they see the potential for disruption against PromptTech, they'll be more inclined to join us."

Mossey, who had been tapping his fingers nervously on the table, spoke up. "What if they don't buy into our story? What if they think we're just a bunch of idealists?"

"We won't know until we talk to them," Kusi said firmly, his resolve unwavering. "We have to convince them of the stakes."

Just then, a figure emerged from the shadows—an individual clad in a sleek, dark jacket and a hood that obscured their features. The Specter had arrived.

"Are you Kusi?" the figure asked, their voice a smooth blend of curiosity and authority.

"I am," Kusi responded, trying to keep his tone steady. "And these are my associates, Juna and Mossey. We reached out because we need your expertise."

The Specter nodded, taking a seat across from them. "You're aware that working with us comes with risks. We don't take kindly to betrayal."

"Neither do we," Kusi shot back, meeting the figure's intense gaze. "We're not here to play games. We're here to expose PromptTech's operations and protect our identities—and the identities of countless others."

The Specter leaned back, seemingly assessing Kusi's sincerity. "And how do you plan to do that? We don't have time for half-measures."

Kusi took a deep breath, feeling the weight of the moment. "We have information about a black market for memories and individuals being erased from existence. We want to gather evidence, expose the truth, and build a coalition to fight back."

The figure's expression remained inscrutable. "That's a tall order. PromptTech has a stranglehold on this city. What makes you think you can disrupt their operations?"

"We've seen it firsthand," Juna interjected, her voice steady. "People are suffering. Memories are being commodified, and dissent is being erased. We're fighting not just for ourselves, but for those who have been silenced."

The Specter considered her words, the tension in the air palpable. "If you're serious, you'll need a plan—something that can draw attention. You need evidence that can't be ignored."

"We're willing to do whatever it takes," Kusi said, determination evident in his tone. "We need your help to infiltrate their systems and gather proof of their operations."

"Let me make one thing clear," the Specter replied, leaning forward. "PromptTech is not just an adversary; they are a behemoth. If you want to take them down, you need to be prepared for the consequences."

"Whatever it takes," Mossey echoed, his voice resolute.

The Specter studied them closely before nodding slightly. "Very well. I'll provide you with resources and contacts within the underground network. But you'll need to move quickly; they're tightening their grip."

As they discussed their next steps, Kusi felt a spark of hope igniting within him. They were no longer isolated; they were part of something larger. The Specter's guidance would be instrumental in their fight against PromptTech.

"We'll need to gather intelligence on their memory extraction facility," Kusi said, scribbling notes on a napkin. "If we can get inside and retrieve evidence of the operations, it could be enough to rally public support."

The Specter nodded. "I can arrange for a distraction. While PromptTech's security is focused elsewhere, you'll have a narrow window to infiltrate the facility."

Juna's eyes lit up. "What kind of distraction?"

"I have a few contacts who can create a diversion," the Specter explained. "A coordinated disruption will draw their attention away from you, but it'll only last for a short period."

Kusi exchanged glances with Juna and Mossey. "When do we start?"

"Tomorrow night," the Specter replied. "Be ready. I'll send you the details."

As they concluded the meeting, Kusi felt a mix of excitement and dread. The stakes were higher than ever, and while the plan felt solid, he couldn't shake the feeling that they were stepping into the lion's den. On their way back, the weight of uncertainty hung heavily over them. "Do you really think this will work?" Juna asked, her voice filled with concern.

"We have to believe it will," Kusi replied, trying to quell his own doubts. "If we don't, then we're already lost."

Mossey, ever the pragmatist, offered a more grounded perspective. "And if we fail? What then?"

Kusi felt the familiar pang of fear, but he pushed it aside. "We won't fail. We can't. Too many lives depend on us."

That night, Kusi found it difficult to sleep, his mind racing with the possibilities of what lay ahead. He tossed and turned, thoughts swirling like a tempest in his mind. The next day would set everything in motion, and he had to be ready.

The faint glow of dawn crept through his window, casting long shadows across the room. He rose early, determined to prepare himself mentally and physically for the challenges ahead.

He spent the morning reviewing the information they had gathered on PromptTech, pouring over every detail. The more he learned, the more he understood the vastness of their operations—their reach extended far beyond what he had initially imagined. They were a machine, and he and his friends were mere cogs attempting to disrupt its function.

Later that day, Kusi met with Juna and Mossey to go over their plan one last time. "We need to be synchronized," he said, pacing the small room. "Every second will count. When we get the signal, we move in."

"What if something goes wrong?" Mossey asked, his brow furrowed with concern. "We need a backup plan." Kusi nodded, acknowledging the wisdom in his words. "If we get caught, we need to stay calm. We can't let them know what we're after. We'll play it cool until we find an opportunity to escape."

Juna chimed in, her voice steady. "And if we do find the evidence we're looking for?"

"Then we'll make it public," Kusi declared, his heart pounding. "We'll expose PromptTech for what they are. We'll show everyone the truth behind their façade."

As night fell, the anticipation hung thick in the air. Kusi felt a surge of adrenaline coursing through his veins as they prepared to execute their plan. They gathered their gear, ensuring they had everything they needed for the infiltration.

When the time finally came, Kusi's heart raced as they received the Specter's message—a signal indicating that the distraction was in place. "This is it," he said, glancing at Juna and Mossey. "Stay focused. We can do this."

They moved swiftly through the darkened streets, the thrill of the impending operation driving them forward. As they approached the PromptTech facility, Kusi's breath caught in his throat. This was the moment they had prepared for—the moment they would either reclaim their identities or fall victim to the shadows.

With a deep breath, Kusi led the way, ready to navigate the darkness and uncover the truth lurking within the heart of PromptTech. The battle for their memories—and their futures—was about to begin.

Chapter 26: Fallen Shadows

The night was thick with tension as Kusi, Juna, and Mossey approached the towering façade of PromptTech's extraction facility. The oppressive silence seemed to swallow them whole, the only sound being the distant hum of machinery and the faint echoes of their footsteps. Kusi's heart pounded in his chest, the enormity of their mission weighing heavily on his shoulders.

"Remember the plan," Kusi whispered, his voice steady despite the fear bubbling beneath the surface. "We stick together. No heroics."

Juna nodded, her determination palpable. "We've come too far to turn back now."

Mossey shifted uneasily, his gaze darting around the shadows. "I just hope the distraction holds long enough for us to get what we need."

As they neared the entrance, Kusi gestured toward a side door, half-hidden by overgrown vines. "That's our way in," he said, leading the way. The door creaked ominously as they pushed it open, revealing a dimly lit corridor lined with flickering lights.

They stepped inside, their movements careful and deliberate. The air was thick with a metallic scent, a reminder of the technology that lay beyond the walls. Kusi felt a mix of excitement and dread; this was the moment they had trained for, but it also felt like stepping into the maw of a beast.

"Keep your eyes peeled," he warned, glancing back at his companions. "We don't know how deep their security runs."

They crept through the narrow hallway, the sound of their breathing the only indication of their presence. Each step brought them closer to the core of PromptTech's operations—the extraction room. Kusi's mind raced as he recalled the layout he had studied, every detail etched into his memory.

Finally, they reached a heavy door marked with a high-security lock. Kusi knelt before it, pulling out a small device gifted by the Specter—a hacking tool designed to bypass PromptTech's security systems. "Let's hope this works," he murmured, his fingers trembling as he connected the device.

The device emitted a low beep as Kusi focused on the screen. Lines of code scrolled rapidly, and he felt a rush of adrenaline as the lock began to crack. Just then, the lights flickered, and an alarm blared, filling the corridor with a deafening sound.

"Dammit!" Mossey shouted, looking back toward the entrance. "We've been made!"

"Stay calm!" Kusi urged, his heart racing. "Just a few more seconds!"

With a final beep, the lock clicked open, and Kusi pushed the door wide, ushering his friends inside. "Go! We need to find the memory storage unit!"

They rushed into the room, the sight before them chilling. Rows of sleek, sterile machines lined the walls, each one housing a pod filled with a shimmering liquid. Kusi could see shadows moving within, a haunting reminder of the lives trapped in limbo.

"Look!" Juna pointed to a central terminal displaying a network of connections and files. "We can access the memory logs from there!"

Kusi moved swiftly to the terminal, typing furiously as he bypassed the security protocols. The screen illuminated with data—names, dates, and fragmented memories that flickered like ghosts. His heart sank as he scrolled through the entries, each one a testament to lives erased.

"Here!" he exclaimed, pointing to a file labeled "Dissenters." "This is what we need!"

As Kusi downloaded the data onto a small drive, Juna suddenly froze, her gaze fixed on one of the pods. "Kusi, look!" she whispered, her voice trembling.

Inside the pod, a woman floated, her features hauntingly familiar. "It's Araba!" Juna gasped, stepping closer. "We have to get her out!"

"No, we can't," Kusi replied, panic rising. "We need to get the evidence first. If we free her now, we risk being caught."

But the anguish in Juna's eyes was unmistakable. "We can't leave her here!"

In that moment, Kusi felt the weight of the world on his shoulders. He had come to save himself and his friends, yet seeing Araba trapped stirred a fierce urgency within him. He glanced at Mossey, whose expression mirrored his own turmoil.

"Fine," Kusi finally said, his voice firm. "But we have to move quickly. We'll get the evidence, but we can't leave her behind."

With swift movements, Kusi approached the control panel for the pod. "Let's hope this works."

He tapped the controls, his heart racing as he initiated the release sequence. The pod hissed and released a cloud of mist as it opened, revealing Araba's unconscious form. Kusi reached in, carefully lifting her out as Juna rushed to support her.

"We have to go now!" Mossey urged, glancing at the door as alarms blared louder. "They'll be here any second!"

With Araba in their arms, they raced back toward the entrance, Kusi's mind focused solely on escape. The tension in the air crackled as footsteps echoed behind them, the sound of guards closing in.

"Keep moving!" he shouted, adrenaline fueling his speed. They burst through the side door and into the cool night air, but the sound of pursuit echoed behind them.

They dashed into the shadows, seeking cover as Kusi's heart pounded in rhythm with their hurried breaths. "This way!" he called, leading them into a narrow alley, praying they wouldn't be caught.

Once they were safely hidden, Kusi dropped to his knees, exhaustion washing over him. "We made it," he gasped, looking at Juna and Mossey, then glancing down at Araba.

"She needs medical attention," Juna said, her voice trembling with emotion.

Kusi nodded, a wave of relief crashing over him. "We'll get her to safety. We have what we need to expose PromptTech."

As they regrouped, he felt a flicker of hope igniting within him. They had taken a step into the abyss, but they had also found a glimmer of light amidst the darkness.

They would fight back, reclaim their identities, and ensure that the truth would no longer be silenced.

Chapter 27: Echoes of the Past

As dawn broke over the city, the first rays of sunlight pierced through the smog, casting an ethereal glow on the remnants of the night's chaos. Kusi stood at the edge of an abandoned rooftop, surveying the sprawling metropolis below. The weight of their recent actions pressed heavily on his shoulders, mingling with the adrenaline still coursing through his veins. Araba lay in a makeshift bed, her unconscious form a stark reminder of the danger they faced.

Juna and Mossey joined him, their expressions reflecting the uncertainty that loomed over them. "What now?" Juna asked, her voice barely above a whisper.

Kusi sighed, rubbing his temples. "We regroup. We need to analyze the data we extracted from PromptTech and figure out how to expose their operations. But we also need to keep a low profile. They'll be hunting for us."

Mossey frowned, crossing his arms. "And what if they find us first? We've already drawn attention."

Kusi turned to face his friends, determination hardening his resolve. "We'll prepare for that. We need allies—people who can help us get this information out. The more we can expose PromptTech, the harder it will be for them to silence us."

Juna nodded, her spirit reigniting. "We have to find a way to communicate with the outside world. We can't do this alone." As they began to discuss their next steps, Kusi felt a surge of hope. They had faced the abyss and emerged, but the shadows of uncertainty still lingered.

In a dimly lit room within their hideout, Kusi, Juna, and Mossey gathered around a small holographic projector. The data from PromptTech glowed on the surface, revealing a tangled web of connections that made Kusi's head spin.

"Look at this," he said, pointing to the screen as images of individuals, their memories, and the intricate web of transactions appeared. "This is the black market operation—people's memories being sold, erased, and implanted like commodities."

Juna leaned closer, her brows furrowing. "And look at this," she added, highlighting a section of the data. "These are names of high-profile clients—government officials, corporate leaders. They're complicit in this!"

Mossey's eyes widened as he scrolled through the files. "We could blow the lid off this whole operation if we release this information. But how do we get it out without getting caught?"

Kusi pondered for a moment before a thought struck him. "There's a journalist, Talia. She's been investigating PromptTech for years. If anyone can help us, it's her."

Juna nodded, a glimmer of hope igniting. "We need to reach out to her. If we can get her to report this, it'll draw public attention."

"But how do we contact her without revealing our location?" Mossey asked, concern etched on his face.

"We'll have to use a secure communication channel," Kusi replied. "I know a way to bypass their surveillance systems. We just need to be quick and careful."

With their plan set, they prepared to move out, gathering supplies and arming themselves with makeshift weapons. Kusi felt a mixture of excitement and dread as they stepped back into the chaotic streets, the city alive with the hustle and bustle of morning.

They navigated through back alleys, avoiding the main thoroughfares where surveillance drones hovered overhead. The air was thick with tension, and Kusi's heart raced as they approached the safe house where Talia was known to operate.

"We need to keep our heads down," he reminded them, glancing around for any signs of danger. "If we get caught now, it'll be over before we can even make our case."

They arrived at the nondescript building, its facade blending into the surroundings. Kusi knocked on the door, his pulse quickening. A moment later, Talia opened it, her expression shifting from surprise to recognition.

"Kusi?" she said, stepping aside to let them in. "What are you doing here?"

"Things have gotten complicated," he replied, glancing back at the street. "We need your help. PromptTech is deeper in this than we thought."

As they settled into the small, cluttered living room, Kusi laid out the details of their findings. Talia listened intently, her eyes widening as the reality of the situation sank in.

"This is huge," she said, her voice a mix of excitement and concern. "If this information gets out, it could change everything."

"Exactly," Kusi replied. "But we need to do it carefully. We can't let them catch wind of what we're planning."

Talia nodded, her mind racing with possibilities. "I can start preparing an exposé. I have contacts who can help disseminate the information securely. But you need to stay hidden until we're ready."

As they strategized, Kusi felt a sense of camaraderie building between them, the weight of their mission uniting them against a common enemy. But he also felt the lingering threat of PromptTech, their reach extending far beyond what he had anticipated.

"We need to keep Araba safe," Juna reminded them. "She's still vulnerable."

Kusi glanced at her, guilt creeping in. "I should have done more to protect her. We can't let her become a pawn in their game."

Talia raised an eyebrow. "You're right to be cautious. If they know you're alive and trying to expose them, they'll go after everyone connected to you."

With their plan in motion, they spent the next few hours drafting a strategy for the exposé. Kusi felt the tension in the air, each word they typed echoing the urgency of their mission.

Suddenly, a loud crash shattered the stillness, followed by the unmistakable sound of footsteps approaching. Kusi's heart raced as he exchanged panicked glances with Juna and Mossey.

"They've found us!" he hissed. "We need to hide!"

They scrambled to find places to conceal themselves, Kusi ducking behind a large bookshelf as the door burst open. Shadows flooded the room, and Kusi's heart sank as he recognized the figures entering—the PromptTech enforcers, their faces masked and their intent clear.

"Search the place!" one of them barked, a cold edge in their voice.

Kusi held his breath, every muscle tense as they scoured the room. He could feel the adrenaline pulsing through him, the fear of being caught mingling with the determination to protect what they had worked so hard to uncover.

As the enforcers drew closer, Kusi's mind raced. They couldn't let their mission end here. He glanced at the others, seeing the same fire igniting in their eyes.

Just as the enforcers reached the bookshelf, Kusi felt a surge of courage. He pushed himself forward, stepping out from his hiding place.

"Hey!" he shouted, catching their attention. "Over here!"

In that moment of distraction, Juna and Mossey sprang into action, creating chaos as they fought against the enforcers. Kusi joined in, adrenaline fueling his movements as they fought their way toward the exit.

"Go!" he shouted to Talia, pushing her toward the door. "Get out while you can!"

With the enforcers hot on their heels, Kusi, Juna, and Mossey raced into the street, their hearts pounding as they navigated through the crowd. The city around them blurred, the noise of their escape drowning out everything else.

Once they were safely hidden in an alley, Kusi leaned against the wall, breathing heavily. "We made it," he gasped, disbelief washing over him.

But Juna's expression was grim. "What if they come after us? What if they find Talia?"

Kusi swallowed hard, the reality of their situation crashing down. "We have to keep moving. We can't let them break our resolve."

As they fled into the labyrinth of the city, Kusi felt the weight of fractured realities pressing down on him. They had taken a step deeper into the abyss, but they were not alone. Together, they would fight against the shadows, reclaim their identities, and expose the truth that lay hidden beneath the surface

Chapter 28: Fragments of Truth

Kusi leaned against a graffiti-covered wall, trying to catch his breath. The adrenaline from their narrow escape still pulsed in his veins, but now the gravity of their situation sank in. Juna and Mossey stood nearby, scanning the streets for any sign of pursuit.

"Do you think they followed us?" Juna asked, her voice laced with anxiety.

Kusi shook his head, though uncertainty gnawed at him. "They were too focused on Talia. We need to regroup and rethink our approach."

As they made their way through the underbelly of the city, Kusi felt a mix of hope and dread. The data they had gathered from PromptTech was a powerful weapon, but it was also a burden. They were now targets, marked by those who wished to silence them.

They slipped into an old, rundown café, the kind that served as a refuge for those trying to escape the city's relentless scrutiny. The smell of stale coffee filled the air as they settled into a secluded booth in the back.

"We need a plan," Mossey said, glancing around nervously. "We can't just wait for them to come after us."

Kusi nodded, his mind racing. "We need to expose PromptTech, but we also need to protect ourselves. If we can find a way to leak the data without revealing our identities, we might have a fighting chance."

Juna pulled out her tablet, tapping away as she searched for potential allies. "What about the underground network? They could help us disseminate the information securely."

Kusi considered her suggestion. The underground network was known for its resilience against corporate oppression. They had helped countless individuals and organizations evade the grasp of powerful entities.

"Let's reach out to them," Kusi replied. "But we have to be cautious. If PromptTech is monitoring communication channels, they could trace us back."

Juna and Mossey exchanged glances, their expressions a mixture of determination and fear. Kusi felt a surge of pride for his friends. Despite the looming threats, they were willing to fight.

Just as they began to strategize, the café door swung open, drawing Kusi's attention. A figure stepped inside—a woman with striking silver hair and piercing blue eyes. She moved with an air of confidence, scanning the room as if assessing potential threats.

Kusi's instincts kicked in. He recognized her from news reports: Lila Murphy, a renowned activist known for her fierce opposition to corporate corruption. If anyone could help them, it was her.

"Stay here," he whispered to Juna and Mossey, standing up to approach Lila.

As he neared her, she caught his gaze and smiled, though her eyes held a depth of understanding that suggested she was aware of the dangers lurking in the shadows. "Kusi," she said, her voice smooth like silk. "I've been hearing whispers about you. It seems you've stirred quite the storm."

Kusi nodded, feeling a mix of apprehension and excitement. "We need your help, Lila. PromptTech is deeper in this than anyone realizes. We have evidence that could expose them, but we need a secure way to disseminate it."

Lila studied him for a moment, her expression serious. "The risk is immense, Kusi .PromptTech won't hesitate to eliminate anyone who threatens their empire."

"I understand the dangers," he replied, a fire igniting within him. "But if we don't act, countless lives will be destroyed. We can't let them continue erasing people's identities."

She considered his words, and Kusi could see the wheels turning in her mind. "All right. I'll help you, but we must be strategic. The underground network has resources we can utilize, but we have to ensure our communications are secure."

Returning to his table, Kusi shared the news with Juna and Mossey. "Lila's on board. She knows people in the underground network who can help us."

"Great!"Mossey said, relief flooding his features. "What's the next step?"

"Lila suggested we meet with a contact of hers," Kusi explained. "Someone who can help us anonymize the data before we release it."

As they finalized their plan, Kusi couldn't shake the feeling that they were walking a tightrope. One misstep could spell disaster.

Hours later, they found themselves in a dimly lit warehouse on the outskirts of the city. The air was thick with tension, and Kusi could hear the distant hum of machinery. Lila led the way, her demeanor commanding as they approached a small group of individuals gathered around a flickering holographic display.

"This is our contact, Ash," Lila introduced, gesturing to a tall figure cloaked in a dark hoodie. "They have extensive experience in data anonymization."

Ash raised their head, revealing a face obscured by shadows. "I know what you're dealing with, Kusi. PromptTech is ruthless. If we're going to do this, we need to move quickly and quietly."

They gathered around the holographic display as Ash outlined the plan. "We'll create a secure channel to release the data. It'll be encrypted, and I can help you set up anonymous profiles to prevent tracing back to you."

Juna leaned closer, her brows furrowing. "What if they detect the leak before it goes live?"

"That's a risk we'll have to take," Ash replied, their voice steady. "But we can minimize it by staggering the release over multiple channels. It'll make it harder for them to pinpoint the source."

Kusi felt a surge of hope. "Then let's do it. We can't afford to wait any longer."

As they worked late into the night, Kusi felt the weight of their mission pressing down on him. The shadows seemed to whisper secrets, warning him of the dangers that lay ahead. He was acutely aware that they were weaving through a web of deceit, each choice carrying the potential to unravel everything they had fought for.

Finally, after hours of collaboration, they stood on the precipice of a breakthrough. Ash finalized the encryption protocols, and Kusi felt a mixture of exhilaration and dread.

"This is it," Ash said, their eyes gleaming with determination. "Once we hit send, there's no turning back."

Kusi exchanged glances with Juna and Mossey, the gravity of the moment settling over them like a shroud. "Are we ready?"

"Let's do it," Mossey said, steeling himself.

With a trembling hand, Kusi pressed the button to initiate the release. The data began to flow, cascading through the secure channels they had set up. A wave of adrenaline surged through him, mingling with the fear of what would come next.

As the information spread, Kusi felt a sense of liberation wash over him. They were breaking the silence, tearing down the veil that had shrouded PromptTech's corruption. But even as he reveled in the moment, he couldn't shake the feeling that they were still in the eye of the storm.

Suddenly, an alert flashed on Ash's console, and the room fell silent. "We've got incoming," Ash said, urgency lacing their voice.

Kusi's heart raced. "What do you mean?"

"They're onto us. We need to move, now!"

Panic set in as the reality of their situation hit hard. They had released the data, but in doing so, they had drawn the ire of a powerful enemy. The enforcers would be coming for them, and time was running out.

"Everyone, out!" Lila commanded, her voice cutting through the chaos. "We have to regroup and get out of sight before they close in."

Kusi grabbed Juna and Mossey, their breaths quickening as they rushed toward the exit. The warehouse felt like it was closing in on them, the walls echoing their racing hearts.

As they burst into the night, the cool air hit Kusi like a wave. They sprinted through the darkened streets, adrenaline propelling them forward. The shadows danced around them, and Kusi could feel the danger lurking just behind.

They navigated through alleyways and back streets, their escape fueled by desperation. Kusi's mind raced with thoughts of the future. They had taken a bold step, but what awaited them on the other side of this veil of illusion?

Finally, they reached a secluded spot, the city's noise fading into the background. They paused to catch their breath, the adrenaline slowly subsiding.

"We did it," Juna said, her voice shaky but filled with hope. "The data is out there."

Kusi nodded, a mix of relief and uncertainty flooding through him. "But it's not over yet. We have to stay vigilant. PromptTech won't let this go unpunished."

As they regrouped, Kusi felt a renewed sense of purpose. They were no longer mere players in someone else's game. They had taken control of their narrative, and no matter what came next, they would face it together.

Chapter 29: Threads of Destiny

Kusi, Juna, and Mossey took refuge in an abandoned subway station, the air heavy with the scent of rust and stale water. Dim emergency lights flickered overhead, casting eerie shadows on the walls. They had narrowly escaped PromptTech's grasp, but the data release weighed heavily on Kusi's mind. He knew the corporation would retaliate.

"We need to assess the fallout from the leak," Juna said, her eyes darting around the darkened station. "The longer we stay in the shadows, the more time they have to hunt us down."

Mossey nodded, his face pale. "What do we do now? We can't stay here forever."

Kusi leaned against the cold concrete wall, trying to collect his thoughts. "We need to find a way to turn this into an advantage. If we can rally public support against PromptTech, we might have a chance."

They huddled together, discussing their options. The underground network they had tapped into was vast and filled with potential allies. "We need to reach out to those who've been affected by PromptTech's actions," Kusi suggested. "If we can unite them, we'll have the strength to fight back."

Juna's eyes lit up. "What about the activist groups? They're already vocal against corporate tyranny. We can connect with them and amplify our message."

"Good idea," Mossey chimed in. "But we need to be careful. If we broadcast our intentions too loudly, we'll draw unwanted attention."

Kusi nodded, feeling the weight of responsibility on his shoulders. "We'll use encrypted channels and secure messengers. We'll reach out to the leaders of these groups, present our evidence, and strategize."

As they planned their next steps, a figure emerged from the shadows—a tall, slender man with a weathered face and sharp eyes. "I heard you might need some assistance," he said, his voice low and gravelly.

Kusi tensed, instinctively reaching for the hidden knife at his waist. "Who are you?"

"Name's Darian," the man replied, raising his hands in a gesture of peace. "I've been watching your fight against PromptTech. I'm with the Collective."

"The Collective?" Juna echoed, her curiosity piqued.

"They're a group dedicated to resisting corporate control. I can help you connect with others who share your goals," Darian explained. "But it won't be easy. PromptTech has eyes everywhere."

Kusi weighed the man's offer carefully. "How do we know we can trust you?" he asked, his tone guarded.

Darian smiled, revealing a missing tooth. "Trust is a luxury we can't afford, but we have a common enemy. If you're serious about this fight, I can provide the contacts and resources you need."

After a moment of deliberation, Kusi nodded. "All right. We're in. But we need to move fast. The longer we wait, the more vulnerable we become."

Darian led them through the labyrinthine tunnels of the subway station, sharing whispers of a growing movement against PromptTech. "We've been monitoring their activities, gathering intel on their operations. We're ready to strike, but we need a coordinated effort."

In the dim light of the subway, they strategized with Darian. He introduced them to key players within the Collective, including tech specialists, former employees of PromptTech, and others who had suffered under the corporation's oppressive reign.

"We'll need to create a network of safe houses," Darian advised. "People need to feel secure before they come forward with their stories. We can't just rely on the leaked data; we need real testimonies."

As they mapped out their plan, Kusi felt a renewed sense of purpose. The threads of their destinies were intertwining, creating a tapestry of resistance. They were no longer isolated fighters; they were part of a larger movement.

As the days passed, Kusi, Juna, Mossey, and Darian worked tirelessly to connect with various activist groups. They set up encrypted communication channels, spreading the word about their cause. Slowly but surely, they began to gather momentum.

During this time, Kusi took on the role of a spokesperson, sharing his story and the evidence they had uncovered. He found strength in the faces of those who listened—people who had lost loved ones, careers, and even their identities due to PromptTech's ruthless practices.

At one gathering, Kusi stood before a small crowd, the weight of their hopes resting on his shoulders. "We are not just fighting for ourselves. We are fighting for everyone who has been silenced, for those whose memories have been stolen. Together, we can reclaim our identities and take back our lives!"

The crowd erupted into cheers, their voices rising like a tide of defiance. But amidst the celebration, Kusi felt a shadow lingering in the back of his mind. PromptTech was not going to sit idly by while their operations were threatened. The corporation would retaliate, and Kusi knew it.

That night, as Kusi lay awake in the safe house, he couldn't shake the feeling that they were on borrowed time. The tension in the air was palpable, and he could sense the impending storm.

Suddenly, a noise outside interrupted his thoughts—a low rumble that grew louder, accompanied by the distant sound of sirens. Kusi bolted upright, adrenaline surging through him. "Something's happening," he whispered to Juna, who was already awake.

Mossey shot up from his makeshift bed, panic etched on his face. "What's going on?"

Kusi hurried to the window, peering through the grimy glass. In the distance, flashing lights illuminated the darkened streets. "It looks like they're raiding the area. We need to move!"

Without hesitation, they gathered their belongings, ready to escape. As they stepped out into the chaos, Kusi felt a mixture of fear and determination. They had come too far to back down now.

As they maneuvered through the alleyways, Kusi caught glimpses of the PromptTech enforcers, their dark uniforms contrasting sharply with the flickering neon lights of the city. It was a battleground, and they were caught in the crossfire.

"We need to find a way to regroup," Juna shouted over the cacophony of sirens and shouts. "If we can reach one of the safe houses, we might stand a chance."

"Follow me!" Kusi urged, leading the way into the labyrinth of backstreets. The adrenaline surged through him as they navigated the shadows, their hearts racing with every step.

As they ducked into an alley, Kusi felt the weight of their fight resting on his shoulders. The odds seemed insurmountable, but he couldn't let despair take hold. They had ignited a spark of resistance, and that flame needed to be nurtured.

In the distance, he spotted a figure waiting in the shadows—Darian. Relief washed over him as he beckoned them over.

"We have to move fast," Darian urged, his voice urgent. "PromptTech is ramping up their efforts. We can't stay here much longer."

Kusi nodded, the reality settling in. The threads of their destinies were about to be woven into something greater, but the battle ahead would test their resolve like never before.

Chapter 30: Beneath the Surface

Kusi, Juna, Mossey, and Darian navigated the darkened streets, the sounds of chaos fading behind them as they made their way to one of the Collective's hidden safe houses. It was a dilapidated building on the outskirts of the city, long abandoned and forgotten by most. As they approached, Kusi couldn't shake the feeling of being watched, every sense on high alert.

"Stay close," Kusi whispered, glancing over his shoulder. "We can't afford to be caught now."

Darian led the way, pushing open the creaking door and ushering them inside. The air was stale, filled with dust motes dancing in the dim light. It felt as though they had stepped into another world—a sanctuary for those who dared to resist.

Once inside, Kusi took a moment to absorb their surroundings. The walls were lined with faded posters of past protests and rallies, the remnants of a vibrant community dedicated to fighting against corporate oppression. A makeshift table in the center of the room held an array of old monitors, each displaying different feeds from the city, allowing them to monitor the situation outside.

"Welcome to the heart of the Collective," Darian said, gesturing around the room. "This is where we plan our movements, gather intel, and coordinate with other groups. We may not have much, but we have each other."

Kusi felt a renewed sense of hope as he looked at the faces around him. This was a network of individuals united by a common goal—a rebellion against PromptTech's tyranny. "What's our next move?" he asked, his voice steady.

"We need to spread the word about what PromptTech is doing," Darian replied. "If we can expose their actions to the public, we might spark more interest and support for our cause."

Mossey chimed in, "We can leverage social media platforms and encrypted messaging apps. Many people are unaware of the truth behind memory trading. If we can get enough evidence out there, we might be able to rally more allies."

Juna nodded in agreement, her determination shining through. "We can also reach out to journalists and bloggers who have been critical of PromptTech in the past. They have the audience we need to amplify our message."

As the group gathered around the table, Kusi felt a rush of adrenaline. They discussed strategies, crafting messages that would resonate with the public and highlight the dangers of memory manipulation. It was a delicate balance—spreading the truth without putting themselves in more danger.

Darian tapped a few keys on the monitor, bringing up news articles and social media posts that showcased the growing discontent among the populace. "People are beginning to wake up to PromptTech's influence," he said, excitement bubbling in his voice. "But we need to give them a push. We can't let fear silence us."

Kusi leaned forward, inspired by the energy in the room. "Let's create a viral campaign. Short videos, impactful graphics, and personal stories. If we can humanize the victims of memory erasure, people will start to care."

As they brainstormed ideas, the atmosphere shifted from despair to determination. Each suggestion built upon the last, igniting a fire within them. Kusi felt invigorated, ready to take on the world and expose the truth.

But beneath their enthusiasm lay an undercurrent of tension. Kusi couldn't shake the feeling that danger lurked just outside their sanctuary. The recent raid by PromptTech's enforcers had only intensified his instincts.

Later that night, as the group finalized their campaign plans, a loud crash echoed from the street outside. Kusi's heart raced as he exchanged worried glances with Juna and Mossey. "What was that?" Juna whispered, her eyes wide.

"Stay here," Kusi instructed, his voice low and urgent. He crept to the window, peering through the grime. Outside, a squad of PromptTech enforcers flooded the area, their dark uniforms a stark reminder of the oppressive power they faced.

Kusi quickly turned back to the group. "We need to move. Now."

Panic erupted as they scrambled to gather their belongings. Darian's voice cut through the chaos, "We have a back exit. Follow me!"

They rushed through the narrow hallways, Kusi's heart pounding in rhythm with their hurried footsteps. The oppressive weight of the building felt like a suffocating cage, and the urgency of their escape pushed them forward.

As they reached the back door, Kusi hesitated. "We can't just run without a plan. If we get caught, it's over."

Darian placed a hand on Kusi's shoulder, grounding him. "We'll regroup at another safe house. There are other members of the Collective nearby. We can't let them capture us here."

With a deep breath, Kusi nodded, pushing down his fear. They slipped out into the night, the chill of the air invigorating yet unsettling. The streets were eerily quiet, as if the city itself held its breath, anticipating what was to come.

Navigating through the shadows, they moved cautiously, their senses heightened. Kusi led the way, determined to keep them safe. He could feel the adrenaline coursing through him, propelling him forward despite the danger that loomed around every corner.

As they turned down a narrow alley, the sound of footsteps echoed behind them. Kusi's heart dropped. "We're being followed!" he hissed, his instincts kicking in.

"Run!" Juna shouted, pushing forward.

They sprinted down the alley, the sounds of pursuit growing louder. Kusi's breath came in ragged gasps as he urged his legs to move faster. They couldn't afford to be caught—not now, when they were so close to exposing PromptTech's sinister machinations.

"Over here!" Darian shouted, gesturing to a doorway leading into a nearby building. They ducked inside just in time, the heavy door slamming shut behind them.

Inside, the darkness enveloped them, and Kusi strained to listen for any signs of their pursuers. He could hear the distant thuds of footsteps outside, the faint sounds of voices searching for them.

They huddled together in the cramped space, the dim light barely illuminating the room. It was a storage area, filled with old furniture and discarded items, creating a makeshift hiding place. Kusi felt the tension in the air as they waited, holding their breaths.

After what felt like an eternity, the footsteps faded, and the voices grew distant. Kusi glanced at his companions, relief washing over him. "I think they're gone."

Juna let out a shaky breath. "We can't keep running like this. We need a solid plan."

Kusi nodded, feeling the weight of their situation pressing down on him. "We need to find a way to strike back at PromptTech. We have the information; now we just need to find the right moment to use it."

As they sat in the darkness, Kusi's mind raced. He thought of the people who had suffered at the hands of PromptTech, their memories erased, their identities stolen. "We need to make this personal," he said, determination igniting within him. "If we can humanize our message, people will be more likely to stand with us."

Mossey spoke up, his voice filled with conviction. "We can gather testimonials from the victims. If we share their stories, we can show the world the reality of what's happening."

"That's it!" Kusi exclaimed, the idea crystallizing. "We'll organize a series of interviews. We can compile them into a documentary-style video, showing the human impact of PromptTech's actions."

With their plan taking shape, the group began to strategize how to gather testimonials without drawing attention to themselves. They discussed safe locations, encrypted communication methods, and how to maintain secrecy while ensuring they connected with those who had been affected.

Kusi felt a renewed sense of purpose. They weren't just fighting against a corporation; they were fighting for the memories and identities of those who had been lost. As they began to form a coherent strategy, the shadows around them seemed to recede, replaced by a flicker of hope.

But as they prepared to leave the hidden space, Kusi couldn't shake the feeling that their journey was only just beginning. The stakes were higher than ever, and the battle ahead would be unlike anything they had faced before.

Chapter 31: The Web of Lies

The air was thick with tension as Kusi and the others made their way through the labyrinth of alleys and hidden pathways, each step laden with purpose. They had a plan now, but the reality of what lay ahead was daunting. Kusi felt the weight of responsibility pressing on his shoulders, a constant reminder of the lives at stake.

As they approached a discreet café that served as another front for the Collective, Kusi took a deep breath, trying to steady his racing heart. The establishment, dimly lit and adorned with eclectic art, was a gathering place for those who sought refuge from the oppressive gaze of PromptTech. It buzzed with low conversations, whispers of dissent echoing against the walls.

Kusi spotted a table in the corner where several familiar faces were gathered. Among them was Mira, a sharp-witted journalist known for her investigative pieces on corporate corruption. If anyone could help amplify their message, it was her.

"Over here," Kusi called, beckoning to his group. They navigated through the scattered tables, settling down beside Mira, whose keen eyes scrutinized their expressions.

"Looks like you've been through the wringer," Mira observed, concern etched in her features. "What's going on?"

Kusi wasted no time, outlining their plan to expose PromptTech's heinous practices. He explained their idea of gathering testimonials, focusing on the human impact of memory erasure. The café's low hum faded into the background as they engaged in a heated discussion, strategizing how to get their message out to the public.

"I can help with the narrative," Mira said, her enthusiasm evident. "If we frame this as a story of survival against corporate greed, we can draw in a larger audience. But we need solid evidence—proof that PromptTech is behind the memory manipulation."

Mossey chimed in, "We have some leads on ex-employees who can testify about the internal workings of the company. They're scared, but if we can assure them of their safety—"

"I can use my connections in the media," Mira interrupted. "If we can create a compelling article alongside the video, we can generate a lot of buzz. We need to present this as a larger issue affecting society as a whole."

As the conversation unfolded, Kusi felt a renewed sense of determination. They began to map out a plan, coordinating their efforts to reach out to potential witnesses and gather evidence. Mira jotted down notes, her focus unyielding.

"We'll need to work fast," Mira warned, glancing around the café as if anticipating an attack. "PromptTech has eyes everywhere. The moment they catch wind of what we're doing, they'll come after us."

Kusi nodded, fully aware of the risks involved. "We'll keep everything under wraps until we're ready to launch. The last thing we need is to tip them off."

Just then, the door swung open, and a gust of wind swept through the café. Kusi felt a chill run down his spine as he glanced at the entrance. A figure entered, cloaked in shadows, scanning the room with a keen gaze. The newcomer seemed out of place amidst the warmth of the café, an air of danger radiating from him.

Kusi's instincts kicked in, and he turned his attention back to the group, lowering his voice. "Stay alert. I don't like the look of that guy."

As the figure moved deeper into the café, Kusi's heart raced. He couldn't shake the feeling that their safe haven was about to be compromised. Just then, the stranger approached their table, his demeanor calm but with an intensity that sent shivers down Kusi's spine.

"Mind if I join you?" the man asked, his voice smooth and measured. There was an unsettling familiarity in his gaze, as if he knew more than he was letting on.

Mira raised an eyebrow, her wariness apparent. "Who are you?"

The man smiled, a hint of mischief in his expression. "Name's Kade. I've heard whispers of your little operation and thought I might be able to help."

Kusi exchanged glances with Juna and Mossey, uncertain of whether to trust this stranger. "What do you know about us?" Kusi pressed, his tone defensive.

Kade leaned closer, lowering his voice. "Let's just say I have my ear to the ground. I know about your plans to expose PromptTech, and I know you're looking for allies. I can connect you with people who have access to crucial information about their operations—information that could blow the lid off this whole thing."

Kusi felt a mix of intrigue and caution. "And what's in it for you?"

Kade grinned, his eyes glinting with something akin to ambition. "Let's just say I have my reasons for wanting to see PromptTech taken down a peg. I'm not interested in being a cog in their machine anymore."

Mira leaned back in her chair, studying Kade with narrowed eyes. "How do we know you're not working for them?"

Kade chuckled softly. "You don't. But if you're serious about this, you'll have to take some risks. I can provide intel, but you need to trust me."

The atmosphere at the table shifted as they considered Kade's offer. Kusi felt a growing sense of unease. "What kind of intel are we talking about?"

"Details about the internal structure of PromptTech, their memory manipulation technology, and the locations of key facilities," Kade replied confidently. "This isn't just corporate espionage; this is a chance to save lives."

Kusi's mind raced. Could they trust this man? He weighed the potential benefits against the risk of betrayal. "We'll need time to think about it," he finally said, trying to maintain control of the situation.

Kade shrugged, unfazed. "Take your time. But remember, every moment you hesitate is another moment PromptTech tightens its grip. I'll be around if you change your mind."

With that, he stood and moved toward the exit, leaving a trail of uncertainty in his wake. The group sat in silence, grappling with the implications of his proposition.

After a moment, Kusi broke the silence. "We can't ignore this. If Kade has the information he claims, it could be the key to exposing PromptTech and rallying more support for our cause."

"But what if he's playing us?" Mossey countered, his concern evident. "We can't afford to trust just anyone."

"I get that," Juna interjected, her voice firm. "But we're running out of options. If we want to make a real impact, we need to take risks."

Kusi nodded, feeling the weight of their decision. "Let's reach out to Kade and see what he has to offer. But we'll keep our guard up. Trust is earned, not given."

As they finalized their plans, Kusi felt a sense of resolve wash over him. They were standing on the precipice of something monumental, a chance to take down PromptTech and reclaim the memories and identities of those who had been lost.

The stakes were higher than ever, and the path ahead was fraught with danger, but Kusi knew they couldn't turn back now. The fight for their lives—and the lives of countless others—had just begun.

Chapter 32: The Gathering Storm

The sun dipped below the horizon, casting long shadows across the cityscape as Kusi and his team gathered in their makeshift headquarters. The dimly lit room, cluttered with outdated technology and hastily drawn maps, felt both like a sanctuary and a trap. They had reached a critical juncture, and the air buzzed with anticipation and anxiety.

Kusi stood at the front, his expression resolute. "We need to make contact with Kade. He might be our best shot at getting the intel we need to take down PromptTech." He scanned the faces of his companions—Mossey, Juna, and Mira—all displaying varying degrees of concern and determination.

Mira leaned forward, her brow furrowed. "If we're going to meet him, we should choose a location that's secure. We can't risk him leading us into a trap."

"Agreed," Juna replied, her voice steady. "There's an old warehouse on the outskirts of the city. It's abandoned, but it's close enough to the heart of things that we can keep an eye on it without raising suspicion."

Mossey nodded, his fingers tapping rhythmically against the table. "I'll scout it out first. We can't afford any surprises."

As Mossey prepared to leave, Kusi turned to Mira. "Have you made any progress on the article?"

"Absolutely," she replied, her enthusiasm palpable. "I've started gathering testimonials from some of the people affected by memory manipulation. If we can weave their stories into the narrative, it will give our cause a human face."

Kusi felt a surge of hope. "Good. We need to build momentum. If we can show the public the true consequences of PromptTech's actions, we can rally more support."

After Mossey departed, Kusi and Juna began laying out their strategy. "We'll need to coordinate everything carefully. If Kade really has information that can dismantle PromptTech's operations, we must be ready to act quickly."

Juna nodded. "I can reach out to some contacts within the underground networks. They might be able to help us amplify our message when the time comes."

As night enveloped the city, Kusi's mind raced with possibilities. He couldn't shake the feeling that time was slipping away, that PromptTech was always one step ahead. He glanced out the window, his gaze scanning the streets below. A chill crept up his spine as he noticed a pair of figures loitering near the entrance of the building. They were dressed in dark clothing, their eyes hidden beneath the hoods of their jackets.

"Juna," Kusi whispered, pointing toward the window. "Do you see those two? Something feels off."

Juna moved closer to peer through the glass. "They've been standing there for a while. It could be a coincidence, but we should be cautious."

Kusi's heart raced. "We need to make sure we're not being watched. I'll check the back entrance while you keep an eye on the front."

As Kusi slipped out of the room, he felt the adrenaline coursing through him. He navigated the narrow hallways of the building, his senses heightened. Every creak of the floorboards felt amplified, every whisper of the wind a potential threat.

When he reached the back door, Kusi paused, scanning the area for any signs of danger. Just as he was about to step outside, he heard the unmistakable sound of footsteps behind him. He turned quickly, ready to confront whoever had followed him.

To his surprise, it was Mossey, his expression taut. "Kusi, we need to talk. There's something you need to see."

"What is it?" Kusi asked, urgency flooding his voice.

Mossey glanced around before leaning closer. "I scouted the warehouse. It's not abandoned. There are people inside—more than I expected. They're armed."

Kusi felt his stomach drop. "Are they with PromptTech?"

"I don't know," Mossey replied. "But I overheard them talking about a shipment coming in. It sounded like they're moving something important."

Kusi's mind raced as he processed the information. "We need to reconsider our approach. If Kade is involved with those people, this could be a setup."

Mossey nodded in agreement. "We can't afford to be reckless. We need to gather more intel before we make any moves."

Returning to the main room, Kusi relayed the news to Juna and Mira. "Mossey spotted a group in the warehouse. We can't go in blindly. We need to gather more information before making contact with Kade."

Mira looked thoughtful. "Maybe we can set up surveillance. If they're moving something significant, we need to know what it is."

"Good idea," Juna said. "I can get my hands on some old equipment from my contacts. We can set up a watch without getting too close."

As they worked together to devise a new plan, Kusi felt the weight of the world on his shoulders. They were racing against time, and every moment spent in hesitation felt like a step closer to disaster.

Once the plan was established, the team split up to prepare. Kusi and Juna headed out to secure the surveillance equipment, while Mira remained behind to continue her research on PromptTech and gather more testimonies.

While they were out, Kusi couldn't shake the feeling that they were being watched. The streets were darker than usual, and shadows seemed to cling to every corner. He and Juna moved quickly, their senses on high alert, the weight of their mission pressing heavily on them.

Later that night, they returned to their headquarters, the equipment in tow. Kusi felt a strange mix of anticipation and dread as they set up the surveillance gear. They stationed the cameras to provide the best angles of the warehouse entrance while ensuring they remained hidden.

As they waited for dawn, Kusi shared his thoughts. "If we're going to take them down, we need to be ready to act on any information we gather. We can't afford any slip-ups."

Juna nodded, her eyes glinting with determination. "We'll be ready. We have to be. Too many lives are at stake."

In the darkness, Kusi glanced at the flickering monitors, his resolve solidifying. The storm was gathering, and they were about to step into the eye of it. The truth lay just ahead, but so did the danger.

As the first light of dawn broke through the horizon, Kusi felt a sense of urgency wash over him. They were on the cusp of something monumental, and every heartbeat echoed the risk they were taking. He silently vowed to himself that they would expose the truth, no matter the cost.

As the sun rose, illuminating the warehouse and the world beyond, Kusi knew they were about to enter a new phase of their battle against PromptTech—a phase fraught with danger but rich with the potential for change.

Chapter 33: Threads of Truth

The sun peeked through the cracks of the warehouse's weathered facade, spilling light onto the cold concrete floor. Kusi and his team huddled around the monitors, anticipation buzzing in the air. Each pixel on the screen reflected not only their immediate mission but also the lives of countless individuals caught in the web of memory manipulation.

Mira adjusted the focus of the camera, her fingers deftly navigating the controls. "We've got a clear view of the entrance. If anything moves, we'll know it." Her voice carried a mix of determination and anxiety.

Mossey leaned against the wall, arms crossed. "Let's hope it's Kade and not a swarm of PromptTech goons. I'm not in the mood for a firefight today."

"Agreed," Juna replied, her gaze fixed on the monitors. "But we need to be prepared for anything."

Kusi nodded, his heart pounding with a blend of fear and hope. "We need to stay sharp. If Kade shows up, we need to extract as much information as possible."

As the minutes stretched into hours, the tension in the room grew palpable. Each creak of the warehouse echoed like a distant gunshot, amplifying their collective anxiety. Kusi paced the floor, glancing between the monitors and the team, mentally rehearsing the questions they needed to ask Kade.

"What if he doesn't show?" Mossey asked, breaking the silence. "What if we're just wasting our time?"

"We can't think like that," Juna interjected. "Kade's been in this game long enough. He knows the stakes. If he has information about PromptTech, he'll find a way to get it to us."

Mira's brow furrowed. "We also need to consider that he might not be entirely trustworthy. We can't let our guard down, even for a moment."

Kusi took a deep breath, letting the weight of their mission settle into his chest. "We'll cross that bridge when we come to it. For now, we need to remain focused and vigilant."

Just as Kusi finished speaking, the sound of footsteps echoed outside the warehouse. He and the others exchanged glances, their hearts racing as they leaned closer to the monitors. The figures of two men emerged from the shadows, their movements deliberate.

"It's them!" Mossey exclaimed, pointing at the screen. "Kade's here!"

As the men approached, Kusi's pulse quickened. The taller of the two had a familiar swagger, a confident stride that spoke of experience in the underground. Kade stopped just outside the entrance, scanning the surroundings before stepping inside.

"Keep the cameras rolling," Kusi instructed, gripping the edge of the table. "Let's see what he has to say."

Kade entered the warehouse, his eyes adjusting to the dim light. He wore a leather jacket that had seen better days, and his face bore the marks of countless encounters in the underbelly of the city. The other man, shorter and stockier, remained close to Kade, his eyes darting around the room with suspicion.

"Is this where the magic happens?" Kade's voice echoed through the vast space, a mixture of sarcasm and intrigue.

Kusi stepped out from the shadows, his expression firm. "You could say that. We need to talk."

Kade raised an eyebrow, a smirk playing on his lips. "I'm listening. But I'll warn you, I don't have all day."

Kusi gestured for Kade to follow him deeper into the warehouse, where they could speak more privately. The tension in the air was thick as they gathered around an old crate, the flickering lights casting ominous shadows on their faces.

"We know about the shipment," Kusi began, his voice steady. "We need to know what's in it and why it's important to PromptTech."

Kade leaned against the crate, crossing his arms. "You're digging into dangerous territory. You might want to reconsider your approach."

"Is that a warning?" Juna interjected, her tone sharp. "Because we don't have time for games. People's lives are at stake."

Kade studied them for a moment, his expression shifting to one of seriousness. "Alright, let's cut to the chase. PromptTech is moving a shipment of memory cores—advanced tech that allows them to manipulate memories on a much larger scale. They're planning something big, and it involves erasing dissenters on a mass level."

Kusi felt a chill run down his spine. "How do you know this?"

"I have my sources," Kade replied cryptically. "But you need to understand that this isn't just about you or me. This is about a war for control over consciousness itself. If they succeed, they'll erase anyone who poses a threat to their power."

Mira took a step closer. "What can we do to stop them?"

Kade glanced at her, a flicker of admiration in his eyes. "You're not just looking for answers; you're ready to fight. I like that. But you need to gather more intel before making your move. There's a rendezvous point tonight where they'll be distributing the memory cores. If you can infiltrate that meeting, you might get what you need to expose their plans."

"And if we get caught?" Mossey asked, concern etched on his face.

"Then you'll have a problem," Kade said, his tone turning serious again. "But if you're smart about it, you'll blend in. The people at the meeting won't be expecting trouble."

Kusi weighed Kade's words carefully. "If we go in, we'll need a solid plan. We can't just wing it."

"I can help with that," Kade replied, a hint of eagerness creeping into his voice. "I know the layout and the players involved. But you need to trust me. I can't do this without your support."

Juna exchanged glances with the others before nodding. "We'll work together. But know this: if you betray us, we won't hesitate to expose you."

Kade raised his hands in mock surrender. "Understood. I have my own stakes in this game."

With the new information in hand, Kusi and his team set to work devising a plan. They gathered their gear, ensuring they had everything they needed for the infiltration. Kusi felt a surge of adrenaline as they discussed strategies, each member contributing their strengths to the mission.

As night descended upon the city, Kusi's heart raced. This was it—the moment that could change everything. They would confront PromptTech directly and expose their sinister plans. The weight of the mission hung heavy in the air, but Kusi felt more alive than ever.

As they made their way toward the rendezvous point, Kusi couldn't shake the feeling that the stakes had never been higher. They were entering the lion's den, a place filled with danger and deception. But for the first time in a long time, Kusi felt the threads of truth weaving together, guiding them toward their purpose.

"We're almost there," Kusi said, his voice steady. "Remember, we stick to the plan. No matter what happens, we stay united."

With each step, Kusi felt a mix of fear and determination. They were about to face the unknown, and whatever lay ahead could either be their greatest triumph or their most devastating defeat. The storm was brewing, and they were ready to face it head-on.

Chapter 34: The Escape

The city pulsed with life as Kusi and his team navigated through the labyrinthine alleys, shadows dancing against the crumbling walls. The distant hum of neon lights illuminated their path, but the darkness felt alive, concealing dangers lurking just beyond sight. Kusi's heart raced as anticipation mixed with dread.

"Stick to the plan," he reminded them as they approached the rendezvous point. "We go in, gather intel, and get out. No heroics."

Mira nodded, her expression resolute. "We can do this. We're not just after information; we're here to take a stand."

"Remember, our objective is to blend in," Juna added, her voice steady. "Follow my lead, and don't draw attention."

Kusi felt a rush of pride for his team. Each member brought unique skills, and together they formed a force strong enough to challenge the dark machinations of PromptTech. But as they rounded the corner, the atmosphere shifted, a tangible tension crackling in the air.

The rendezvous point was an abandoned warehouse, its façade marked by years of neglect, yet tonight, it radiated an unsettling energy. Flickering lights spilled from the cracked windows, illuminating a crowd gathered inside. Kusi's instincts sharpened as he peered through a gap in the door, assessing the situation.

"Looks like they're already here," he whispered, spotting several figures dressed in suits that screamed corporate authority. Among them were individuals Kusi recognized—people rumored to have ties to PromptTech's shadowy dealings.

"Let's get closer," Mossey suggested, glancing back at the team. "We need to hear what they're saying."

They crept closer, finding a vantage point behind some old crates stacked haphazardly. As they settled in, Kusi strained to hear the hushed conversations. A man with slicked-back hair stood at the forefront, his voice cutting through the chatter.

"Tonight, we're discussing the final stages of Project Erasure," he announced, commanding attention. "This is not just about controlling the populace; it's about erasing any potential threats to our future. With the new memory cores, we'll be able to influence public perception on a massive scale."

Kusi exchanged glances with Juna, both of them grappling with the enormity of what was unfolding before them. The implications of such power were staggering, and the ethical ramifications echoed through Kusi's mind. Memories—both personal and collective—were the essence of identity, and to manipulate them was to play god.

As the discussion continued, another figure, a woman with piercing eyes, stepped forward. "And what about the dissenters? We can't allow them to organize against us. We need to ensure that anyone who poses a threat is dealt with swiftly."

Kusi felt a chill run down his spine. The mention of dissenters hit too close to home. He thought of the countless individuals who had been erased or silenced, their lives reduced to mere data.

"Leave that to me," the man replied with a sinister grin. "The new cores will not only erase memories but also implant false ones.

We can turn them against each other, sow discord, and create an illusion of stability. By the time they realize what's happening, it'll be too late."

"Is it foolproof?" the woman pressed, skepticism lining her tone.

"Nothing is foolproof, but with our resources, we can ensure the outcome is favorable," he assured her. "We're about to change the game entirely."

Kusi felt a surge of anger, a visceral need to act. He leaned in closer to Juna, whispering urgently, "We can't let this happen. We need to expose them now."

"Agreed," she replied, determination blazing in her eyes. "But we need proof. We can't just charge in without evidence."

Mossey shifted restlessly, his hands clenched into fists. "What if we hack into their system? If we can access the data they're transferring tonight, we'll have everything we need to blow this wide open."

Kusi considered the idea, weighing the risks. "It's a gamble, but it might be our best shot. We need to act fast before they disperse."

With a plan in motion, they quietly made their way around the perimeter of the warehouse, looking for an entry point that wouldn't draw attention. Kusi's mind raced with strategies, each step bringing them closer to the truth but also deeper into danger.

They found a side door slightly ajar, the metallic creak loud in the stillness. Kusi held his breath as they slipped inside, the dim light revealing a hallway lined with doors. He gestured for them to follow him, every instinct alert to the potential threats around them.

"Stay close," he murmured, leading the way. "We need to find their main control room."

As they navigated through the maze of corridors, Kusi felt a sense of urgency pressing down on them. The stakes were higher than ever, and they were on the precipice of uncovering something monumental.

Finally, they arrived at a heavy door marked with security protocols. Kusi pulled out his handheld device, fingers flying over the interface as he bypassed the lock. The door clicked open, revealing a dimly lit room filled with screens displaying real-time data streams and surveillance footage.

"Bingo," Mossey whispered, his eyes wide with excitement. "This is where they keep everything."

Mira quickly moved to one of the terminals, typing furiously as she began to sift through the files. "I'll extract what I can, but we need to be quick."

Kusi stood watch by the door, his heart pounding in his chest. They were on borrowed time, and the longer they stayed, the greater the risk of being discovered.

Mira's eyes widened as she uncovered a file labeled *"Project Erasure Protocol."* "This is it! This outlines their entire plan—everything they're doing and who they're targeting!"

"Download it," Kusi urged, glancing nervously at the door. "We need that data to take to the media."

As she continued to work, the tension in the room escalated. Kusi could feel the weight of their mission pressing down on him, knowing they were on the brink of something powerful and dangerous.

Suddenly, alarms blared throughout the building, red lights flashing ominously. "We've been compromised!" Mira shouted, her fingers racing across the keyboard. "I'm almost done, but we need to move!"

"Let's go!" Kusi commanded, leading the charge as they sprinted for the exit. The sounds of footsteps echoed behind them, shouts reverberating through the corridors.

"Down this way!" Juna shouted, guiding them toward an emergency exit. Kusi could feel his pulse quicken, adrenaline flooding his veins as they burst through the door into the cool night air.

But as they reached the outside, they were met with chaos. PromptTech's security teams swarmed the area, vehicles pulling up and lights flashing. Kusi's mind raced as he searched for an escape route.

"Over there!"Mossey pointed to an alleyway lined with dumpsters and shadows. "We can lose them in the maze of streets!"

They darted into the alley, the adrenaline propelling them forward. Kusi's heart pounded in his chest, each step feeling heavier as the realization of what they had just accomplished settled in.

"We did it! We got the data!" Mira exclaimed, breathless but exhilarated.

"Not yet," Kusi replied, keeping his voice low. "We need to find a safe place to regroup and plan our next move. They won't stop coming after us."

As they navigated through the dark streets, Kusi couldn't shake the feeling that the worst was still ahead. They had exposed a fragment of the truth, but the full extent of PromptTech's plans loomed ominously on the horizon.

In the safety of an abandoned building, they finally paused to catch their breath. Kusi's mind raced with the possibilities that lay ahead. They had the information they needed, but the battle was far from over. PromptTech would come for them, relentless and unforgiving.

"We need to get this data to the right people," Juna said, her expression determined. "This isn't just about us anymore. It's about everyone they're planning to erase."

Kusi nodded, a newfound resolve igniting within him. "We'll make sure everyone knows the truth. It's time to bring this corporation down."

As they prepared to disseminate the information, Kusi couldn't help but feel the weight of their mission. They were about to step into the spotlight, and the repercussions could be monumental. But they had come too far to turn back now.

In the shadows, they would rise, fueled by the truth and united in their fight against the darkness threatening to consume them all.

Chapter 35: A Revelation

Kusi stared at the flickering screen, the digital map revealing the hidden layers of the city as he plotted their next move. The data they had extracted from PromptTech was potent, revealing not only the details of Project Erasure but also the names of key operatives involved. Each name felt like a tether to the lives that had been lost or altered. It ignited a flame of purpose within him.

"Tonight, we make our voices heard," Kusi declared, looking around at his team, their faces illuminated by the harsh glow of the monitor. "We've gathered enough evidence to expose PromptTech's operations. We need to get this to the media, but we can't just hand it over. We need a strategy."

Juna nodded, her expression fierce. "We should organize a press conference. Gather everyone who's willing to listen, and we can stream it online. The public needs to see the truth."

"Agreed," Mossey chimed in, leaning forward, excitement bubbling in his voice. "We need to leverage social media, get this information out to the masses quickly. The more people know, the harder it'll be for PromptTech to silence us."

Mira's eyes sparkled with determination. "We should reach out to grassroots organizations. There are people out there fighting against corporate oppression who will rally with us. We need allies."

Kusi felt the adrenaline rush through him. The momentum was building, and they were no longer just survivors—they were warriors in a battle against an oppressive regime.

As the team began brainstorming ideas, Kusi pulled out his communicator, preparing to reach out to trusted contacts. "We need to spread the word fast. I'll reach out to Alice; she's been working with activist groups for years. If anyone knows how to mobilize a crowd, it's her."

"Good idea," Juna replied. "And I can contact the journalists I've worked with in the past. If they know what's at stake, they'll help us get this into the right hands."

As they formulated their plans, Kusi couldn't shake the feeling of urgency pressing down on him. They were on the brink of a major revelation, and the longer they delayed, the more time PromptTech had to counteract their efforts.

Hours passed as the team worked tirelessly, reaching out to connections and building a network of allies. Kusi felt a flicker of hope; the wheels were in motion, and momentum was growing. Each message sent, each contact made, felt like a step closer to unraveling the web of lies that had ensnared so many lives.

Just as they were finalizing details for the press conference, Mira's communicator beeped, cutting through the intensity of their planning. She glanced at the screen, a mix of confusion and concern crossing her features.

"It's Alice," she said, her voice laced with urgency. "She wants to meet us—now."

"Where?" Kusi asked, instinctively knowing that this wasn't a casual request.

"At the old subway station on Fifth," Mira replied. "She said it's urgent and that we need to come prepared."

Kusi exchanged glances with his team, a sense of foreboding settling over them. "Let's go. If Alice thinks it's urgent, we need to hear what she has to say."

They made their way through the shadowy streets, the atmosphere thick with tension as they approached the derelict subway station. Kusi felt a chill run down his spine, the darkness swallowing them as they descended into the underground.

The air was damp and heavy, the distant sounds of dripping water echoing through the dimly lit tunnels. As they moved deeper, Kusi's senses heightened, every instinct telling him they were stepping into unknown territory.

"Stay alert," he whispered, eyes scanning their surroundings. "We don't know what we're walking into."

They arrived at a small platform, illuminated by flickering lights overhead. Alice stood at the far end, her silhouette tense as she awaited their arrival. The moment she spotted them, her expression shifted from anxiety to relief.

"Kusi, thank god you're here," she said, rushing toward them. "I have critical information, but it's not just about PromptTech. It's bigger than we thought."

Kusi's heart raced as they gathered closer, the weight of her words hanging in the air. "What do you mean?" he pressed.

Alice took a deep breath, her voice steady but urgent. "I've been investigating some connections between PromptTech and the government. They're not just operating independently; they're working hand-in-hand to control the narrative, especially around memory manipulation."

Kusi's mind raced, piecing together the implications. "Are you saying they're colluding?"

"Yes," she confirmed, her eyes blazing. "And they've been setting up disinformation campaigns to discredit any dissenters. If we expose PromptTech, we also expose those in power supporting them. But we need to be careful. They're watching everyone involved in this."

Kusi felt the gravity of her words, the enormity of the challenge ahead. "How do we protect ourselves? We're already targets."

Alice glanced around, her voice lowering to a whisper. "We need to create a secure network. Use encrypted communication, keep everything off the grid. And we need to act fast. They know we're onto them."

With Alice's revelations, the urgency heightened. They huddled close, discussing strategies to ensure their safety while also pushing forward with their mission. Kusi felt a renewed sense of determination.

"Let's use this to our advantage," he suggested. "We'll integrate Alice's findings into our presentation. If we can prove the collusion between PromptTech and the government, it'll add a whole new layer to our case."

Juna nodded. "We should also prepare for backlash. If they're as powerful as Alice says, they won't go down without a fight."

"Then we'll be ready," Kusi replied, feeling the fire of resolve burn within him. "We've come this far; we can't back down now."

As they wrapped up their meeting, Kusi felt the weight of the storm brewing on the horizon. The world was shifting, and they were on the cusp of something monumental. But with every move they made, danger lurked in the shadows.

Leaving the subway station, Kusi glanced back at the darkness they had just emerged from. It felt symbolic—a reminder of the battle ahead. They were not just fighting for their identities; they were fighting for a future free from manipulation and control.

With each step, they forged ahead, united in their mission. The storm was gathering, and Kusi could feel the electric tension crackling in the air. The time for action was approaching, and they would face whatever came next together.

Chapter 36: Threads of Conspiracy

As the sun dipped below the horizon, casting shadows over the city, Kusi felt a mix of anticipation and dread. The plans they had put into motion were about to unfold, but he couldn't shake the nagging feeling that they were being watched. He glanced around their makeshift headquarters, a dilapidated warehouse on the outskirts of the city. It was supposed to be a secure location, but with PromptTech's reach, nothing felt truly safe.

"Tonight's the night," Juna said, breaking his thoughts as she entered the room, her eyes shining with resolve. "Alice is coordinating with the activist groups, and the livestream is set. We'll have hundreds, maybe thousands, tuning in."

Kusi nodded, feeling a surge of pride for his team. They had come so far, from a ragtag group of survivors to a united front ready to challenge a powerful corporation. "Let's make sure we're ready. Every piece of evidence we have needs to be airtight. No room for error."

Mira entered next, her expression serious. "I've been working on the presentation. I think we can structure it to highlight not just the evidence against PromptTech but also the broader implications of what they're doing. We need people to understand that this isn't just about memory trading; it's about their very freedom."

"Exactly," Kusi replied, feeling the weight of their mission. "We need to connect the dots for them. If we can make them see how it affects their lives, we can galvanize a movement."

As night enveloped the city, the atmosphere thickened with tension. Kusi paced the floor, his mind racing with possibilities and contingencies. He could almost feel the electricity in the air, a prelude to the storm of revelations they were about to unleash.

"Everyone's in position," Juna said, her voice breaking through his thoughts. "We're ready when you are."

Kusi took a deep breath, grounding himself. "Alright. Let's do this." They gathered around the central screen, the digital map now filled with data points and visuals that illustrated the depth of PromptTech's operations. Each click brought up another layer of evidence, another story of lives altered or erased.

As the livestream began, Kusi's heart raced. He took a moment to collect his thoughts, looking at his team, the people who had become his family through their shared struggle. He could see the determination etched on their faces, each one ready to fight for their cause.

"Welcome, everyone," Kusi began, his voice steady as he faced the camera. "Tonight, we're here to unveil the truth about PromptTech—a truth that has been hidden from you for far too long."

The chat exploded with comments, questions, and support, but Kusi focused on the task at hand. "For years, this corporation has been manipulating memories and erasing dissent. But we're here to expose their operations and fight back against this tyranny."

As he presented their findings, Kusi felt the energy in the room shift. Each revelation landed with impact, the visual evidence showing the stark realities of memory manipulation. The audience's reactions were visceral—shock, outrage, disbelief.

"Alice and I have uncovered connections between PromptTech and high-ranking government officials," he continued, his voice gaining strength. "This is not just a corporate scandal; it's a conspiracy that undermines our very freedom."

He clicked to the next slide, revealing documents and footage that showcased the extent of the operation. "These are real people whose lives have been altered without their consent. This is the cost of complacency."

Kusi could see the audience's engagement growing as the narrative unfolded. "We need you to stand with us. Share this information. Join the movement to reclaim our identities and demand accountability from those in power."

Juna took over, presenting testimonies from individuals affected by PromptTech's actions, their stories weaving a narrative of loss and resilience. As the images flashed across the screen, Kusi could feel the collective anger rising. This was the moment they had been waiting for.

Just as they were reaching the climax of their presentation, an unexpected interruption jolted them. The screen flickered, and an unrecognized logo appeared, filling the screen with a warning: *"Cease and desist. Your actions are being monitored."*

Gasps echoed through the warehouse as Kusi's heart raced. "What the hell is this?" he muttered, his mind racing.

"Someone's hijacking our stream!" Mira exclaimed, frantically tapping on her tablet.

"Cut it off!" Kusi shouted, urgency surging through him. "We can't let them take control."

In the chaos, Juna managed to regain control of the stream, but Kusi could see that their message had already reached the masses. The chat was alive with confusion and anger, people reacting to the threat.

As the stream ended, Kusi felt a mix of exhilaration and dread. They had made their point, but now the stakes had risen dramatically. PromptTech was aware of their efforts, and they would not remain idle.

"We need to get out of here," Kusi urged, adrenaline coursing through him. "They'll come after us, and we have to be prepared."

The team sprang into action, gathering their things and securing the data they had presented. Kusi felt a newfound determination solidifying within him. This was only the beginning of the fight.

As they stepped into the night, Kusi knew they were in for a battle. The storm had gathered, and the confrontation with PromptTech was inevitable. But they were no longer just pawns in a game. They had ignited a fire, and now they would fight to protect their identities and their freedom.

With each step into the unknown, Kusi felt the weight of their mission pressing upon him, but he also felt a flicker of hope. They were no longer alone in this fight. The movement had begun, and together, they would challenge the darkness threatening to consume them.

Chapter 37: Reaching out for Araba

After narrowly escaping the chaos of their livestream, Kusi and his team retreated to a hidden safehouse, an old apartment building that had seen better days. The atmosphere was thick with tension, yet beneath it simmered a current of resolve. They huddled in the dimly lit living room, the faint hum of machinery in the background reminding them of the precariousness of their situation.

"Alright, we need to regroup," Kusi said, pacing the cramped space. "PromptTech knows we're onto them. We have to anticipate their next move." His mind raced, strategizing on how to stay one step ahead.

Juna, her arms crossed, nodded in agreement. "They'll try to discredit us, make us look like conspiracy theorists. We need to fortify our credibility, dig deeper into their operations, and rally more support. People need to see this isn't just about us; it's about everyone."

Mira sat at a makeshift desk, her fingers flying over the keyboard. "I've been combing through our evidence. We have some serious intel, but it's scattered. If we can create a cohesive narrative that connects the dots, we can present a more compelling case to the public."

As they discussed their next steps, Kusi's thoughts drifted to Araba. He hadn't seen her since the presentation, and worry gnawed at him. She had been instrumental in their movement, but Kusi knew the risks they were all facing. They were in a war not just for their memories but for their very lives.

"Has anyone heard from Araba?" Kusi asked, trying to mask the concern in his voice.

"I reached out to her earlier," Juna replied, a hint of apprehension in her tone. "She's safe for now but says she's been receiving threats. PromptTech won't let anyone who knows too much stay in the shadows for long."

Kusi clenched his fists, a wave of anger rising within him. They had already lost so much to PromptTech's machinations, and the thought of losing Araba too felt unbearable. "We have to get to her," he asserted. "If they've targeted her, then we need to ensure her safety. We can't afford to lose our strongest ally."

With a renewed sense of purpose, the team began formulating a plan to reach Araba. They mapped out potential routes and safe havens, drawing upon their network of supporters to secure transportation. Time was of the essence, and Kusi felt the urgency pressing down on them like a weight.

As they finalized their plans, Mira suddenly exclaimed, "Wait! I've found something." The rest of the team turned towards her, intrigued. "I've been digging into PromptTech's financials. It appears they've been funneling money into a project that's been labeled 'Project Deletion.' It sounds ominous."

"What's it about?" Kusi asked, leaning closer.

"From what I can gather, it's an initiative to enhance their memory manipulation technology. They're developing a new system that not only allows them to erase memories but also implant false ones more convincingly. If they succeed, it could change everything—make it easier for them to control the population."

Kusi's mind raced with the implications. "If we can expose Project Deletion, we can show people that PromptTech isn't just manipulating memories; they're rewriting reality. This is bigger than we thought."

Just as they began to strategize on how to expose this new information, Kusi's phone buzzed. It was a message from Araba, her voice clear but laced with urgency: *"They're coming for me. I need help—now!"*

Panic surged through Kusi as he shared the message with the group. "We have to move. They're onto her."

"Do we have time to regroup?" Juna asked, concern etched across her face.

Kusi shook his head. "We can't risk it. We have to go now. Everyone grab what you can. We'll head to her location and extract her before they can reach her."

They hurriedly gathered their belongings and slipped out of the safehouse, adrenaline fueling their every move. The streets felt alive, the usual noise of the city heightened by their urgency. Kusi led the way, his instincts honed from their recent encounters with danger.

As they navigated through the winding alleys, Kusi felt the weight of responsibility settle on his shoulders. Every decision mattered, and the stakes had never been higher. If they failed to reach Araba in time, the consequences could be dire—not just for her but for their entire cause.

Suddenly, a sleek black car sped past them, the driver's gaze fixed on Kusi and his team. "They're onto us!" he shouted, and the team picked up their pace, weaving through the crowds.

Just as they rounded a corner, a second vehicle blocked their path, and masked figures emerged, weapons drawn. "Stop right there!" one of them barked, the menace in his voice clear.

Kusi's heart raced as he turned to his team. "We can't let them take us without a fight." He glanced at Mira, who was already pulling out a small device from her bag. "What do you have?"

"It's a disruptor," she explained, her voice steady despite the chaos. "If I can activate it, it should create a temporary field that disrupts their technology, giving us a chance to escape."

"Do it," Kusi urged, readying himself for a confrontation.

With a determined nod, Mira activated the device, and a wave of energy pulsed through the air. The attackers froze, confusion crossing their faces. In that moment, Kusi and his team sprang into action, darting past their stunned assailants.

"Go! Go!" Kusi shouted, adrenaline surging through him as they sprinted down the alley, urgency propelling them forward.

They raced through the twisting streets, their path a blur of motion and noise. Kusi's mind was a flurry of thoughts, focused on Araba and the fight ahead. He couldn't let fear paralyze him; he had to believe they could reach her in time.

After what felt like an eternity, they approached the building where Araba was hiding. The street was eerily quiet, tension hanging in the air like a storm cloud. "We need to be careful," Juna whispered, scanning the surroundings for any sign of danger.

Kusi nodded, feeling the weight of responsibility pressing down on him. "Stay close and be ready for anything."

As they entered the building, Kusi's heart raced. They climbed the stairs quietly, each step echoing in the silence. The closer they got to Araba, the more anxious he became.

Finally, they reached the apartment where Araba had been hiding. Kusi knocked softly on the door, his heart pounding in his chest. "Araba, it's us. Open up!"

A moment later, the door creaked open, revealing a frightened but determined Araba. Relief washed over Kusi as he stepped inside, pulling her into a tight embrace. "I was so worried," he murmured, feeling her warmth against him.

"I knew you'd come," she replied, her voice steady despite the fear in her eyes. "But we have to move—now."

Before Kusi could respond, the sound of shouts echoed from the stairwell below. "They're coming!" Juna exclaimed, urgency lacing her voice.

"Let's go!" Kusi shouted, leading the group through the narrow apartment and down the back stairs. They needed to escape before PromptTech's enforcers could close in on them.

They slipped through the back exit and into the alley, Kusi's mind racing with plans for their next steps. The streets were dark and unforgiving, but their resolve was stronger than ever. They wouldn't let fear dictate their actions.

As they made their way to a safer location, Kusi's heart swelled with gratitude for his team. Together, they had faced danger time and time again, and each close call only strengthened their bonds. They were not just fighting for their memories; they were fighting for a future free from manipulation.

As dawn broke over the city, Kusi felt a renewed sense of purpose. They were more than a team; they were a movement, a force to be reckoned with. And as long as they stood together, they could confront whatever shadows lay ahead.

With Araba safe and their plans set in motion, Kusi knew that the battle against PromptTech was far from over. But with each step they took, they were one step closer to reclaiming their identities and exposing the truth.

Chapter 38: The Last Stand

The air was thick with anticipation as Kusi, Araba, and their team gathered in an abandoned warehouse on the outskirts of the city. It was a far cry from the chaotic streets they had navigated to reach safety, but the calm was deceptive. They all knew that a storm was brewing, and soon they would face PromptTech in what could be their final confrontation.

Kusi stood at the front, his gaze sweeping over the makeshift command center they had established. Screens flickered with data, maps were spread across tables, and a buzz of urgency permeated the room. His heart raced with a mix of determination and anxiety; the weight of their mission hung heavy on his shoulders.

"Alright, everyone," he began, raising his voice to cut through the chatter. "Today, we take the fight to PromptTech. We've gathered enough evidence about Project Deletion to expose their plans to the world. But we need to act quickly. They won't sit idle while we try to dismantle their operations."

Mira, seated at her laptop, looked up, her brow furrowed. "We've confirmed that they're set to launch a public demonstration of their new memory technology this afternoon. If we can infiltrate that event and expose the truth, we could turn the tide in our favor."

"Good," Kusi replied, his mind racing with possibilities. "But we need to be smart about this. PromptTech will have their security on high alert. We'll need to split into teams to cover more ground."

As they discussed their plan, Araba felt a surge of adrenaline course through her veins. This was it—the moment they had been preparing for. Her memories may have been fragmented, but her resolve was unyielding. They were fighting not just for their own identities but for everyone whose memories had been manipulated.

"We need to get to the main server room," Juna suggested, pointing to the map. "If we can access their system, we can release the data we've gathered directly to the public."

Kusi nodded in agreement. "Mira, you'll lead the tech team. Araba and I will take care of security. We'll distract them while you upload the evidence."

"Are you sure about this?" Araba asked, concern creeping into her voice. "What if something goes wrong?"

Kusi met her gaze, determination shining in his eyes. "We've come too far to back down now. We can do this together. Trust in what we've built."

With the plan in place, the team prepared for their mission. Kusi could feel the weight of the moment pressing down on him as they geared up. Each member had their role, and their success hinged on their ability to work together.

As they moved out, Kusi took a moment to check in with each member, offering encouragement and reminding them of their strength. They were more than a team; they were a family, united in their fight against the oppressive force of PromptTech.

The journey to the event site was filled with tense silence, punctuated only by the sounds of their footsteps and the occasional rustle of equipment. Kusi's heart pounded in his chest, a mix of fear and exhilaration flooding through him.

Upon arriving, they positioned themselves around the perimeter of the venue, a sleek modern building that oozed corporate power. Kusi's eyes scanned the surroundings, noting the guards and security cameras that dotted the entrance. They would have to be quick and efficient.

"Okay, let's do this," Kusi whispered, his voice barely audible above the hum of the city. He led Araba towards the entrance, confidence bolstering his steps.

Mira and Juna moved in tandem with them, keeping to the shadows as they approached a side door marked "Staff Only." Kusi gestured for the others to follow him as he stepped forward, ready to take on whatever challenges awaited them inside.

Inside the building, they were met with a bustling atmosphere of employees and high-ranking executives preparing for the presentation. Kusi's heart raced as they navigated through the crowds, blending in as best as they could.

"Stick to the plan," Kusi reminded everyone through the comms, his voice steady despite the chaos. "We're heading to the server room. Mira, keep us updated."

As they made their way deeper into the building, the tension heightened. Kusi's instincts were on high alert, and he felt a sense of urgency pressing down on him. They had to reach the server room before PromptTech could initiate the demonstration.

Suddenly, alarms blared, and red lights flashed throughout the building. Kusi's heart sank. "They know we're here! Move!"

The group sprinted down the hall, the echo of their footsteps reverberating against the sterile walls. Kusi led the way, adrenaline surging as they pushed forward. He could feel the eyes of PromptTech's enforcers upon them, the hunt was on.

As they reached the door to the server room, Kusi fumbled with the keypad, fingers trembling as he punched in the code they had obtained from a former employee. The door clicked open, and they rushed inside, slamming it shut behind them.

"Mira, get to work!" Kusi shouted, urgency lacing his voice.

Mira immediately set to work on the terminal, her fingers flying over the keys. "I'll need a few minutes to upload everything. Keep an eye on the door!"

Araba and Kusi positioned themselves at the entrance, ready to defend against any incoming threats. The atmosphere was charged with tension as they awaited the inevitable confrontation.

Just as Mira reached the final stages of the upload, the door burst open, and a group of armed security personnel stormed in. Kusi and Araba sprang into action, their instincts taking over.

The confrontation was chaotic, gunfire echoing through the room as Kusi and Araba fought off their attackers. Kusi's heart raced as he dodged a blow, countering with a swift kick that sent one of the guards sprawling.

"Keep going, Mira!" he shouted, adrenaline fueling his every movement.

Araba fought alongside him, her fierce determination evident in every strike. They were a well-oiled machine, moving in perfect sync as they fended off the security team.

But there were too many of them. Kusi could feel the pressure mounting, his body screaming for a break as he fought to protect not just their mission but their lives.

As the fight raged on, Mira's voice broke through the chaos. "I'm done! I've uploaded the files!" she exclaimed, her voice a beacon of hope amidst the turmoil.

"Now, let's get out of here!" Kusi shouted, urgency lacing his voice.

With a final push, Kusi and Araba fought their way to the exit, adrenaline propelling them forward as they navigated the chaos. They burst through the door, the bright light of the outside world flooding their vision.

Kusi led the charge, racing towards the exit as the sounds of the building erupted behind them. The sirens wailed, and the alarms blared, but they didn't stop. They had come too far to turn back now.

As they emerged into the open air, Kusi could feel the weight of the world shifting. They had exposed PromptTech's dark secrets, and there was no turning back. The battle for their identities had reached a tipping point.

"Over here!" Juna shouted, waving them towards a waiting vehicle. The group piled in, urgency propelling them forward as they sped away from the chaos.

As they drove away, Kusi felt a sense of triumph mixed with the reality of what they had just faced. They had taken on a powerful corporation and emerged victorious—at least for now. But the fight was far from over.

"Did we do it?" Araba asked, her voice filled with hope.

Kusi nodded, a grin spreading across his face. "We did. The world will know the truth."

As they drove into the unknown, Kusi realized that this was only the beginning. They had ignited a spark that could lead to a revolution. The battle for their memories, their identities, had turned into a fight for everyone's freedom.

Chapter 39: The Dawn of Truth

The days following their daring escape from PromptTech were a blur of activity. Kusi and his team worked tirelessly to spread the information they had acquired, and the world was beginning to wake up to the reality of memory manipulation. News outlets buzzed with reports of the leaked documents detailing PromptTech's Project Deletion—an operation that had not only erased the memories of dissenters but had also aimed to control the very essence of human identity.

Kusi sat in a small conference room that served as their makeshift headquarters. The walls were plastered with posters of protest slogans, images of the erased, and charts detailing the connections between memory manipulation and societal control. The atmosphere was electric, charged with a sense of urgency and hope.

"Look at this," Mira said, pointing at a screen that displayed a growing wave of public outrage. "Social media is on fire. People are mobilizing, sharing their own stories of memory loss and manipulation."

Araba stood beside Kusi, her gaze fixed on the screen. "It's incredible. I never thought we could make such an impact so quickly."

"It's just the beginning," Kusi replied, determination hardening his voice. "PromptTech will fight back. We need to be ready."

As the days turned into weeks, Kusi and his team established a network of allies—activists, journalists, and former employees of PromptTech who were willing to share their experiences. They formed a council of resistance, united by a shared mission to expose the truth and protect those whose memories had been stolen.

One evening, as they gathered for a council meeting, Kusi felt the weight of responsibility on his shoulders. They discussed strategies, planned protests, and coordinated efforts to gather more evidence against PromptTech.

Juna stood up, her expression serious. "We need to disrupt their operations further. If we can infiltrate one of their memory clinics, we can gather more evidence and possibly rescue some of the individuals trapped there."

Kusi nodded, the idea resonating with him. "I agree. We have to show people what they're really doing behind those closed doors."

As the group brainstormed ideas, Araba felt a sense of belonging wash over her. They were no longer just survivors; they were warriors fighting for a cause greater than themselves.

After several intense discussions, they formulated a plan to infiltrate one of PromptTech's memory clinics located in a remote part of the city. It was heavily guarded, but they had gathered enough intel to identify a security loophole. Kusi felt a sense of purpose surge within him; this was their chance to uncover more evidence and potentially save those whose memories had been erased.

"Let's do a reconnaissance mission first," Mira suggested. "We need to assess the security measures in place before we make any moves."

The team agreed, and Kusi felt a rush of excitement mixed with apprehension. This mission could change everything.

The night was cool and dark as Kusi, Araba, Juna, and Mira approached the clinic. They moved stealthily, their breaths mingling with the chill of the night air. Kusi's heart pounded in his chest, and he felt the thrill of the mission coursing through him.

They reached a vantage point overlooking the clinic, and Kusi pulled out binoculars to survey the area. "Looks like they have a rotating security detail. We'll need to time our movements carefully," he whispered, scanning for any signs of weakness.

Mira nodded, her eyes focused. "There's a delivery entrance around the back that looks less guarded. If we can get in through there, we might find a way to access the records."

"Good call. Let's move," Kusi instructed, leading the way as they stealthily made their way around the building.

Once they reached the delivery entrance, Kusi felt a surge of adrenaline. The door was secured with a keypad, but Juna quickly worked her magic, hacking the system with ease. The door clicked open, and they slipped inside.

The interior of the clinic was eerily sterile, bright lights casting harsh shadows in the hallways. Kusi led the team through the maze of corridors, his instincts heightened. They passed rooms filled with advanced memory manipulation equipment and sleek, cold chairs designed for the procedure.

"Over here," Mira said, pointing to a door marked "Records." Kusi nodded, and they moved toward it, anticipation building within him.

As they entered the room, they were met with rows of monitors displaying patient records. Kusi's eyes widened as he scanned the information on the screens. These were not just names; these were lives affected by the corporation's dark agenda.

"Start downloading everything," Kusi ordered, urgency in his voice. "We need to gather as much evidence as possible."

Just as they began the download, alarms blared throughout the building. Kusi's heart sank. "We need to move, now!"

The team scrambled, urgency fueling their movements as they retraced their steps. But the clinic's security was already closing in. The sound of footsteps echoed in the hallways, a chorus of impending danger.

"Split up!" Kusi shouted, adrenaline surging through him. "We'll meet at the rendezvous point!"

Araba hesitated for a moment, her eyes locking with Kusi's. "I'm not leaving you!"

"We'll find each other," Kusi insisted, urgency lacing his voice. "Trust me!"

With a final nod, they split up, each taking a different route as they navigated the chaos. Kusi sprinted through the hallways, his heart racing. He could hear the guards calling out, the sound growing louder as they closed in.

Kusi turned a corner and skidded to a halt as he nearly collided with a group of security personnel. Heart pounding, he ducked into a nearby room, pressing his back against the wall as the guards rushed past. He held his breath, waiting for the footsteps to fade before cautiously peeking out.

When he was sure the coast was clear, he bolted down another hallway, adrenaline propelling him forward. Every instinct screamed at him to keep moving, to escape the danger that loomed just behind him.

As he navigated the maze of hallways, he felt a mix of fear and determination driving him. They had to expose the truth—there was no turning back now.

Finally, Kusi reached the rendezvous point outside the clinic. He was panting, eyes scanning the darkness for any sign of his team. Moments felt like hours, anxiety gnawing at him as he waited.

Just as doubt began to creep in, he spotted Araba emerging from the shadows, her expression a mix of relief and worry. "Kusi!" she called, rushing toward him.

He pulled her into a tight embrace, feeling a surge of relief. "I thought we lost you!"

"I was right behind you," she replied, breathless. "Did you get everything?"

"Most of it. We'll analyze it back at the hideout," he said, determination hardening his voice. "But we need to get out of here before they find us."

As they made their way to their getaway vehicle, Kusi's mind raced with the information they had gathered. They had taken a significant risk, but it was all part of the greater fight against PromptTech.

Once they were safely in the car, Kusi glanced at the others, who had managed to regroup. "We did it," he said, his voice filled with conviction. "We're one step closer to exposing the truth."

As they drove away from the clinic, Kusi felt a renewed sense of purpose. The battle was far from over, but with each step they took, they were igniting a revolution. The dawn of truth was rising, and they would not be silenced.

Chapter 40: The Final Confrontation

In the wake of their daring escape from the PromptTech memory clinic, Kusi and his team returned to their hideout, a nondescript warehouse tucked away in an industrial area of the city. The atmosphere was charged with anticipation as they prepared to sift through the data they had obtained. They gathered around a makeshift table cluttered with laptops, files, and half-empty coffee cups.

Kusi couldn't shake the feeling of urgency that coursed through him. They had uncovered vital information that could dismantle PromptTech's grip on society, but the stakes had never been higher. As the team worked, the weight of their mission pressed heavily on him.

"Alright, everyone," Kusi began, his voice steady despite the chaos swirling in his mind. "We need to focus on what we found. This data could expose the full extent of PromptTech's operations, but we have to be strategic."

Mira glanced at the screens, her brow furrowed in concentration. "We've got evidence of their human trials and the unethical practices they used to erase memories. We can't just leak it—we need a coordinated plan to maximize its impact."

Araba nodded, her determination evident. "People need to see the human cost of these operations. We can't forget that behind every erased memory is a person."

As they delved deeper into the data, Kusi felt a flicker of hope ignite within him. They had gathered evidence of not only the memory manipulation but also the powerful connections that PromptTech had within the government. This was bigger than they had anticipated. If they could reveal the truth to the public, it could spark a revolution against the corporation.

Hours passed, and the weight of fatigue settled over the team. Kusi pushed through, fueled by adrenaline and determination. They were on the brink of something monumental, and he could feel it in the air.

"Let's set up a press conference," Juna suggested, breaking the tension. "We can invite journalists who are sympathetic to our cause. We need to control the narrative."

Kusi looked around the table, seeing the resolute faces of his friends and allies. "That's the plan. We'll gather as much media coverage as possible, and I'll make sure to have our story ready to go."

As they prepared for the press conference, Kusi couldn't shake the feeling that they were walking into a storm. PromptTech would not take this lying down; they had already proven they would do anything to maintain control. The thought of facing the corporation head-on was daunting, but it was a risk they had to take.

On the day of the press conference, the air crackled with tension. The team set up in a small community center, decorated with banners and placards showcasing their mission. Kusi stood at the podium, his heart racing as he glanced at the small crowd gathering. Reporters buzzed with curiosity, eager to hear what the group had to say.

As the cameras rolled and the first questions began to fly, Kusi felt a surge of confidence. He spoke passionately about the atrocities committed by PromptTech, detailing the stories of those who had suffered at their hands. He watched as the crowd reacted, their faces shifting from skepticism to outrage. "Today, we're here to expose the truth about memory manipulation," Kusi declared, his voice ringing with conviction. "PromptTech has been erasing lives, and we will not stand for it any longer!"

As the conference unfolded, it became clear that the revelations were shaking the very foundations of societal trust in PromptTech. Journalists asked probing questions, and Kusi answered with a mix of facts and emotions, weaving the narrative of human cost into the broader implications of memory manipulation.

But as the momentum built, Kusi felt a prickling sense of danger at the back of his mind. PromptTech would not let this go unchallenged. Just as he wrapped up his statements, a sudden commotion erupted at the back of the room.

The doors burst open, and a group of security personnel stormed in, flanking the entrance with menacing authority. Kusi's heart dropped. He recognized the lead guard—an intimidating figure named Voss, notorious for his ruthlessness.

"Everyone, stay where you are!" Voss barked, his voice cold and commanding. "This press conference is over."

Kusi's instincts kicked in, and he stepped forward defiantly. "You can't silence us, Voss! The truth is out, and you can't erase that!"

Voss's eyes narrowed, and the atmosphere crackled with tension. "You think you can expose PromptTech and get away with it? You have no idea who you're dealing with."

As he spoke, Kusi could see the fear spreading through the crowd. Some reporters began to back away, unsure of what would happen next. Kusi glanced at Araba, who stood firm by his side, her determination unwavering.

"This is about more than just us," she shouted, her voice cutting through the fear. "This is about all the lives you've destroyed!"

A tense standoff ensued as the room filled with uncertainty. The air was thick with the realization that they were on the brink of a confrontation—one that could define the future of their fight.

"Enough of this!" Voss growled, gesturing for his men to move in.

Without hesitation, Kusi took a step forward, adrenaline pumping through his veins. "If you want a fight, you'll get one! We won't let you intimidate us!"

The room erupted into chaos as Kusi and his team moved to protect themselves and the gathered crowd. The clash was swift and fierce, the sound of bodies colliding and voices shouting drowning out the cries of confusion.

Araba fought beside Kusi, her fists flying as they pushed back against the guards. Mira and Juna quickly organized a defense, using tables as barriers to shield the crowd from the encroaching security forces.

As Kusi grappled with one of the guards, he felt a rush of adrenaline—this was it. They were fighting for their freedom, for the people who had been silenced and erased. With a swift kick, he knocked the guard off balance, and the momentum shifted.

Suddenly, a loud crash echoed through the room as one of the barricades toppled over, sending papers and equipment flying. Kusi took the opportunity to push forward, rallying his team and the crowd behind him. "We can't back down! Fight for the truth!"

With renewed determination, the team pressed on, pushing back against Voss and his men. The chaos intensified, and Kusi could feel the tides turning. The crowd began to fight back, emboldened by Kusi's rallying cry. But just as victory seemed within reach, Voss drew a weapon—a sleek, advanced taser designed for subduing crowds. Kusi's heart raced as he recognized the danger. "Araba! Watch out!"

In a moment of instinctual courage, Araba lunged forward, pushing Kusi out of the way as Voss pulled the trigger. The taser fired, and Araba fell to the ground, convulsing in pain.

"NO!" Kusi screamed, rushing to her side. The fight around them faded into the background as he cradled her in his arms, panic washing over him. "Araba, stay with me! Please!"

Voss laughed, a cold, ruthless sound. "You should have known better than to challenge us. This is what happens to those who defy PromptTech."

Kusi's heart shattered as he looked into Araba's eyes, which flickered with pain but still held a glimmer of defiance. "Kusi, don't let this end here. Keep fighting... for all of us."

In that moment, time seemed to freeze. Kusi felt a swell of emotions—fear, anger, and a burning desire for justice. Araba's sacrifice would not be in vain. With a fierce resolve, he pushed himself to his feet, ignoring the chaos around him.

"Everyone, listen to me!" Kusi shouted, his voice breaking through the din. "This is our moment! We can't let them silence us! We need to stand together!"

The crowd began to rally, emboldened by Kusi's words. They pushed back against the guards, using their collective strength to fight for freedom. Voss and his men, overwhelmed by the sheer force of unity, began to falter.

Kusi felt a surge of hope. Araba had ignited a fire within him, and he would not let it extinguish. As the fight continued, he knew they were on the precipice of something monumental—a turning point that could change everything.

When the dust settled, Kusi found himself standing among the remnants of the chaos. The guards had retreated, overwhelmed by the determination of the crowd. He glanced around, searching for Araba, his heart pounding with fear.

But the moment of victory was bittersweet. The realization of the cost of their fight weighed heavily on him. Kusi knelt beside Araba, her breathing shallow but her spirit unyielding.

"Stay with me," he whispered, tears streaming down his face. "We'll get you help."

But Araba smiled weakly, her eyes reflecting strength and pain. "You have to keep going, Kusi. The truth must come out."

As the crowd rallied around them, Kusi felt the weight of their mission more than ever. They had ignited a revolution, but it had come at a

price. He promised himself, as he held Araba's hand, that he would honor her sacrifice.

The battle against PromptTech was far from over, but now, they were armed with the truth—and the world would hear their story. The fight for freedom and identity had only just begun, and Kusi knew that he would stop at nothing to bring justice to those who had suffered.

Chapter 41: A New Dawn

The days following the chaotic confrontation at the community center blurred together in Kusi's mind. In the aftermath, he felt as though he was navigating through a fog, the memories of Araba's sacrifice haunting him. The city was alive with the echoes of their struggle—protests erupted on the streets, igniting a fire of rebellion against PromptTech. Yet, amidst the growing unrest, Kusi felt an emptiness that gnawed at him.

Sitting in the dimly lit warehouse that had become their makeshift headquarters, Kusi sifted through the countless reports, articles, and videos flooding in from the media. The truth was spreading like wildfire, but every time he stumbled upon a photograph of Araba—her radiant smile now a bittersweet reminder—he felt a pang of grief.

Juna entered the room, her eyes scanning the cluttered space before settling on Kusi. "We need to regroup and plan our next move," she said gently, understanding the weight he carried. "The public is responding, but we have to keep the momentum going."

Kusi nodded, his gaze still fixed on the screen. "I know. But I can't shake the feeling that we're just reacting to their moves. We need a strategy—something that will truly cripple PromptTech."

As the team gathered, Kusi felt the energy in the room shift. They had transformed from a group of individuals fighting for their lives into a unified front, driven by a shared purpose. Mira and Juna outlined their ideas for further exposing PromptTech, detailing how they could infiltrate higher levels of the corporation.

"Based on the data we have, we can create a detailed report about the unethical practices—targeting not just the memory manipulation, but the political corruption tied to it," Mira explained, her fingers flying over the keyboard. "If we can get that into the hands of influential figures, we might sway public opinion on a larger scale."

Kusi leaned forward, excitement coursing through him. "And we could organize a series of rallies—spread the word, share stories of those impacted. Let's give a voice to the erased."

Araba's spirit seemed to linger in the air, propelling him forward. He could feel her presence, urging him to fight for the truth they had uncovered together.

As plans began to take shape, the team utilized every resource available. They reached out to journalists who had shown interest in their cause, inviting them to cover the unfolding situation. With each passing day, the resistance against PromptTech grew stronger, fueled by the stories of the erased and the injustices they had uncovered.

As Kusi worked late into the night, he couldn't help but think of the lives they were touching. Each story of loss, each memory erased, painted a vivid picture of the impact of PromptTech's greed. The stories became a catalyst for change, uniting people from all walks of life in a common cause.

Kusi found solace in the moments spent with the team. Juna's laughter echoed through the warehouse, a reminder that even in darkness, there was still light. Mira's dedication inspired him, her relentless pursuit of the truth igniting a fire within him. Together, they were creating a movement that could not be silenced.

One evening, as Kusi pored over data reports, he stumbled upon a series of documents detailing PromptTech's experimental projects. His heart raced as he read through the findings—there were mentions of a groundbreaking technology that could manipulate not just memories but also emotions. It was a chilling revelation.

"This changes everything," Kusi muttered, calling the team together. "If PromptTech has developed a way to control emotions, it could explain why so many people have accepted the corporation's actions without question."

Mira leaned in, her eyes widening. "They could be using this technology to suppress dissent, to keep the population docile. This could be the key to exposing their manipulation on a deeper level."

Kusi felt a surge of determination. "We need to get our hands on this technology. If we can expose it, we can dismantle their entire operation."

They devised a plan to infiltrate PromptTech's main facility, where the experimental technology was being developed. Kusi could feel the adrenaline coursing through him as they mapped out their approach, strategizing every detail of the mission.

"We'll need to be smart about this," Juna cautioned, her brow furrowed. "PromptTech won't take kindly to intruders, especially after everything that's happened. We'll need a distraction."

Mira volunteered to create a diversion, using her hacking skills to trigger an alarm elsewhere in the facility. It was a risky move, but Kusi could see the resolve in her eyes—this was their chance to make a real impact.

The night of the mission arrived, and the atmosphere was electric with anticipation. Dressed in dark clothing, the team moved stealthily through the shadows, approaching the heavily guarded PromptTech facility. Kusi's heart raced as they slipped past the security checkpoints, adrenaline pumping through their veins.

Mira's voice crackled through the earpiece. "I'm in position. Once I trigger the alarm, you'll have about five minutes to get inside before they scramble security."

"Copy that," Kusi replied, his mind racing with thoughts of what they could uncover.

As the alarm blared in the distance, chaos erupted within the facility. Kusi and the team seized the opportunity, slipping through the doors and into the heart of PromptTech. The sterile hallways buzzed with activity, the hum of technology filling the air.

"Follow me," Kusi urged, leading the way through the maze of corridors. They navigated past rooms filled with advanced equipment, each step heightening their resolve.

They finally reached a laboratory marked with heavy security doors. Kusi's heart raced as he initiated a bypass, praying that Mira's distraction was holding. The doors slid open with a hiss, revealing a room filled with screens displaying data—each one detailing the manipulation of memories and emotions.

"This is it," Kusi breathed, stepping into the room. "We need to gather as much information as we can."

As they worked, a chilling realization washed over them. The data wasn't just about manipulation; it detailed methods to erase specific emotions, to implant false memories that could alter perceptions of reality. This was far beyond what they had imagined.

Suddenly, footsteps echoed in the hallway. Kusi's heart dropped as he exchanged frantic glances with his team. "We need to hurry!"

Just as they finished downloading the crucial data, the door burst open, revealing Voss and a group of armed security personnel. "You thought you could come in here and expose us?" Voss sneered, his eyes glinting with malice. "You'll regret this."

"Get back!" Kusi shouted, stepping in front of his team. "You can't silence us anymore!"

A tense standoff ensued, and Kusi could feel the weight of their mission pressing down on him. This was their chance to confront the very embodiment of the corporation's tyranny.

"Your time is up, Voss," Kusi declared, his voice steady. "We're taking this information to the world, and there's nothing you can do to stop us."

Voss's expression darkened, and he signaled his men to move in. "Then you'll have to go through me."

In that moment, chaos erupted once more. Kusi and his team fought back against Voss and his guards, using every ounce of strength they had. The room became a whirlwind of movement—punches thrown, bodies colliding, and the air charged with determination.

With adrenaline coursing through him, Kusi felt the weight of their cause driving him forward. Every strike was fueled by the memory of those who had suffered, and he refused to let them down.

Just as it seemed they were outmatched, Mira emerged from the shadows, having hacked into the facility's security systems. "I've locked the doors! No one's getting in or out!"

Kusi felt a surge of hope. "Now's our chance! We can't let them take this data."

The tide of the fight began to shift as Kusi and his team pushed back against Voss and his guards. They fought as a cohesive unit, their movements synchronized by a shared purpose. Each strike felt like a blow against the corporation that had wronged so many.

As the battle raged on, Kusi locked eyes with Voss. He could see the desperation in his expression—the realization that he was losing control. With a final surge of energy, Kusi tackled Voss to the ground, the two grappling for dominance.

"Your reign of terror ends here," Kusi growled, pinning Voss beneath him. "You've done enough damage to this world."

With a swift movement, Kusi secured Voss's hands behind his back, leaving him incapacitated. The remaining guards, seeing their leader defeated, began to falter, their resolve crumbling.

As the last of the guards surrendered, Kusi felt a rush of triumph. They had fought against the odds and emerged victorious, but the victory came with a bittersweet taste. Araba's absence loomed large in his heart, but he knew her spirit had fueled their fight.

"Let's get this data out to the world," Kusi urged, rallying the team. They hurried to the computers, preparing to send the information to trusted journalists and activists who could help spread the truth.

As the data uploaded, Kusi took a moment to breathe, the weight of their success settling over him. They had exposed the dark underbelly of PromptTech and, in doing so, reclaimed a piece of their identities.

As they made their escape from the facility, Kusi couldn't help but feel a sense of hope. The world was changing, and they were part of that change. The fight wasn't over, but they had ignited a spark—a movement that could no longer be snuffed out.

As they regrouped outside, Kusi felt the weight of the past begin to lift. He glanced at Mira and Juna, the bond they had formed growing stronger with each challenge they faced. Together, they had become a force to be reckoned with.

In the days that followed, the world responded. Protests erupted, and the information they had shared spread like wildfire, calling for accountability and justice. Kusi could see the tide turning—the people rising up to reclaim their voices.

Kusi took a deep breath, feeling the fresh air fill his lungs. He knew the fight would continue, but he was no longer alone. Together, they would forge a new path—one where memories were cherished, not commodified.

And as he stood there, he felt Araba's presence beside him, her spirit guiding him toward a brighter future. In the distance, the sun began to rise, casting a warm glow over the city—a new dawn on the horizon, full of possibilities and hope.

Chapter 42: The Weight of Truth

The air was electric with change, a palpable tension threading through the city as Kusi walked through the streets. News vans lined the avenues, reporters clamoring for interviews and updates, while citizens gathered in groups, discussing the recent revelations about PromptTech. The uprising sparked a fire within the populace, igniting a passion for justice that had long been dormant.

But beneath the surface of this newfound energy lay a complexity that Kusi couldn't ignore. The shadows of their recent battle loomed large, and every face he encountered was a reminder of the personal stakes involved. He could feel the weight of the truth pressing down on him—an immense responsibility to ensure that their victory translated into lasting change.

As he navigated the bustling streets, Kusi's thoughts drifted back to Araba. He had lost her in the fight for truth, and her absence was a constant ache in his heart. But he also felt her spirit guiding him, urging him to stay the course. With each step, he resolved to honor her memory by continuing the fight against the forces that sought to erase the very essence of humanity.

At the makeshift headquarters, the atmosphere buzzed with urgency. Juna and Mira were strategizing, poring over reports and social media reactions. Kusi joined them, eager to be part of the momentum they had built.

"We need to consolidate our efforts," Juna said, her eyes shining with determination. "If we can unify the various groups that have sprung up in the wake of the revelations, we can create a stronger front against PromptTech."

"Agreed," Kusi replied, feeling a sense of purpose wash over him. "Let's reach out to community leaders, activists, and anyone willing to join our cause. We need to ensure that this isn't just a flash in the pan."

Mira nodded, her fingers tapping rapidly on her keyboard. "I've been compiling a list of organizations and individuals who have been vocal against PromptTech in the past. We can leverage their networks to expand our reach."

Kusi felt the adrenaline surge within him as they began to make calls and send messages. He could feel the tide turning, the energy building like a wave ready to crash. This was their moment to harness the spirit of the uprising and channel it into a coordinated movement for change.

As the days turned into weeks, Kusi and his team worked tirelessly to organize rallies and events, calling attention to the issues surrounding memory manipulation and the ethical implications of PromptTech's practices. The message was clear: they would not stand idly by while the corporation continued its machinations.

Kusi found himself becoming a spokesperson for the movement, addressing crowds and sharing stories that resonated with the public. He recounted the experiences of those who had lost their memories, individuals whose lives had been irrevocably altered by the corporation's greed. Each story became a rallying cry, drawing people into the fold.

At one particularly poignant rally, Kusi stood before a sea of faces, each one reflecting the hope and anger that had ignited the movement. "We are not just fighting for ourselves," he proclaimed, his voice ringing out over the crowd. "We are fighting for everyone who has been silenced, everyone whose memories have been commodified. This is our chance to reclaim our identities and our humanity!"

The crowd erupted in applause, the energy infectious. Kusi felt a swell of pride and responsibility as he looked out at the faces before him. These were not just strangers; they were allies in a shared battle, each one a vital part of the movement for truth and justice.

But as the movement gained momentum, PromptTech began to retaliate. Kusi received word that Voss had escaped custody during the chaos at the facility and was rallying his resources for a counteroffensive. The news sent a shiver down Kusi's spine.

"We need to be vigilant," Juna warned during one of their strategy sessions. "Voss won't back down easily. He'll try to discredit us and undermine our efforts."

Mira agreed, her brow furrowed in concentration. "We've already seen their tactics—spreading misinformation, attempting to sow discord among our ranks. We can't let that happen."

Kusi felt a surge of anger at the thought of Voss lurking in the shadows, plotting his next move. "We need to prepare ourselves for whatever he throws our way. We've come too far to let him derail this movement."

They began to develop counter-strategies, creating a communications plan to address any misinformation that might arise. Kusi knew that they had to be proactive; the stakes were too high.

As Kusi delved deeper into the workings of PromptTech, he uncovered disturbing connections between the corporation and influential political figures. The truth revealed a web of corruption that extended far beyond memory manipulation—it was a system designed to keep power concentrated in the hands of the few.

With Mira's help, Kusi began compiling evidence of this collusion, preparing a detailed report to present to the public. They were determined to expose the full extent of PromptTech's influence, revealing the ways in which they had infiltrated every level of society.

"We need to get this information into the right hands," Kusi urged during a team meeting. "If we can expose the corruption at the highest levels, we can rally even more support."

Juna nodded, her resolve unwavering. "We'll coordinate with journalists who have covered PromptTech in the past. They'll know how to handle this information and can help us bring it to light."

In the midst of their preparations, Kusi received an unexpected message from an anonymous source claiming to have insider information about Voss's whereabouts. Skeptical but intrigued, he arranged to meet the informant in a secluded location.

As he waited in a dimly lit café, Kusi's heart raced with anticipation. Would this be a trap, or a genuine opportunity to gain an edge over PromptTech?

When the informant arrived, Kusi was taken aback. It was a familiar face—one he had never expected to see again. "Kusi," the informant said, pulling down the hood of her jacket. "It's me, Zara."

"Zara?" Kusi stammered, disbelief flooding through him. "I thought you were... lost."

"I was, but I managed to escape the corporation's grasp," she replied, her eyes dark with determination. "I have information that could turn the tide in our favor."

Zara revealed that she had been working within PromptTech as a data analyst, privy to confidential information about their operations. "I was able to gather data on Voss's movements and plans," she explained, her voice steady. "He's regrouping and preparing to launch a counteroffensive, but I have intel on where he'll be making his next move."

Kusi felt a surge of hope. "This could change everything," he said, leaning forward. "If we can anticipate his actions, we can stay one step ahead."

Zara nodded, her expression resolute. "I also have access to some of the files that detail PromptTech's experiments. It's more horrifying than you can imagine. If we can expose that data, we'll not only undermine Voss but also show the public the true nature of the corporation."

With Zara on their side, Kusi and his team worked tirelessly to compile the evidence she had provided. Time was of the essence, as Voss's plan was set to unfold in a matter of days. They strategized how to use the information to their advantage, creating a multi-faceted approach to counter Voss's imminent attacks.

As the day of action approached, Kusi felt a mixture of anxiety and determination. This was their chance to confront Voss head-on, to reclaim the narrative and protect the movement they had built.

Kusi gathered the team for one final strategy session before the big day. "We've come so far, but we can't let our guard down now," he emphasized, looking each of them in the eye. "We have the truth on our side, and that's our greatest weapon."

The team nodded, the shared sense of purpose invigorating them. They were ready to face whatever Voss had in store, united by their resolve to fight for justice and reclaim their memories.

As the sun began to rise on the day of the confrontation, Kusi could feel the tension in the air. The team prepared to disseminate the information they had gathered while also anticipating Voss's next move.

Kusi took a deep breath, steeling himself for what lay ahead. "Today is about more than just us," he said, his voice firm. "It's about everyone who has suffered at the hands of PromptTech. We're here to reclaim our identities and bring the truth to light."

As they moved out into the world, Kusi felt a sense of determination wash over him. They were on the brink of a new chapter—a chapter filled with hope, resilience, and the unwavering belief that truth could triumph over oppression.

And as he took his first step into the unknown, Kusi knew that he was ready to face the challenges ahead, fueled by the memories of those who had come before him and those who would follow. The fight was far from over, but they had ignited a spark that could not be extinguished. Today, they would make their stand.

Chapter 43: Tides of Change

As dawn broke over the city, Kusi felt the weight of anticipation heavy in the air. The streets buzzed with a nervous energy, a mixture of hope and anxiety as people prepared for the confrontation with PromptTech. The knowledge they had uncovered was no longer just whispers in dark corners; it was a tidal wave ready to crash upon the shores of complacency.

Gathered in their makeshift headquarters, Kusi, Juna, Mira, and Zara reviewed their final plans. Maps and charts plastered the walls, a visual representation of their strategy to expose Voss and the corporation's machinations. The once-quiet office was now filled with the palpable energy of determination.

"We'll launch our campaign at noon," Juna announced, her voice steady. "We need to hit them where it hurts—their reputation. The more people we can reach, the better our chances of swaying public opinion."

Mira was busy setting up the streaming equipment, her fingers deftly arranging cables. "We'll go live just before the protest begins, showcasing the evidence we've compiled. This isn't just about PromptTech; it's about all of us reclaiming our voices."

Kusi nodded, the gravity of their mission sinking in. "We're not just fighting for ourselves anymore; we're fighting for everyone who's ever had their identity stripped away."

Meanwhile, within the sleek walls of PromptTech's headquarters, Voss was formulating his own plan. The reports of the growing movement had reached him, and he was furious. He had underestimated Kusi and his allies, but that mistake would not be repeated.

Gathering his inner circle of executives, Voss paced before them, his face a mask of rage. "We can't let this uprising gain any more traction. If the public sees us as the enemy, we'll lose everything," he growled, slamming his fist against the table.

One of his aides, a thin man with sharp features, spoke up cautiously. "We could initiate a counter-campaign, framing Kusi and his team as radicals trying to incite chaos. If we can sway public perception, we can undermine their credibility."

Voss's eyes gleamed with a dangerous intensity. "That's a start, but we need something more decisive. We'll use our resources to create a narrative that casts them as threats to national security. If we can tie them to any acts of violence or disturbance, we can discredit their entire movement."

Back at Kusi's headquarters, the team was fine-tuning their strategy as the clock ticked closer to noon. Zara had provided invaluable information about PromptTech's inner workings, including a list of key personnel involved in the corporation's darker dealings.

"We can expose these individuals during the live stream," Zara suggested, her voice carrying a fierce determination. "If people can see the faces behind the corporation, it will make the fight feel more personal."

Kusi felt a surge of inspiration. "Let's make sure to include testimonies from those who have suffered due to memory manipulation. Their stories are the heart of this movement."

As they finalized their plans, Kusi felt the bond between them strengthen. They were no longer just individuals fighting against a corporation; they were a united front, a family forged in the fires of adversity.

As the hour approached, Kusi's heart raced. He glanced at Mira, who was adjusting the camera settings, her focus unwavering. Juna was preparing her notes, while Zara reviewed the list of testimonies to ensure everything was ready.

"Are we ready?" Kusi asked, trying to gauge the group's energy.

Mira looked up, determination in her eyes. "We've got this. Let's give the people what they need to fight back."

Juna nodded, her expression resolute. "It's now or never."

Kusi took a deep breath, feeling the weight of their mission settle over him. "Let's make our voices heard."

As they went live, Kusi felt a rush of adrenaline. The camera light blinked on, illuminating the faces of those who had fought tirelessly for justice.

"Hello, everyone. We are here to speak the truth about PromptTech," Kusi began, his voice steady and strong. "What you're about to see is the reality behind the corporation's facade. This is not just a corporate scandal; this is about our identities, our memories, and our humanity."

Mira cut in, her voice passionate. "We will share stories of those who have suffered due to PromptTech's unethical practices, and we will expose the executives who have profited from the pain of others."

As they presented the evidence—documents, testimonies, and video clips—the response was immediate. Social media erupted with comments, shares, and live reactions as people began to rally behind their cause.

But as the movement gained traction, Voss's counter-campaign was already underway. News outlets began running stories that portrayed Kusi and his allies as a fringe group, radicalizing the narrative to paint them as a danger to society.

"We need to counter this narrative," Juna urged as they monitored the coverage. "If people see us as a threat, they'll turn against us."

Kusi felt frustration bubbling within him. "We have to combat their lies with the truth. Let's gather more testimonies and stories from people affected by PromptTech's practices."

With the clock ticking, they worked diligently to gather additional evidence and testimonials, knowing that the fight for truth was far from over.

As they prepared for the evening rally, the atmosphere crackled with energy. Kusi could feel the passion of the crowd as they gathered, a sea of faces united in their demand for justice.

Standing before the crowd, Kusi felt a sense of purpose surge within him. "This is our moment! Together, we can reclaim our memories and our identities. We will not be silenced!"

The crowd erupted in cheers, their voices rising in unison. It was a chorus of hope, a rallying cry that resonated throughout the city.

As the rally reached its peak, Kusi caught sight of a familiar figure in the crowd—Voss, hidden among the throngs, a sinister smile playing on his lips. The realization sent a jolt of adrenaline through him. Voss was watching, and Kusi could feel the weight of the impending confrontation looming.

Juna noticed Kusi's change in demeanor. "What's wrong?" she asked, her brow furrowing in concern.

"Voss is here," Kusi replied, his voice low. "We need to be ready for whatever he has planned."

As the rally continued, Voss stepped forward, his presence commanding attention. "This is a misguided movement!" he shouted, his voice dripping with disdain. "You are all being manipulated by Kusi and his band of misfits! They seek to sow chaos, not justice!"

Kusi felt the anger boiling within him. "We're not here to create chaos! We're here to reclaim our voices and hold you accountable for your actions!"

The crowd began to chant Kusi's name, their support reinforcing his resolve. But Voss wasn't done. He gestured to a group of security personnel flanking him. "If you don't cease this insurrection, we will take action to restore order!"

The atmosphere shifted, tension hanging thick in the air. Kusi knew they had to stand firm against Voss's intimidation tactics. "We will not be silenced!" he declared, his voice rising above the din. "We are here to fight for justice, for every person who has been harmed by your greed!"

As the crowd rallied behind him, Kusi felt the tide of fear begin to shift into empowerment. This was their moment to demonstrate their strength, to stand united against the forces that sought to control them.

The rally turned into a full-blown protest, a manifestation of anger and hope that reverberated through the city. Kusi felt a surge of determination as he witnessed the resolve of his fellow citizens. They were rising, refusing to back down in the face of oppression.

In that moment, Kusi understood that they were not just fighting against PromptTech; they were fighting for a future where memories and identities were cherished, not exploited. And as he stood amidst the crowd, he knew that together they would forge a new path, one built on truth, justice, and the unbreakable bond of shared experience.

As the sun set, casting an orange glow over the gathering, Kusi felt a renewed sense of hope. They were not merely a group of individuals; they were a movement—a powerful force for change that could not be extinguished. Together, they would dismantle the systems of oppression and rebuild a world where memories were celebrated, and identities were reclaimed. The fight was far from over, but the dawn of a new era was on the horizon.

.

Chapter 44: Shadows of Revelation

In the days following the protest, the city simmered with tension. The rally had become a catalyst for change, igniting discussions in homes, cafés, and workplaces about the ethical implications of memory manipulation and the oppressive grip of corporations like PromptTech. Kusi and his allies felt the momentum of their movement, but with that momentum came a heavy burden of responsibility.

Kusi sat in the makeshift headquarters, surrounded by Juna, Mira, and Zara, as they processed the aftermath. News channels were rife with reports of the protest, showcasing both support for their cause and vehement opposition from Voss and PromptTech. The narrative was shifting, but it was far from settled.

Juna sighed, her fingers tracing the rim of her coffee cup. "The media is framing us as a revolutionary force, but they're also giving Voss a platform to push back. He's going to fight dirty."

Mira, scrolling through her tablet, looked up with a serious expression. "Voss has already started his counter-offensive. He's discrediting our movement by labeling us as extremists. We need to respond, and fast."

Zara nodded in agreement, her voice firm. "We have to keep the focus on the stories—the people who have suffered because of

PromptTech's practices. Their voices need to be louder than any corporate spin."

Kusi felt a surge of determination. "Let's organize a series of community forums. We can invite those affected by memory trading to share their stories. It will not only humanize our movement but also give the public a chance to connect with the real impact of PromptTech's actions."

As the group brainstormed, Kusi couldn't shake the feeling that Voss was planning something more sinister. The corporate mogul was known for his ruthless tactics, and Kusi understood that their movement was a direct threat to his empire.

Days turned into weeks as Kusi and his team worked tirelessly to plan the forums. They secured venues, contacted individuals willing to share their experiences, and promoted the events across social media. The response was overwhelming; people were eager to join the fight against PromptTech, motivated by their own experiences or the stories they had heard.

The first community forum was held in a local community center, the room filled to capacity with individuals from all walks of life. Kusi stood at the front, addressing the crowd with a mix of excitement and apprehension.

"Thank you all for being here today," he began, his voice steady. "We are here to listen, to share, and to stand together against the injustices that have plagued our lives because of PromptTech's greed."

As the first speaker—a woman named Elia, whose memories had been manipulated by the corporation—stepped up to the microphone, a hush fell over the room. She spoke with raw honesty about her experiences, detailing the disorientation of waking up one day with memories that felt foreign and painful.

"I lost my family's history, my sense of self," Elia said, her voice trembling. "They erased parts of me, and I've been searching for answers ever since."

The audience was captivated, the power of her story resonating deeply within them. Kusi watched as heads nodded in understanding, tears glistening in the corners of eyes. This was what they had hoped for—a genuine connection forged through shared experiences.

As the forum progressed, more voices emerged, each testimony building on the last, weaving a tapestry of loss, hope, and resilience. Kusi felt the atmosphere shift; what began as individual stories became a collective cry for justice.

Later that evening, Kusi and his team gathered in their headquarters to reflect on the forum's impact. The room buzzed with excitement and energy as they discussed the responses they had received on social media and in the community.

"We reached more people than I anticipated," Juna noted, her eyes shining with enthusiasm. "The hashtags are trending, and people are sharing their own stories online. This movement is gaining traction!"

Zara, scrolling through her phone, frowned. "But Voss isn't sitting idly by. He's ramping up his smear campaign. We need to anticipate his next move."

"Let's not react hastily," Kusi cautioned, sensing the urgency in the air. "Instead, let's gather more evidence, more stories. The more we can arm ourselves with truth, the stronger we'll be against whatever he throws at us."

As Kusi dove deeper into gathering evidence, he found himself increasingly drawn to a particular aspect of PromptTech's operations—its connection to the black market for memories. He knew that if they could expose this network, it would be a devastating blow to Voss and his corporation.

Kusi reached out to Zara, who had been digging into PromptTech's past dealings. "I think we need to look into the origins of their memory trading practices," he said, pacing the room. "There has to be something linking them to the illegal trade."

Zara nodded, her expression thoughtful. "I can dig into the corporate records, see if there are any red flags. If we can find evidence of their involvement in the black market, it could turn public opinion against them even more."

The next few days were filled with late nights and intense research. Kusi, Juna, Mira, and Zara spent countless hours poring over documents, connecting the dots between PromptTech and the black market. They began to uncover a web of deception that hinted at a far-reaching conspiracy.

One evening, as Kusi was reviewing some files at a local café, he noticed a shadow lurking outside. The figure looked familiar, and his instincts kicked in. He slipped out of the café, heart racing, and approached the figure cautiously.

It was a man he recognized—a former employee of PromptTech who had gone missing months ago. "I know who you are," Kusi said, his voice low. "What are you doing here?"

"I have information," the man whispered urgently, glancing around nervously. "They know you're digging into their past. You need to be careful. They're watching."

Kusi felt a chill run down his spine. "What do you know?"

"I was part of a team that worked on memory manipulation technology for PromptTech. We had to keep it under wraps—what they were doing was illegal, unethical. If you expose them, they'll come after you. They don't take kindly to traitors."

The man hesitated, looking over his shoulder as if expecting someone to appear at any moment. "I have documents—proof of their involvement in the black market. But you need to act fast. They're onto me. I'm leaving tonight."

Kusi felt the weight of the situation press upon him. "Meet me here in an hour. I'll have a way to get the documents to safety."

As the man vanished into the shadows, Kusi raced back to the café, adrenaline coursing through his veins. He had to warn the team and prepare for whatever was coming.

Back at the headquarters, Kusi relayed the encounter to Juna, Mira, and Zara. "We need to be ready for a fight," he said, urgency lacing his tone. "PromptTech knows we're closing in on the truth. They'll stop at nothing to protect their interests."

"Let's set up security measures," Juna suggested, her voice steady. "We need to ensure that if they come for us, we have a plan."

Mira nodded, her determination evident. "We'll also ramp up our outreach. If we can mobilize more people, it'll make it harder for Voss to silence us."

As night fell, Kusi's heart raced. He returned to the café, anxious but hopeful that the information could be the key to their victory. The man arrived, his face pale with fear.

"Here," he said, thrusting a flash drive into Kusi's hands. "This contains everything—the documents that prove PromptTech's ties to the black market and illegal memory manipulation. You have to expose them."

Kusi nodded, a sense of purpose igniting within him. "Thank you. You've done a brave thing by coming forward."

Just as they began to leave, Kusi felt a sudden tension in the air. A group of men approached, their expressions cold and calculating.

The former PromptTech employee stiffened, fear written across his face.

"They found me," he whispered. "Run!"

In an instant, Kusi turned, bolting for the exit, his heart pounding as he and the former employee dashed down the alley, adrenaline propelling them forward. Behind them, shouts rang out, footsteps pounding on the pavement as the men pursued them.

Kusi and the man sprinted through the labyrinth of alleyways, the city's night lights flickering like stars above them. Kusi's mind raced with thoughts of the documents in his possession—evidence that could turn the tide in their fight against PromptTech.

"Where do we go?" Kusi gasped, glancing over his shoulder as the shouts grew closer.

"Follow me! I know a place," the man urged, his breath coming in ragged gasps.

They turned a corner, ducking into an abandoned warehouse. Inside, the echoes of their footsteps bounced off the walls as they pressed deeper into the shadows. The man led Kusi to a small office at the back, quickly locking the door behind them.

"Stay quiet," the man whispered, his eyes darting around the room. "They could be looking for us."

Kusi's heart raced as they crouched in silence, the weight of the flash drive heavy in his pocket. He could feel the tension building in the air as they waited, straining to hear any signs of pursuit.

After what felt like an eternity, the footsteps faded, and they cautiously made their way back outside, their senses heightened. Kusi knew they had to get the information to safety and share it with the world, but the danger was far from over.

As they emerged into the moonlit streets, Kusi couldn't shake the feeling of impending doom. PromptTech was more dangerous than he had ever imagined, and their relentless pursuit made it clear that they would do anything to protect their secrets.

"Let's get to the headquarters," Kusi urged, his voice resolute. "We need to prepare for the storm that's coming."

Together, they sprinted through the city, their minds racing with possibilities and strategies. Kusi felt a newfound strength in his resolve. They were no longer just fighting for themselves—they were fighting for everyone who had suffered under PromptTech's manipulative grasp.

As dawn broke over the city, Kusi and his team gathered in the headquarters, their spirits ignited with purpose. The documents from the flash drive would serve as the foundation for their next move—a direct confrontation with Voss and his empire.

"This is our moment," Kusi declared, the fire of determination blazing in his eyes. "We have the proof we need to expose PromptTech for what it truly is. We'll take this fight to the public and ensure that no one can turn a blind eye to the truth."

The room erupted in applause, the team united in their mission. They were ready to face whatever challenges lay ahead, knowing that the fight for justice was only just beginning.

.

Chapter 45: Shattered Illusions

The atmosphere in Kusi's headquarters was electric with anticipation as the team gathered around a central table cluttered with documents, laptops, and digital screens displaying a myriad of information. The flash drive had opened a Pandora's box of secrets about PromptTech, revealing not just their illegal memory manipulation operations but also their deep ties to a network of shadowy figures involved in the black market trade of memories.

Kusi stood at the head of the table, his expression serious. "We have a mountain of evidence here, but we need to organize it in a way that the public can understand. This isn't just about us—it's about everyone who has been wronged by PromptTech."

Zara, poring over the documents, nodded. "I can create infographics to illustrate how PromptTech has exploited vulnerable individuals. Visuals will help convey the impact of their actions."

Mira, her fingers flying over the keyboard, chimed in, "I can draft a press release and a series of social media posts. We need to create a buzz around this information before Voss can spin it."

Juna, who had been quiet until now, leaned forward, her brow furrowed in thought. "We should also consider a video campaign.

Testimonials from those affected can humanize our cause and make it harder for PromptTech to dismiss us as extremists."

Kusi felt a swell of pride for his team. Each member was contributing unique ideas, a testament to their resilience and determination to expose the truth.

In the following days, the team worked tirelessly, compiling evidence and crafting a comprehensive media strategy. They organized a press conference to unveil their findings, timing it perfectly to maximize media coverage.

As the day of the press conference arrived, Kusi felt a mix of excitement and anxiety. The stakes had never been higher; the success of their movement hinged on how effectively they could communicate their message.

Standing at the podium, Kusi took a deep breath, scanning the crowd of reporters, activists, and curious onlookers. "Thank you for being here today," he began, his voice steady but passionate. "Today, we are not just revealing the truth about PromptTech—we are standing together to demand justice for all those who have suffered due to their unethical practices."

As he spoke, Kusi detailed the evidence they had uncovered, including testimonies from individuals whose memories had been manipulated or erased. He shared stories of lives torn apart, families fractured, and identities lost in the wake of corporate greed.

Midway through his speech, Kusi introduced Elia, the woman whose story had resonated deeply during the community forum. She stepped up to the podium, her expression fierce and resolute.

"I lost more than just memories," she said, her voice unwavering. "I lost my identity, my connection to my family.

PromptTech has played god with our lives, and it's time we hold them accountable. We will no longer be silent!"

The crowd erupted in applause, the power of her words igniting a fire within everyone present. Kusi felt a surge of hope; they were building a movement that could no longer be ignored. But as Kusi basked in the moment, he knew Voss wouldn't remain passive. PromptTech's public relations machine would swing into action, spinning narratives and attempting to discredit their movement.

Later that evening, as the team celebrated the success of the press conference, a news alert popped up on Kusi's phone. *"PromptTech Responds: CEO Voss Dismisses Claims as Baseless and Misleading,"* it read.

Kusi felt a knot tighten in his stomach. "They're going to try to turn this around on us. We need to prepare for their backlash."

Gathered in their headquarters once more, the team discussed their strategy. Zara laid out the timeline of events, detailing how they could counter PromptTech's attacks.

"If we can anticipate their moves, we can undermine their narratives before they even hit the news," Zara said, her finger tracing the timeline. "We should also amplify our outreach—get more people involved in sharing their stories."

Mira, nodding vigorously, added, "Let's create a dedicated website where people can submit their experiences with PromptTech. We can curate these stories and share them on our social media platforms to keep the momentum going."

Juna looked thoughtful. "And we need to connect with other activists and organizations. The more allies we have, the stronger our voice will be."

Kusi reached out to various activist groups, inviting them to join the cause. He was surprised at the overwhelming response;

many organizations that had been fighting against corporate greed and unethical practices rallied to their side.

As the coalition grew, Kusi realized they were no longer just a small group of activists. They had transformed into a formidable force, united in their mission to expose PromptTech's corruption and demand justice for those affected.

One day, as Kusi was meeting with new allies, a familiar face entered the room. It was the former PromptTech employee who had first contacted him in the alley.

"I've been doing some digging of my own," he said, his eyes bright with determination. "I managed to obtain more documents—information about PromptTech's plans for a new memory implant technology that they're testing in secret."

Kusi leaned forward, intrigued. "What do you mean?"

"They're planning to launch it as a revolutionary breakthrough in memory enhancement, but it's all a cover for their ongoing manipulation of people's memories. They want to create a market for memories they can erase and sell back to individuals—essentially creating a never-ending cycle of exploitation."

Kusi felt a surge of anger. "We need to expose this. If the public finds out they're not just manipulating memories but also profiting off their erasure, it could shift everything."

With the new documents in hand, Kusi and his team set to work again. They organized another press conference, determined to unveil the shocking truth about PromptTech's plans. The stakes were higher than ever, and Kusi knew they needed to tread carefully.

As the day of the conference approached, the tension in the headquarters was palpable. The team spent countless hours preparing their speeches, ensuring that every detail of the information would resonate with the public. When the day finally arrived, Kusi stood at the podium once more, surrounded by his team and the former employee. He took a deep breath, looking out at the sea of reporters and cameras.

"This is a pivotal moment," Kusi began, his voice steady. "Today, we reveal the truth not just about PromptTech's past but about their plans for our future. This isn't just a fight for justice—it's a fight for our humanity."

As Kusi detailed the new revelations, he saw the shock and disbelief in the faces of the reporters. The tide was beginning to turn.

> He unveiled the documents, showing the connections between PromptTech's memory manipulation technology and their plans for profit. "PromptTech is not just a corporation; it is a parasite feeding off the memories of individuals. They are testing new technologies that could permanently alter who we are for their gain."

The room buzzed with murmurs as Kusi continued. "We will not allow this to happen. We will stand united against this exploitation and fight for the rights of every individual who has been affected."

As he concluded his speech, Kusi raised his voice, fueled by passion. "This is not just our battle—it is a collective fight for our identities, our memories, and our rights as human beings. Together, we will not only expose PromptTech but dismantle the systems that allow such exploitation to exist!"

The applause was deafening, the crowd energized and united. Kusi felt a swell of hope; they were not just telling their story—they were creating a movement that could change the future.

But even as he celebrated, Kusi knew the challenges ahead were monumental. Voss would retaliate, and the fight would only grow fiercer. As he left the podium, he felt a sense of foreboding wash over him; the struggle was far from over, and the battle lines had been drawn. The aftermath of the press conference would set in motion a series of events that would test their resolve, pushing Kusi and his team to their limits. But as they regrouped in the aftermath, he felt a newfound strength in their unity.

Kusi gathered his team, his expression determined. "We've taken a significant step forward, but we must remain vigilant. Voss will not back down easily. We need to stay one step ahead and prepare for whatever he throws at us."

Juna nodded, her eyes filled with determination. "Let's keep the pressure on. The more we can keep the public engaged and informed, the harder it will be for Voss to manipulate the narrative."

As they strategized, Kusi felt a surge of hope. They were no longer just fighting for themselves; they were fighting for everyone who had been silenced by corporate greed. They would continue to pull on the threads of truth, weaving a tapestry of resistance that would be impossible for PromptTech to unravel.

Chapter 46: The Final Gambit

The news of PromptTech's unethical practices had sent shockwaves through the public, and Kusi's team found themselves at the heart of a growing movement. Protests erupted across the city, and people flooded the streets, demanding justice for those whose memories had been stolen. But Kusi knew that Voss wouldn't go down without a fight.

As the protests continued to gain momentum, an unexpected message came through their secure communication channel. It was from a source within PromptTech, one they hadn't heard from before. The message was brief but alarming: *"Voss is planning something big. He's desperate. Be ready."*

Kusi read the message aloud to the team, who were huddled in their command center. Juna crossed her arms, her expression tense. "What could it mean? If Voss is truly desperate, there's no telling what lengths he might go to."

Mira, who had been monitoring social media activity, looked up from her screen. "Whatever it is, we need to prepare. He'll likely try to discredit us or divert the public's attention."

Kusi nodded, his mind racing. "We need to stay ahead of him. Let's double down on our efforts to expose every aspect of his operation. If he's planning a move, we'll make sure it's too late for him to succeed."

The next day, headlines blared with shocking accusations against Kusi and his team. Major media outlets, clearly influenced by PromptTech, reported that Kusi had falsified evidence, accusing him of being a criminal mastermind exploiting the public's emotions for his gain. The timing was perfect for Voss—just as the protests reached a fever pitch, the public was bombarded with questions about Kusi's integrity.

Juna slammed a fist onto the table in frustration. "This is classic corporate smear tactics. They're trying to turn the narrative against us."

Kusi remained calm, though inwardly he was seething. "We knew this was coming. They want to shake the public's trust in us. We need to hit back harder."

Mira suggested a countermeasure. "Let's release a statement refuting these claims, but more importantly, let's leak the most damning evidence we have. If we release the full extent of what we've uncovered, it'll make Voss's accusations look like desperate lies."

Kusi agreed with Mira's plan, but Zara raised a concern. "If we release everything now, we lose our leverage. What if there's something we don't know yet? What if Voss has another trick up his sleeve?"

Kusi considered her words carefully. There was always a risk in playing all their cards at once. But time was running out, and the public's trust was a fragile thing. He knew that if they didn't act soon, they could lose everything.

"We're doing it," Kusi said finally, his voice firm. "We'll release the documents. The public deserves to know the full truth, and we'll deal with whatever comes next."

The team worked quickly to compile the most explosive revelations from their investigation. They released the documents to the public, detailing PromptTech's involvement in illegal memory manipulation, black market trading, and human rights abuses. The evidence was overwhelming, and it reignited the public's outrage.

As the truth spread, the backlash against Voss and PromptTech was swift and brutal. Protesters swarmed PromptTech's headquarters, demanding accountability. The company's stock plummeted, and several high-profile executives resigned, attempting to distance themselves from the unfolding scandal.

But Voss remained silent, refusing to step down. His arrogance was evident, and Kusi knew that the final confrontation was approaching.

Kusi's team received another message from their anonymous source within PromptTech. This time, the message contained critical information: Voss was planning a last-ditch effort to salvage his empire. He had gathered a group of powerful allies, individuals with influence over the media and government, and was preparing to unveil a new initiative—one that would distract the public from the scandal and reframe the narrative in his favor.

Kusi gathered the team. "This is it. Voss is making his move. We need to be ready."

Mira frowned. "What exactly is he planning? And how can we stop him?"

The source had provided details of a major press conference Voss was planning to hold, where he would unveil a so-called revolutionary advancement in memory technology. It was a move designed to capture the public's imagination and shift focus away from the corruption they had uncovered.

Juna's eyes narrowed. "If we let him do this, he might regain control of the narrative. We can't let that happen."

Kusi agreed. "We need to disrupt the conference, expose him in real time. We have to be there when it happens."

The day of the press conference arrived, and Kusi's team was ready. They had infiltrated the venue, blending in with the crowd of reporters and tech enthusiasts.

The auditorium was filled with tension. PromptTech's top executives, including Voss, sat on stage before a sea of reporters and onlookers. Their attempt at damage control had spiraled out of their hands, and what was meant to be a press conference turned into a public crucifixion. Whispers and murmurs filled the air as journalists furiously scribbled notes, eyes locked on Voss.

Voss stood tall, trying to project the same confidence that once commanded respect. But his voice faltered. As he began his speech, Kusi and Araba, sitting among the audience, knew that this was it—this was the moment when PromptTech's empire would fall.

The public had been made aware of the company's crimes. The explosive data leak revealed every detail of their illegal operations—the memory wipes, the disappearances, and the human rights violations committed for profit. The evidence was undeniable. And now, the world watched as Voss tried to justify the unjustifiable.

"I... We at PromptTech have always sought to push the boundaries of technological innovation," Voss stammered, his usual bravado replaced by unease. "But some... unfortunate actions have been taken out of context..."

The audience was not buying it. Boos began to ripple through the crowd. Someone shouted, *"You erased people's lives!"* Another yelled, *"You've destroyed families!"*

Voss's eyes darted across the crowd, desperately searching for an exit strategy.

Suddenly, from the back of the room, a group of activists burst through the doors, holding signs and chanting. Their voices echoed through the auditorium: *"Justice for the erased!"* Security rushed to control the situation, but it was too late. The crowd's energy had shifted. The protestors had ignited something—an unrelenting anger that could not be subdued.

In the midst of the chaos, Voss made a desperate move. Kusi saw him edge toward the side of the stage, his eyes fixed on the nearest exit. He was going to run. Araba nudged Kusi, both recognizing what was about to happen.

"He's not going to get away," Kusi muttered under his breath, his pulse quickening.

Just as Voss took his first step toward the exit, the crowd surged forward, blocking his path. Security struggled to maintain control as the crowd pressed closer to the stage. The protestors' chants grew louder, drowning out any hope Voss had of speaking. There was nowhere to go.

Realizing he couldn't flee, Voss stood frozen, his face a mask of panic. The once-powerful CEO, who had wielded his influence like a weapon, was now trapped by the very people he had exploited.

It was then that law enforcement arrived. Officers stormed the stage, grabbing Voss by the arms. The sight of him in handcuffs sent a wave of satisfaction through the crowd. Phones were raised high, capturing every second of the fall of PromptTech's once-mighty leader.

As Voss was dragged off the stage, Kusi and Araba watched in silence. This was the moment they had fought for—the public takedown of the man responsible for so much suffering.

Reporters scrambled to get closer, cameras flashing as Voss was forced into the back of a police vehicle. His face, once a symbol of control, was now plastered with fear and defeat. The crowd roared as the doors slammed shut behind him.

This was only the beginning.

In the days that followed, the world watched as the trial of PromptTech's executives began. The courtroom was packed, every seat filled with spectators hungry for justice. On one side, victims and their families sat, their faces etched with pain and determination. On the other, Voss and his collaborators, their arrogance stripped away, sat like shadows of their former selves.

The prosecution laid out its case with brutal precision. Witness after witness took the stand, each one recounting the horrors they had endured at the hands of PromptTech. The erased, or their surviving family members, told their stories of lives shattered, memories stolen, and identities lost.

One victim's mother spoke through tears, holding up a picture of her daughter who had been erased, her existence wiped from every record. "They erased her like she never existed," she sobbed. "I've lived every day knowing my daughter is out there, somewhere, but she doesn't remember who she is."

The defense's arguments were weak, their attempts to downplay the atrocities futile. Voss, pale and haggard, sat silently, his eyes downcast. There was no defiance left in him.

When the verdict was read, it was as if the entire world held its breath. Voss and several other top executives were found guilty on all charges—corruption, human rights violations, and conspiracy. The judge's voice rang through the courtroom as the sentences were delivered.

"For his role as the mastermind behind the memory manipulation and the exploitation of countless individuals, Voss is hereby sentenced to life imprisonment without the possibility of parole," the judge declared.

The courtroom erupted in a mix of cheers and sobs. Justice had been served, but the scars of PromptTech's actions would last forever.

For the collaborators, the sentences ranged from 50 years to life, depending on their level of involvement. Each one was led away in handcuffs, the weight of their crimes hanging over them like a dark cloud.

Kusi and Araba exchanged a look of quiet victory. The battle was won, but the work of healing was just beginning.

Chapter 47: The Shutdown

As news of the trial verdict spread, the world's attention shifted to the imminent shutdown of PromptTech. The media was ablaze with coverage. Headlines flashed across every screen: *"PromptTech Crumbles," "Justice Delivered,"* and *"The End of an Empire."* News anchors debated the fallout while citizens celebrated in the streets. The once untouchable corporation had fallen, and now it was time for the final act.

Across the country, television and radio stations broadcast the government's official announcement: *"PromptTech, effective immediately, will cease all operations. Law enforcement and regulatory agencies have been dispatched to secure all company premises. Any attempt to obstruct this process will be met with legal consequences."*

The weight of the announcement sent ripples through the population. PromptTech had been so deeply intertwined with everyday life that its shutdown felt surreal. Employees, many of whom had no knowledge of the company's illegal activities, were left in shock, unsure of what came next.

At dawn the following day, police vehicles surrounded PromptTech's global headquarters. Helicopters buzzed overhead, and a massive crowd gathered to witness the downfall of the corporation that had ruled their lives for so long. Dozens of officers, in full tactical gear, lined the perimeter, ensuring that no one could enter or leave without authorization.

News vans lined the streets, cameras rolling, capturing every moment. It was a spectacle—one that would be broadcast live to millions of viewers. The sight of the once-powerful building, now a fortress under siege, was enough to send a clear message: this was the end.

As the police entered the building, journalists reported the scene: "The PromptTech headquarters, a symbol of power and influence, is now a crime scene. Authorities are inside, seizing documents, servers, and anything else that could further implicate the company in its heinous crimes."

The crowd outside cheered. Banners and signs waved in the air, carrying slogans like *"Justice for the Erased!"* and *"No More Memory Manipulation!"* Protestors, activists, and regular citizens alike had come together to witness history being made.

Within the sprawling halls of the once-mighty corporate giant, law enforcement worked swiftly to shut down operations. Offices were sealed, equipment confiscated, and confidential files pulled from locked cabinets. Computers were shut off, their hard drives taken into evidence. The nerve center of PromptTech was dismantled, piece by piece.

Kusi stood just outside the building, watching the scene unfold. He had refused any press interviews for the day. This wasn't a moment for him to bask in the glory of their victory. It was a moment of reckoning.

"Do you think this is really the end?" Araba asked, standing beside him, her eyes scanning the crowd.

Kusi remained silent for a moment, taking in the magnitude of the situation. "For now, yes," he finally replied, his voice heavy with the weight of everything they'd been through. "But power doesn't just disappear. It shifts. Someone else will try to pick up the pieces eventually."

The shutdown of PromptTech was more than just the fall of a company—it was the collapse of an entire system that had exploited people for years. In cities across the world, the public reacted with a mix of relief and celebration. For the families of those erased, this was a bittersweet moment. The company responsible for their loss was gone, but the damage it had done could never be undone.

Candlelight vigils were held in several cities, honoring the memories of those who had been erased. The names of the victims were read aloud, one by one, as people gathered to remember those who had been lost to PromptTech's greed.

In one particularly moving scene, a mother, holding a picture of her erased child, whispered, *"This is for you, my love. You may be gone, but you're not forgotten."* Tears welled in the eyes of those around her, the collective grief palpable in the air.

Meanwhile, the streets of major cities were filled with celebrations. Music blared, and people danced, holding up signs that read *"Freedom from Memory Slavery"* and *"Victory for the Erased!"* It was a moment of unity, where strangers embraced, and hope filled the air.

News stations around the world reported on the shutdown in real-time. Footage of the police swarming PromptTech's headquarters was broadcast on every channel. Analysts weighed in on the fallout, speculating about what this meant for the future of the memory trade.

"This is a historic moment," one commentator declared. "PromptTech's shutdown is a warning to any company that believes they can exploit human lives for profit. But make no mistake, this will have far-reaching consequences for industries that rely on memory manipulation."

The debate raged on, but one thing was certain: PromptTech's era of control was over. The headlines the next morning would cement it as one of the most significant corporate takedowns in history.

As the police continued their operation, one final act marked the symbolic end of PromptTech. The company's logo—a sleek, modern design that had once represented technological dominance—was removed from the top of the building. The crowd erupted in applause as it was lowered to the ground, a powerful symbol of the company's demise.

Araba watched as the logo was dismantled, her thoughts drifting to the lives that had been affected. "Do you think they'll ever really heal from this?" she asked.

"Some will," Kusi said. "But for others, the scars will remain."

As the last police vehicle left the premises, and the building stood stripped of its identity, Kusi felt a strange sense of closure. This was it—the final nail in the coffin of PromptTech. He had started this journey to seek justice for those who had been erased, and now, that justice had been served.

But the road ahead would not be easy. There were still challenges to face, and the system that allowed PromptTech to thrive still existed. For now, though, Kusi took a deep breath and allowed himself to feel the weight of their victory.

Chapter 48: The Restoration

In the aftermath of PromptTech's shutdown, the government swiftly moved to address the devastation caused by the corporation's malfeasance. A press conference was held by the President, standing before a crowd of reporters with the national flag fluttering in the background.

"PromptTech's crimes will not go unpunished," the President declared, her voice solemn yet determined. *"Today, we are announcing a comprehensive package of reparations and support programs for those affected by their actions. The victims and their families have suffered greatly, and it is our duty to provide them with the assistance they deserve."*

The compensation plan included direct financial reparations to the families of those who had been erased. It was a monumental step, one that acknowledged the human toll of PromptTech's greed. The media buzzed with the announcement, with headlines like "Government Rolls Out Historic Compensation for PromptTech Victims" and "Justice and Healing: A New Era of Accountability Begins."

A national fund was established, backed by the government and contributions from various philanthropists, to ensure that the victims could rebuild their lives. Families who had lost loved ones to the memory manipulation practices were compensated based on the severity of their losses, and memorials were planned to honor those who had been erased.

"It's not just about money," the President continued. "*It's about restoring dignity, and rebuilding trust between the people and the systems that should protect them.*"

The support didn't stop with financial compensation. The government launched a series of programs aimed at reintegrating the erased individuals who were still alive but had lost their identities. A network of specialized rehabilitation centers was created to help them regain a sense of self. Each center had psychologists, memory experts, and social workers dedicated to assisting individuals in recovering or reconstructing their memories.

Families were reunited with their erased loved ones, though the process was often emotionally complex. Some victims could never fully regain their former lives, but the government vowed to stand by them every step of the way.

One such scene played out in a small rehabilitation center where a woman, who had been erased years ago, stood face-to-face with her sister for the first time. Tears streamed down their faces as they embraced, holding on to each other tightly, neither willing to let go.

"I thought I'd lost you forever," the sister whispered.

"I don't remember everything," the erased woman replied, her voice fragile. "But I know you. I remember this feeling."

It was these moments—of reconnection, healing, and hope—that began to restore the fabric of a society torn apart by PromptTech's greed.

At the heart of the government's restoration plan was the idea that communities needed to be rebuilt. Entire neighborhoods had been devastated by the loss of loved ones and the emotional scars left behind. As part of the reparations, local councils and community groups were provided with funding to create spaces for collective healing.

In one town, a group of volunteers worked together to build a memorial park dedicated to those who had been erased. A vast wall, engraved with the names of the victims, stood in the center of the park. Flowers and candles were laid at its base as a quiet tribute to the lost. The park became a place where people could gather, reflect, and remember.

"This is our way of honoring them," one volunteer said, standing before the wall. "We may never forget what happened, but we can find a way to move forward together."

Community centers also opened across the country, providing spaces for therapy, support groups, and workshops on memory recovery. These centers became havens for those who had been affected, offering not just professional help but a sense of belonging.

For Kusi, the restoration phase was bittersweet. He had spent so much time exposing PromptTech's crimes that now, with the company gone, he wasn't sure what his next steps would be. Yet, as he stood at the opening of one of the rehabilitation centers, watching families reunite, he knew that his fight for justice wasn't over.

Araba stood beside him, her own journey far from complete. The memories she had lost might never fully return, but she had begun to build a new life. With Kusi's help, she had managed to uncover fragments of her past, pieces that had allowed her to regain some sense of self.

"It's strange, isn't it?" she said quietly. "All of this... It feels like the end, but also like a beginning."

Kusi nodded. "We've come a long way. But there's still work to be done. People need to know they're not alone. That we're all in this together."

Araba smiled softly. "I think you've always known that."

Kusi shrugged. "I'm just doing what needs to be done."

The government's response to PromptTech's actions didn't end with compensations and rehabilitation. Lawmakers introduced sweeping reforms to ensure that no company could ever exploit people in the same way again. The memory industry, once a booming sector of the tech world, was now under strict scrutiny. New laws were passed, banning certain types of memory manipulation and ensuring that individuals' cognitive rights were protected.

Corporations that had once thrived alongside PromptTech were quick to distance themselves from the scandal, publicly declaring their support for the new regulations. Some companies even pledged to fund additional support programs for those who had been affected.

PromptTech's assets, which had been seized by the government, were repurposed to fund research into ethical uses of memory technology. Scientists and ethicists worked together to find ways to use these technologies for good, ensuring that they could never again be used as tools of exploitation.

As time passed, the scars of PromptTech's reign began to heal, but the memory of what had been lost lingered. The government organized a national day of remembrance, honoring the victims of the memory manipulation scandal. On that day, people across the country paused to reflect on the lives that had been erased and the lessons learned from the tragedy.

Families gathered at memorials, lighting candles and sharing stories of their loved ones. It was a day of mourning, but also one of healing and solidarity.

Kusi attended the ceremony at the largest memorial in the capital city. As he stood before the wall of names, he felt the weight of all that had transpired. The fight had been long and difficult, but now, at last, there was a sense of closure.

"They won't be forgotten," Kusi whispered, his voice filled with quiet resolve. "Not now. Not ever."

Though the restoration process was long and fraught with challenges, it marked the beginning of a new era. People who had been erased were finding their way back, families were healing, and communities were rebuilding. The shadow of PromptTech's crimes would never fully fade, but it had brought about a reckoning—one that would ensure a better, more just future for everyone.

For Kusi, Araba, and those who had fought to expose the truth, it was a victory. But it was also a reminder of the work still left to be done. The world had changed, and now it was up to them to ensure that such horrors never happened again.

Also by Eric Agyemang Duah

The AI Uprising
The AI Uprising
Perfect Prompting - A Comprehensive Guide for Professionals
The AI Messiah
The AI Messiah
The Memory Traders - Echoes of the Erased

Watch for more at https://linkedin.com/in/promptech.